SLOW BURN

BRENDA JACKSON

St. Martin's Paperbacks

This is a work of fiction. All of the characters, organizations, and events portrayed in this novel are either products of the author's imagination or are used fictitiously.

SLOW BURN

Copyright © 2007 by Brenda Streater Jackson.
Excerpt from *Her Little Black Book* copyright © 2007 by Brenda Streater Jackson.

Cover photo of woman © Bobby Quillard
Cover photo of man © MTPA Stock/Masterfile

ISBN: 0-312-94049-1
EAN: 978-0-312-94049-2

Printed in the United States of America

St. Martin's Paperbacks edition / November 2007

St. Martin's Paperbacks are published by St. Martin's Press, 175 Fifth Avenue, New York, NY 10010.

10 9 8 7 6 5 4 3 2 1

Praise for BRENDA JACKSON and the MADARIS SERIES

UNFINISHED BUSINESS

"Jackson is a master at juggling two plots at a time, and *Unfinished Business* proves no exception. A perfect balance of tension and chemistry is created as Christy and the somewhat domineering Alex battle unknown criminals—as well as their unresolved attraction to each other."   *—Romantic Times BOOKreviews*

"Hot and sexy."   *—Romance Reader at Heart*

THE MIDNIGHT HOUR

"A super-hot hero, a kick-butt heroine, and non-stop action! Brenda Jackson writes romance that sizzles and characters you fall in love with."   —Lori Foster, *New York Times* bestselling author

"*The Midnight Hour* is a roller-coaster read of passion, intrigue and deceit."   —Sharon Sala, *New York Times* bestselling author

"With a taut, over-the-top romantic thriller, Jackson revisits her popular Madaris Family and Friends series...Jackson smoothly alternates between several points of view and throws in a number of plot twists...Jackson [has a] knack for creating characters with emotional depth and distinct voices...[a] tension-packed read."   *—Publishers Weekly*

"Jackson has written another compelling drama about the Madaris family and their friends."   *—Booklist*

"Action, mystery, and sensuality propel *The Midnight Hour* forward. Jackson forces readers to step outside the romantic suspense box and enter an elusive world of undercover agents and crime lords. Victoria and Drake are memorable characters who will provide hours of enjoyment for even the most cynical of readers."   *—Romantic Times BOOKreviews*

"Drake and Tori are tough, passionate, loyal, and attractive protagonists. Their courage and fire and their strong feelings for each other can't help but appeal to readers. So, too, will the non-stop action; there are no dull moments in *The Midnight Hour*."   *—Romance Reviews Today*

Dear Readers,

It is hard to believe that *Slow Burn* is my fiftieth book.

I can vividly recall how I felt after publishing my very first novel and how excited I was about becoming a romance author. I made a pledge to myself . . . and to my readers, to write stories not only about love but also about deep emotions, fulfillment, and commitment. And it seems so fitting that my very first book, and my fiftieth book, are books about the Madaris family.

I never dreamed when I penned Justin and Lorren's story nearly twelve years ago and introduced the Madaris family for the first time that what I was doing was taking readers on a compelling journey where romance, passion, and true love awaited them at every turn. I had no idea that the Madaris family and their friends would become people you felt like you knew and who you would come to care so much about. The Madaris men have become your heroes because they represent those things you desire—men whose looks can not only take your breath away, but who have the ability to make you appreciate the fact that you are a woman.

I loved writing Slade and Skye's story and I especially enjoyed getting the chance to revisit with those Madaris men and their friends, as well as introducing you to two additional cousins, Quantum and Jantzen Madaris. My next Madaris book, which will be coming your way in November 2008, will concentrate on rodeo super-star, Luke Madaris. See what happens when Luke meets a woman who becomes the one temptation he can't seem to resist.

I am proud to announce that all the books in the Madaris Family and Friends Series are being reprinted, starting with Justin and Lorren's story, *Tonight and Forever*, in December

2007. The reprinted books will have new book covers designed especially for each of my Madaris men in a Special Edition Collectors Series. Now you have the opportunity to collect the entire set.

For a complete listing of all the books in this series as well as the dates they will be available in a bookstore near you, please visit my Web site at—www.brendajackson.net.

I also invite you to drop me an e-mail at WriterBJackson @aol.com. I love hearing from my readers.

I want to thank all of you for your support through the years. You are responsible for me reaching this very important milestone in my career. And I want to say in my fiftieth book the very same thing I said in my first book—*"My greatest satisfaction from my writing will come when I know that I have brought a smile to some reader's face and pleasure to their day through my books."*

All the best,
Brenda Jackson

SLOW BURN

THE MADARIS FAMILY

Milton Madaris, Sr. and Felicia Laverne Lee Madaris

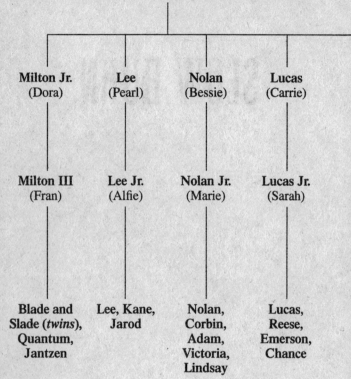

Milton Jr. (Dora)	Lee (Pearl)	Nolan (Bessie)	Lucas (Carrie)
Milton III (Fran)	Lee Jr. (Alfie)	Nolan Jr. (Marie)	Lucas Jr. (Sarah)
Blade and Slade (*twins*), Quantum, Jantzen	Lee, Kane, Jarod	Nolan, Corbin, Adam, Victoria, Lindsay	Lucas, Reese, Emerson, Chance

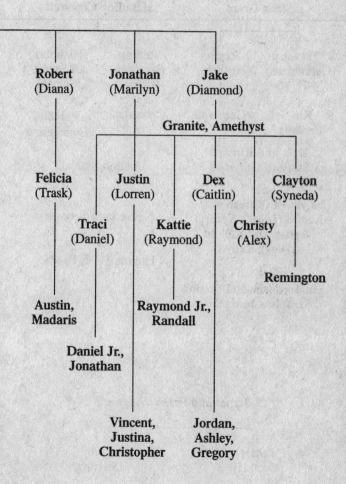

FRIENDS OF THE MADARIS FAMILY

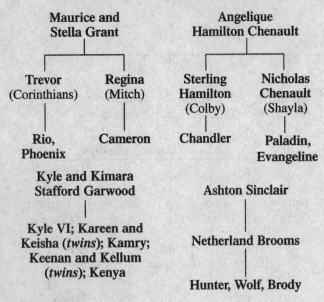

Maurice and Stella Grant
- **Trevor** (Corinthians)
  - Rio, Phoenix
- **Regina** (Mitch)
  - Cameron

Angelique Hamilton Chenault
- **Sterling Hamilton** (Colby)
  - Chandler
- **Nicholas Chenault** (Shayla)
  - Paladin, Evangeline

Kyle and Kimara Stafford Garwood
- Kyle VI; Kareen and Keisha (*twins*); Kamry; Keenan and Kellum (*twins*); Kenya

Ashton Sinclair
- Netherland Brooms
  - Hunter, Wolf, Brody

Trent Jordache and Brenna St. Johns Jordache
- Zane

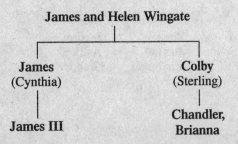

James and Helen Wingate
- **James** (Cynthia)
  - James III
- **Colby** (Sterling)
  - Chandler, Brianna

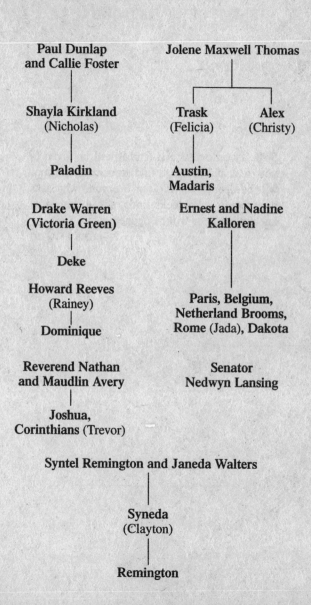

Paul Dunlap
and Callie Foster
|
Shayla Kirkland
(Nicholas)
|
Paladin
|
Drake Warren
(Victoria Green)
|
Deke
|
Howard Reeves
(Rainey)
|
Dominique
|
Reverend Nathan
and Maudlin Avery
|
Joshua,
Corinthians (Trevor)

Jolene Maxwell Thomas
|
Trask   Alex
(Felicia)   (Christy)
|
Austin,
Madaris
|
Ernest and Nadine
Kalloren
|
Paris, Belgium,
Netherland Brooms,
Rome (Jada), Dakota
|
Senator
Nedwyn Lansing

Syntel Remington and Janeda Walters
|
Syneda
(Clayton)
|
Remington

So I say unto you: Ask and it will be given to you; seek and you shall find; knock and the door will be opened to you. For everyone who asks receives; he who seeks finds; and to him who knocks, the door will be opened.

—LUKE 11:9–10

CHAPTER 1

Slade Madaris opened the door and was suddenly entranced by the woman he found standing there. He inhaled. Then exhaled. He repeated the process several times before forcing himself to speak. "May I help you?"

He saw the glint of surprise in her eyes and thought they were beautiful eyes. Warm and expressive. "You aren't Dr. Justin Madaris, are you?" she asked in a soft voice with a New England accent.

Her question made a grin tug at his lips. "No, I'm not Dr. Madaris. I'm his cousin. Do you need to see the doctor?" It wouldn't be the first time someone had come to the front door instead of following the sign and going around the back to where Justin had built a separate facility for his medical practice.

"Yes. No." As if to explain her hasty response, she smiled and said, "This is not a medical call. I'm here to see both Dr. and Mrs. Madaris."

Her smile did something to Slade's insides, actually made his heart skip a beat. "I see," he said, watching her nervously nibble on her lip. He wondered what had her so tense. He continued to watch the torture she was giving her mouth and thought they had to be the most kissable pair of lips he'd ever seen on a woman.

Deciding he'd seen enough and any more would push him to do something outlandishly bold—something his twin brother, Blade, would not hesitate to do—like pulling her into his arms and kissing her, Slade sighed heavily, then pushed away from the door frame and took a step back. "Then won't you come in while I let them know they have a visitor?"

"Yes, thank you."

Skye Barclay walked into the house feeling slightly off-key. If this man was an example of how they grew them in Texas, then she had lived in the wrong state all her life. He was simply gorgeous. And his eyes were so sinfully dark and alluring that she couldn't help the warm surge that began coursing through her.

She put his age in the early thirties, no more than thirty-two or -three, and he had to be every bit of six feet three or more and was dressed in a pair of neatly starched well-worn jeans, a belt with a wide brass buckle, and a white chambray shirt. In her opinion he was the epitome of just what a Texan man should look like, all the way down to his booted feet.

And then there was his face. The man was as ruggedly handsome as any man had a right to be. In addition to the gorgeous pair of eyes, he also had a pair of lips that made you think of stolen kisses on a hot summer night and a pair of dimples that were responsible for the shiver she suddenly felt inching up her spine. His dark hair was cut low and neatly trimmed around his head, and his firm jaw more than complemented the rest of his striking features.

"Would you like something to drink while we wait?"

The man's question recaptured Skye's attention. She gave him a bemused look. "Wait?"

"Yes. Justin and Lorren are out riding. I've sent a text message letting them know they have a visitor."

"You did?"

"Yes."

She glanced around feeling somewhat embarrassed. She was acting like a sixteen-year-old noticing the opposite sex for the first time, instead of the twenty-six-year-old woman that she was. She'd been too busy checking him out to notice he'd used his cell phone. The one he was now placing back into the pocket of his jeans. Doing so made the denim material stretch tight across muscular thighs. She fought to hold back the little moan that threatened to escape her throat. She'd never reacted this way to a man before. Certainly not to Wayne.

"Introductions are in order, don't you think?" he asked, smiling and offering her his hand. "I'm Slade Madaris."

She took his hand, and the moment their hands touched she felt a tingling sensation flow through every part of her body. She cleared her throat and said, "And I'm Skye Barclay."

His smile deepened. "Skye?" At her nod, he said, "I like that. It's different."

"Thank you. My mother named me after someone she once knew."

"And where are you from, Skye? Although I have to admit that your accent gives you away. You're a New Englander, right?"

She chuckled. "Yes. I'm from Augusta, Maine."

Slade nodded. "The capital city. I've been there once, to a political fund-raiser a few years ago with my uncle Jake."

"Jake Madaris?"

Slade lifted a brow. "Yes, one of my grand-uncles. Do you know him?"

She figured that now was not the time to let Slade know that her private investigator had given her a preliminary report on certain members of the Madaris family and Jake Madaris' name topped the list since he was so widely known on a national level. "I don't know him personally," she replied honestly. "But you don't have to be from Texas to know who he is. Everyone knows he married Hollywood actress Diamond Swain a few years ago and they have two children." A teasing glint shone in her eyes when she then added, "See, I'm caught up on my entertainment trivia."

Slade thought her chocolate-brown eyes held a warmth

that nearly stole his breath. "You did pretty good. Their four-year-old son is Granite and their one-year-old daughter is Amethyst." Then without missing a beat he said, "And you never did give me an answer about that drink. Do you want one while we wait?"

She shook her head. "No, thank you. I'm fine."

It was on the tip of Slade's tongue to say yes, she definitely was fine and in all the right places, but he knew such a comment would be inappropriate. Because of the number of projects Madaris Construction, the company he co-owned with Blade, had acquired in the last few years, he had basically put his social life on hold. The woman standing before him was making him think that maybe it was time for it to get reactivated. Every nerve in his body was coming to life just by looking at her. In all his thirty-two years he'd never felt remotely attracted to this degree toward a woman before, and he wasn't quite sure just what to make of it. Blade was the playa in the family, the one who assumed it was his God-given right to have any woman he wanted.

Slade studied Skye thinking her age couldn't be any more than twenty-five and she was no taller than five feet, three inches, with what he considered a perfect face: the coloring that reminded you of dark coffee with a smidgen of cream; full lips; high cheekbones; eyes the color of rich chocolate; and copper brown hair styled in twisted curls that stopped short of touching her shoulder blades. Her makeup, if she was wearing any, was light, and instead of lip coloring her lips shone from a touch of gloss.

She was wearing a floral top and matching skirt that complemented her petite figure, and a pair of flat leather shoes that seemed more for comfort than for show—although he thought they looked cute on her small feet. There was something about her that reminded him of a prissy, prim and proper lady. It was there in the gracefulness of her walk and the correctness of her talk. She was yet to slaughter a single verb.

"Would you like to have a seat then, Skye?" he heard himself asking.

Before Skye could answer, a smiling couple practically breezed into the room. From the genuine warmth in the handsome man's incredibly dark eyes that connected to Skye's—which were so much like Slade's—she immediately got a comfortable feeling. And the woman by his side, whose smile was just as radiant as her beauty, sent out an air of friendliness. Skye knew from the private investigator's report that Dr. Justin Madaris was forty-six. She immediately thought he wore his age well. Except for the sprinkling of gray at his temple, he looked younger than his years, and he appeared to be in great physical shape.

Skye's gaze then moved to zero in on Lorren Madaris. At thirty-six she was definitely a beauty with her nutmeg complexion, dark brown hair that fell in soft curls to her shoulders, and eyes the color of rich caramel.

The first thing Skye picked up on was that they appeared happy together, very much in love, which was evident by the way Dr. Madaris was still holding his wife's hand.

"Hello. I'm Dr. Madaris and this is my wife, Lorren. Slade said you wanted to meet with us."

Dr. Madaris' words pulled Skye's thoughts back to the business at hand. She knew that in order to make them understand the reason for her visit she would have to tell them everything, which meant revealing information she herself just recently had discovered.

Sighing deeply, she took a step forward. "Yes, I'm Skye Barclay," she said, offering both individuals her hand and immediately feeling the genuine warmth she had detected earlier radiating from their touch. "And I've traveled from Maine to meet with the both of you," she continued. "It seems the three of us share a common interest in something. Or should I say someone."

She saw a puzzled look appear in their eyes, and a quick glance at Slade, who was standing not far away, showed that same perplexed look in his gaze as well. It didn't go unnoticed that Lorren Madaris instinctively moved closer to her husband's side and he placed an arm protectively around her waist. Slade had taken a step to stand closer to the couple, sending a silent affirmation that as Madarises they stuck together. When Skye thought of just how disjointed her family was, she couldn't help but admire such loyalty.

"And who might that someone be, Ms. Barclay?" Dr. Madaris asked in a clear yet non-intimidating voice.

Skye inhaled deeply. She had rehearsed this part many times over the past few weeks, since finding out the truth of her birth and deciding to make the journey to Texas. But now that the time had come, she was feeling more than slightly nervous. What if Dr. and Mrs. Madaris were not the pleasant couple they seemed? What if once she told them of the nature of her visit they saw her as a threat to their well-ordered life?

"Ms. Barclay?"

She knew that everyone in the room was waiting for her response, and an ingrained need pushed her to give them one. "Vincent."

It was Lorren Madaris who spoke, and the question seemed to tremble off her lips in a soft tone. "Our son Vincent?"

"Yes. Vincent Madaris, your oldest son. I recently discovered that he's my brother."

CHAPTER 2

Skye held her breath for a few tense moments while the other three people in the room stared at her, as if they were trying to make sense out of what she'd said.

Then with a smile that she felt was both gracious and sincere, Justin Madaris cleared his throat and then gestured to a sofa and several chairs, "In that case I think we should sit down and discuss your recent discovery."

She released a deep sigh as she crossed the room to take one of the chairs. The doctor and Mrs. Madaris sat close together on the sofa, and she noted Slade's tall, muscular frame settling in the chair across from hers. He had introduced himself as Justin's cousin, but evidently he didn't consider himself a distant cousin, since by taking the chair and not excusing himself he was making a clear statement that he felt he had every right to remain and listen to whatever it was she had to say.

"Now then," Lorren Madaris said in a soft voice while holding tight to her husband's hand. "Tell us about your discovery."

Skye nervously smoothed the fabric of her skirt across her thighs. She quickly glanced over at Slade. He was staring at her. But then a glance at the Madarises indicated they were staring as well. Everyone was staring and waiting.

The air surrounding her seemed to thicken, and breathing took an effort. But she forced herself to speak. "I discovered a little over a year ago that I was adopted. My parents never told me."

"How did you find out?" The question was asked by Dr. Madaris.

"I stopped by my parents' home one afternoon to visit. They didn't hear me enter and were in the living room discussing me with Aunt Karen, my father's sister. She was trying to convince them it was time to tell me the truth, that I'd been adopted. She thought I had a right to know and that I *should* know, considering the fact that I was getting married within the year."

"You're engaged to be married?" Slade asked, quickly glancing down at her hand and then returning his gaze to hers. She immediately became captured by his intense stare. To break eye contact she glanced at her own hand that was now minus the engagement ring she had worn for a year and a half. She returned her gaze to his. "No. Not anymore."

She decided not to bother them with the details of how Wayne Bigelow had made good his threat last week to call off their wedding if she continued to pursue what he considered a foolish move in flying out to Texas and meeting her brother. Wayne had given her an ultimatum, either him or Vincent.

"You hadn't suspected you were adopted?" Lorren asked.

Skye shook her head. "No, I hadn't had a clue and no reason to think so. It had been a well-kept secret and I was too shocked to ask my parents anything that day. It was another two weeks before I approached them with what I'd overheard."

"And that's when they told you the truth?" Dr. Madaris asked.

"Yes." *But not before they lied and told me I'd heard wrong,* she decided not to add. She also decided it wouldn't be worth mentioning how they'd joined forces with Wayne asking that she not look for her biological mother. The three of them saw her doing so as disrespecting her adoptive parents.

"So what happened next?" Slade inquired.

"I hired a private investigator," she said. *Against my parents' and my fiancé's wishes.* "It took him almost nine months to finally get back with me, and it was then that I found out that my mother had given birth to me when she was sixteen, given me up for adoption, and later gone to college and met the man she married and they had two children."

"And how old are you, Ms. Barclay?" Justin Madaris asked.

"I'm twenty-six."

Lorren gazed at her husband before asking, "And who was your biological mother?"

"Kathy Lester. And she was married to John Lester. They had two children, Vincent and Candice. Kathy, John, and Candice were killed in a car accident almost twelve years ago. Vincent survived the accident."

When Lorren nodded, Skye inhaled deeply and then continued. "It took me several more months to find out what had happened to Vincent. I learned he had first become a ward of the State of Texas since he had no living relatives. Then I discovered that at the age of six he had been adopted by the two of you."

Lorren smiled proudly. "Yes, we adopted Vincent on his sixth birthday and he's been ours ever since. He's so much a part of us that we often forget he's adopted. That might have been what happened in your parents' situation. Over the years the word '*adoption*' had no meaning in the relationship. In our case, of course Vincent knows he's adopted, and remembers his parents and sister, although he was only five when the accident happened. He remembers the happy times he spent with them, and when he was younger he spoke of them."

"But he doesn't anymore?" Skye asked curiously.

"No, he hasn't mentioned them in a long time. We were able to obtain some of their possessions for Vincent, like family pictures, and I think that helps because he has visuals that he can see whenever he wants."

Skye's stomach fluttered at the thought that someone had a picture of her biological mother. That had been the one thing the private investigator hadn't been able to obtain.

As if reading the sudden look of longing in her gaze and understanding it, the older woman asked when she met Skye's eyes, "Would you like to see the pictures, Skye?"

Skye smiled as a happy thrill shot to every part of her body. This was almost too much to hope for. "Yes, please. If you don't mind."

Lorren waved such a thought away as she stood. "Of course we don't mind. I'm sure all of this, finding out you were adopted and have a brother, had to have been an awesome experience for you."

"Yes, it was," she said softly. *And the impact could have been softened if I'd gotten support from my parents and fiancé,* she thought. But it was as if the very idea of her finding out the truth had bothered her parents for some reason. And as for Wayne, what had been important to her just hadn't mattered to him. From the day they'd started dating, it had always been all about him. She had put up with it only because her parents thought the two of them were a perfect match and she'd always wanted to please her parents.

"Would anyone care for something to drink while I'm up?" Lorren asked.

"Yes, sweetheart, a glass of wine would be nice," Justin said, smiling at his wife. "I'll pour the drinks while you get those albums."

Standing, he glanced over at Slade and Skye. "Would the two of you care for anything?"

Skye, who'd felt her throat drying up earlier, said, "Yes. I'd like a glass of wine, too. Thanks."

"Same here, Justin," Slade replied.

While Justin walked over to a bar set up in the corner of the room, Skye glanced over at Slade. Once again she was captured by his intense stare. A part of her wondered if he'd somehow known she'd deliberately left out parts of the information she'd share with everyone?

"What about your father?"

She blinked upon realizing Slade had spoken. "My father?"

He nodded. "Yes, your biological father. Have you tried locating him as well?"

Slade's words filled her mind, and she tried concentrating on them and not on him. An atmosphere of sensuality surrounded him, to a degree she definitely wasn't used to in a man. She struggled to calm the unfamiliar emotions rising within her as she responded to his question. "No, although I'd like to. But it seemed to take forever to get the information on my mother and more than anything I wanted to know about her first."

Skye thoughtfully nibbled on her lower lip. She didn't want to think how her parents would feel if she began getting information on her biological father as well.

"Here's your drink, Skye."

She glanced up and looked into the eyes of a smiling Justin Madaris. She accepted the wineglass he handed to her. "Thank you."

At that moment Lorren Madaris returned with several large photo albums. She smiled over at Skye. "I think John Lester's favorite pastime was taking pictures of his family, and I'm thankful for that," she said, handing the albums over to Skye. "And I know this has to be a very special moment for you, one you might want to experience alone. We're going into the kitchen for a while to give you your privacy."

"Thank you." Once again Skye was appreciative of the woman's understanding and insight. Somehow Lorren Madaris understood her need to see the pictures for the first time alone. It would be like unveiling a part of her history. She would be seeing photos of her mother, sister, and brother. They were another family she hadn't known existed.

She watched Justin and Lorren turn to leave. Lorren stopped and sent Slade, who hadn't moved out of his chair, a questioning look. "Slade?"

He glanced at Lorren and Justin before moving his gaze to Skye. Skye felt her skin tingle when he stared at her for a second before giving her a soft smile. "I'm staying with her," he said simply.

Skye's heart stuttered at his words, and when Justin and

Lorren glanced back at her, seeking confirmation that it would be okay for him to remain, she nodded. For some reason she wanted Slade to stay. "Yes, that's fine," she said softly.

After Justin and Lorren left the room, Skye glanced over at Slade. He still hadn't moved out of the chair, and his encouraging smile sent a wave of goose bumps over her skin. "Go ahead and look at the photos, Skye. I'm going to be right here, if you need me."

His words touched her. He didn't know her. He had met her less than an hour ago, yet Slade Madaris had done something in that time frame that Wayne hadn't done in all the years he'd known her. Slade was making himself available to her. Unselfishly. Somehow he understood the impact seeing the photos might have on her and hadn't wanted to leave her alone. She was overwhelmed by such thoughtfulness and caring coming from a total stranger.

"Thank you," was the only thing she could think to say, too filled with emotion to say anything else at the moment.

She noticed her hands trembling as she opened the first photo album. Her heart caught immediately. She swallowed hard. The very first photo was that of her mother, standing alone under a huge sycamore tree. She was smiling for the camera, for her husband. As Skye studied the picture, the first thought that came to her mind was, *I favor her a lot. We have the same oval face, the same dark brown almond-shaped eyes, and the same-shaped lips.*

There was no doubt in Skye's mind that she was this woman's child. She inhaled deeply at the thought that Kathy Lester had been the one who'd given birth to her. Her biological mother.

As Skye continued to slowly turn the pages, she knew this first album was one that John Lester had put together as a loving tribute to the wife he adored. And from the way Kathy Lester was smiling back into the lens of the camera, one would know that she loved her husband as well. No matter what mistake she'd made at sixteen, Kathy had found true love and happiness in later years with John Lester.

Skye couldn't help but wonder if her mother had told John about her, about the child she'd given up for adoption at sixteen. A part of Skye wanted to believe that she had. She wanted to believe her mother and her husband had shared a relationship based on love and trust and there hadn't been any secrets between them.

Skye then wondered if it had been a hard decision for Kathy to make in giving her up. Had she held her in her arms before doing so? Or did she have domineering parents who had left her no choice in the matter? Parents who'd made the decision for her.

Skye closed the first album and placed it aside and opened the second. She was tempted to glance over at Slade, but she knew he was there, quietly sitting in the chair, sipping his wine and watching her. The first photo she came to nearly made her heart stop. It was a family portrait, probably the last one the four members of the Lester family had had taken together. Kathy Lester looked radiant and gorgeous, her husband handsome, and her two children were beautiful.

Skye studied the face of the little boy in the photo, who couldn't have been more than four when the picture had been taken. Like his mother's, his face was oval, his eyes dark brown and almond shaped. But he had the smile and dimples of his father.

Her gaze then moved to the little girl who was probably not quite two yet. Skye's breath caught at how much the little girl favored her when she'd been that age. She stared at the photo, thinking of the loss of her mother and sister, their husband and father. Vincent. The four had lost one another in a way that could never be changed. And in a way she had lost them, too. Everyone but Vincent. A shiver of happiness ran through her knowing there was now more than a possibility that she could meet the brother she never knew she had.

"Are you okay, Skye?"

Slade Madaris' voice filled the room. It was deep, sexy, concerned. A long pause ensued before she finally said, "Yes, I'm okay."

But even as she was saying the words, she swiped at the tears that came into her eyes and she knew she was headed toward an emotional meltdown, one she'd tried fighting since discovering she'd been adopted. But she couldn't fight it any longer. Although she tried holding them back, the tears kept coming.

Suddenly, the album was taken out of her hand. She felt herself being pulled up from the chair, and her throat seemed to squeeze shut when large, strong arms wrapped around her, pulled her close to a solid, muscular frame. She automatically leaned into Slade, totally mesmerized not only by his touch but by his tenderness. He was comforting her and she clung to him, as if he were the life preserver she desperately needed in this massive storm she was going through.

More tears came and he wrapped her tighter into his warm embrace. Her mind became blurry. She didn't want to question why Slade was giving her—a woman he didn't know—so much attention. All she cared about was the fact that he was doing so.

"That's it. Let it all out, Skye. Cry for each of them. Cry for your loss. Theirs. It's okay."

She squeezed her eyes shut, and did just what he suggested. She cried for her loss. She wanted to let go of the hurt, the pain, and the betrayal, but the latter was hard because even now a part of her felt there were things regarding her adoption that her parents weren't telling her, were deliberately keeping from her.

But she didn't want to think about any of it now. At the moment all she could think about was being held in the arms of a man who was becoming less and less of a stranger.

Slade Madaris was fast becoming her hero.

CHAPTER 3

Skye wasn't sure how long she stood there, wrapped in Slade's arms. But she knew her tears had stopped, her trembling had ceased. Yet he continued to hold her, and she made no attempt to step back. She got comfort being held by him. She heard the steady and strong beat of his heart, inhaled his manly scent, and marveled in his warm embrace. He continued to hold her tight to him; then, he eased away slightly while maintaining his hand at her waist and asked quietly, "Do you want to go for a walk?"

She looked up at him. "Yes."

"I'll let Justin and Lorren know."

He walked away from her and she heard the sound of the door opening and closing. She inhaled deeply and glanced around, actually noticing her surroundings for the first time. The room was neatly decorated and the furniture was sturdy and solid, which immediately reminded her of Slade.

Numerous questions flooded her mind. Just who was Slade Madaris? His name had never come up in any of the reports from the private investigator she'd hired, but then, from what she'd gathered, the Madaris family was a rather large one.

A shiver snaked up her spine when the door opened again and he was standing there, smiling. He crossed the room to her. "Ready?"

She met his gaze and nodded. "Yes."

He tucked her hand in his before grabbing a wide-brimmed

hat off the rack. Moments later he led her out through the French doors.

With the Stetson on his head, Skye thought Slade Madaris looked even more like a cowboy and could easily be one of those male models who posed for western wear. And he walked with the grace, style and ease of a man who was confident with who he was and where he was going.

She couldn't help but admire that in him. Wayne had constantly needed assurances from her, someone to constantly stroke his ego and would get annoyed with her those times she didn't. His parents, as well as her own, treated him like a king and he'd expected her to follow suit. She could imagine the disaster she would have faced eventually if the wedding had taken place as planned.

Skye followed Slade along the brick walkway, grateful she had worn low shoes. Then he opened a wrought-iron gate and her breath caught.

When she'd first driven up the long driveway, she'd thought the massive ranch-style structure was simply beautiful, and now, seeing the beauty of the land it encompassed, she thought that it was doubly so. And what touched her more than anything was the marker that had been erected at the turnoff. Justin had named the ranch in honor of his wife. It was called Lorren Oaks.

Skye and Slade continued walking. It was a beautiful day, the last week in May, and the poignant scent of bluebonnets filled the air. Her fingers entwined in his reminded her that he was close. Not only that, but they were connected. But she didn't need that as a reminder. His sheer presence beside her was overpowering.

"So, Skye Barclay, what exactly do you do back in Augusta?"

His voice flowed over her like warm honey and she tilted her head and glanced up at him. "I'm an accountant for a real estate firm. What about you? What do you do here in Ennis?"

He smiled. "I'm an architect. My twin brother and I—"

"You have a twin brother?"

He grinned. "Yes. His name is Blade and he's eight minutes older, but we aren't identical twins. Blade and I own a construction company in Houston. I'm here visiting Justin and Lorren for a few days, doing some work for them. They're enlarging the place and want me to design it."

Skye glanced back at the massive ranch house and then back at Slade. "Enlarging it? You're kidding, right?"

He chuckled. "No. They're adding what one would think of as mother-in-law quarters for Lorren's foster mother. Mama Nora is well up in age and has finally agreed that her house in town is too much for her and plans to sell it and move in with Justin and Lorren."

"Lorren has a foster mother?"

"Yes, like Vincent, Lorren's parents were killed in a car accident when she was a kid. I believe she was eight or nine at the time. And without any living relatives she became a ward of the state. Mama Nora and her late husband, Paul, were Lorren's foster parents. In fact, they were foster parents to several kids."

Skye nodded. No wonder Lorren had understood her need to see the photos in those albums, her need to connect to the mother she hadn't known.

"So what are your plans, Skye, regarding Vincent? What happens after you meet him?"

She shrugged. "That depends on Justin and Lorren. They'll know better than anyone if Vincent is ready for me to be a part of his life. I'm sure he doesn't know anything about me, and I'm concerned how he might feel upon discovering that his mother gave up a child for adoption at the same age he is now."

A part of Slade understood her concern. "You're right that Justin and Lorren would be the ones to know whether Vincent is ready to handle something like that, but a part of me thinks that he is. He was only five when he lost his parents, and although I'm sure they'll always have a permanent place in his heart, I also know that he considers Justin and Lorren his parents. No matter who he was before, Vincent is definitely a Madaris now. And at sixteen he's far more mature than most young people his age. He's secure in his parents' and family's love, and it shows. He does well in school, is selective with his friends, and is family oriented to a fault. He's a great kid."

Skye smiled. "I really do hope that I can meet him."

"I'm sure you will. He's at school now and won't be home for a few more hours if he doesn't have soccer practice."

She glanced over at Slade, surprised. "He plays soccer?"

"Like he was born for the game."

A giggle bubbled up in Skye's throat upon hearing that. "Umm, isn't that interesting. I played soccer while in high school as well, and I got offered a scholarship to play in college."

"Did you take it?"

She shook her head, remembering her disappointment. "No, my parents wouldn't let me. They felt they could afford to send me to college without the help of a scholarship. Besides, the university I wanted to attend was somewhere in Florida and they felt that was too far from home."

"So where did you attend college?"

"The University of Maine, right there in Augusta. But I did get to live on campus." She decided not to add that she had appreciated being away from her parents' prying eyes. To say that Tom and Edith Barclay had been the epitome of strict parents would be an understatement.

"So what do you think of this place?" Slade asked when they stopped walking.

She glanced around before smiling up at him. "I think Lorren Oaks is simply beautiful."

Besides the massive ranch house, they had passed a barn that housed several horses, and the part of the ranch where Justin's medical facility was located. A cluster of oak trees lined the walkway that led to several corrals. The scenery was beautiful, and it was a nice day for a walk. She was glad Slade had invited her. She could imagine Vincent living here, learning to ride horses and taking walks along these paths.

"Ready to go back?"

Somehow the thought of going back was a downer. She liked being out here in the fresh open sky with him. "Yes, and thanks for taking the time to take me for a stroll," she said. "It was very kind of you to do so."

"No problem. I could tell your heart was pretty heavy and that you needed to get out, breathe in a bit of fresh air."

"I did and I feel a lot better now."

"There is one thing I want to ask you about, though, before we head back."

"Yes?" She looked up at him. They had stopped walking and were facing each other. His eyes held her captive, and his hands were still holding hers. He was a handsome man with a beautiful smile. She studied his features, fascinated.

"You mentioned things had ended between you and your fiancé and that you were no longer engaged. Is there a possibility the two of you might work things out and get back together?"

Skye breathed in deeply, not sure why he was asking but knowing she would tell him the truth. She reflected on the last conversation she'd had with Wayne and all the cruel things he'd said. And not for the first time she wondered why her parents thought he was the perfect match for her when it was plain to see that he was not.

She shook her head. "No, there's no possibility that Wayne and I will get back together. There won't ever be a wedding between us."

Slade nodded, and without saying anything further, they began walking back toward the ranch house.

Lorren Madaris met them at the entrance to the wrought-iron gate with a huge smile on her face. "I hope the two of you are hungry, since I took the liberty to prepare lunch for everyone."

Slade grinned. "That sounds like a winner to me. If you ladies will excuse me, I'm going to wash up."

He walked away, leaving them alone. Skye didn't answer Lorren immediately because, quite frankly, she didn't know what to say. Things were certainly not going the way her parents and Wayne had warned her they would. They claimed Justin and Lorren would see her interference in their lives as a threat to their adopted son and would not want her and Vincent to get to know each other. They also felt that because of Jake Madaris' wealth and personal connection to key political figures, the Madarises would make her life a living hell. Her parents and Wayne wanted her to let what was in the past remain in the past and look forward to a future with Wayne.

"Skye? Are you all right?"

She met Lorren's gaze. "Yes. No." She inhaled deeply, knowing her answers were probably confusing the woman. "What I mean is that I really don't know. You and Dr. Madaris are certainly not taking this the way I thought you would."

Lorren chuckled as she tucked a curl behind her ear. "And how did you think we would take it? You've fully explained how Vincent is your brother and we believe you. We have no reason not to."

"And you don't see my coming here as a threat?"

Lorren chuckled again. "Of course not. Why would we? We see you as someone who, for the past year or so, has been seeking answers, which led you here to meet the brother you hadn't known you had. Vincent is not a child. He's sixteen years old, so I doubt you'd want to stake any guardianship claim on him at that age. Besides, a judge would let Vincent decide who he would want to live with until he's eighteen. No, Justin and I don't see you as a threat. But what I do see when I look at you is someone who's ecstatic about finding her brother but who's afraid to show it for some reason."

Skye inhaled deeply. Lorren's assessment was right on the money and Skye wondered how she'd known. "What makes you think that?" she asked softly.

"Umm, just a hunch. I was raised in a foster home and although I made numerous friends among the others who lived there with me, one in particular who to this day I consider my very dearest and closest friend, I would have been ecstatic, jumping for joy, totally elated, if someone would have shown up one day claiming to be a brother or sister I hadn't known about. It would not have mattered to me if they would have been an outside child of my father or a child my mother had given up for adoption. Just the thought that the person was related to me in some way would have sent me skyrocketing past heaven."

"B-but what if Vincent doesn't feel that way? What if he sees my appearance as an invasion into what he has here with the two of you and your other children?"

Lorren shook her head. "He won't. I know my son, Skye. He's a very mature young man who's too secure in our love for him to think that way. Besides that, he's a lot like Justin. Vincent is a deeply caring individual and he loves family."

Lorren got quiet for a few minutes and then she added, "I can remember distinctly the first day I met Vincent. Justin and I were dating and he invited me to go camping with him one weekend. He was a volunteer at the Children's Home Society and had planned to take a few of the little guys along. All of them were absolutely precious, but there was something about Vincent that immediately captured my heart. He was the youngest in the group and the most withdrawn. Justin later explained what had happened to his family and my heart went out to him because I had lost my parents the same way, in an automobile accident. I think I fell in love with him that day, and when Justin and I married one of the first things I wanted to do was make Vincent our son. We adopted him before we'd been married three months. In all the ways that matter he's ours, but I'm realistic and secure enough in our relationship with him to accept that he has other family as well."

Skye wondered why her own parents couldn't be as secure in their relationship with her. Why did they feel her uncovering information about her biological parents meant that she didn't care as much for them? "Thanks for sharing that with me, Mrs. Madaris."

Lorren smiled. "Please call me Lorren, and I have a feeling that in the future we'll be seeing a lot of each other."

Skye smiled. She hoped what Lorren said was true.

Slade flipped open his cell phone the moment he walked out of the guest bathroom. "Yes?"

"It's Blade. Luke's here. When are you coming home?"

Slade shook his head, grinning. Blade hated talking on mobile phones, so his words tended to be short and to the point. "My work here is almost finished and I was planning to return this weekend, but I'll let you know on that."

"If your work is almost done, what's keeping you there?"

It was an ongoing joke in the Madaris family that Blade had ways like their cousin Clayton, who was Justin's youngest brother. Both had a tendency to ask a lot of questions. Sometimes Slade wondered why Blade hadn't followed Clayton's footsteps and become an attorney instead of the engineer that he was.

"Slade, I asked what's keeping you there?"

Slade glanced across the way to where he saw Skye still talking to Lorren. He then thought about the revitalization of his social life. "Just a minor detail. How long will Luke be in town?" Luke Madaris was another cousin their age and was well-known on the circuits as a rodeo star. Because of his busy schedule, his trips back home were infrequent.

"Luke's going to be here for at least a week. Great-Gramma Laverne sent for him."

"Why?"

"Someone mentioned to her that he won't be making the family reunion in July due to some rodeo show. She wants him to look her in the face and tell her he won't be coming."

Blade then chuckled and added. "As usual, she's claiming this is her last reunion and wants to see all her children, grands, great-grands, and great-great-grands."

A slow smile spread across Slade's lips. It was hard to believe that at three years short of facing ninety the matriarch of the Madaris family was still as feisty as ever. "You know what's going to happen, don't you, Blade?"

"Yes. Luke's going to drop whatever plans he's made and be at that reunion. Do you blame him?"

"No." And that was the truth. The last thing anyone with a lick of sense would want was to get on Felicia Laverne Madaris' bad side. Besides, if Luke was to miss the family reunion this year and something did happen to their great-grandmother before the next reunion, Luke would be fearful the old gal would come back and make his life a living hell until his dying day.

"Something else you ought to know," Blade was saying.

"What?"

"Great-Gramma Laverne dreamed about fish last night. Everyone is hoping it's not Syneda."

Slade laughed. Syneda was their cousin Clayton's wife. The family thought that Clayton and Syneda's four-and-a-half-year-old daughter, Remington, was a handful, and the thought of them adding another child to their already chaotic household was too much to think about.

"Have you ever considered that with your track record, twin brother, her fish dream could possibly mean that one of your—"

"Don't even think it, Slade. I'm too careful for that. Besides, I do women. Not babies. Luke and I will look for you this weekend. If something comes up and you can't make it back, let us know."

Blade then clicked off the line.

A few minutes later, Slade was opening the French doors to join Justin, Lorren, and Skye on the veranda for lunch.

"We thought you'd gotten lost," Justin said, grinning.

Slade chuckled as he sat down at the table. "I got a call from Blade letting me know that Luke's in town. Great-Gramma Laverne sent for him."

"Poor Luke," Lorren said, grinning.

"Who's Luke?" Skye asked curiously, and hoped she wasn't out of place for doing so.

Evidently she wasn't, since Justin didn't waste time answering her. "Lucas, who we all call Luke, is one of my cousins and he's the same age as Blade and Slade, just a few months younger. He's a well-known rodeo star around these parts."

"Really?" she asked, taking a sip of her iced tea.

"Yes, really," Slade said, smiling, liking the sound of her voice whenever she talked. "Have you ever been to a rodeo?"

She shook her head. "No. I've watched one on television, though."

Slade laughed. "That doesn't count. You have to see one live, from inside the arena. That's the only way you can really get your adrenaline pumping. If you hang around long enough I'll make it my business to take you to one," he said simply.

His words surprised Skye. From the tone of his voice she had no doubt that he meant it, and where she came from such a statement would constitute a planned date. "Thanks, Slade, I'd like that. And I hope to be around awhile, that is, if Justin and Lorren approve."

Justin reached across the table and captured Lorren's hand in his. "Lorren and I have no reason not to approve. I think Vincent will be excited when he finds out he has a sister."

"Even one who's ten years older?" she asked, still not sure of the situation.

Justin chuckled. "Yes, even one who is ten years older."

Skye bit into the delicious chicken salad sandwich Lorren had prepared, thinking that she really hoped so. Everyone seemed to believe that Vincent would be fine in meeting her, and she just hoped they were right.

She felt Slade's eyes on her and glanced over at him. Her stomach jittered a little when their gazes connected. There was this attraction between them. She had felt it from the first, the moment he had opened the door. She idly took a sip of her tea, and instead of concentrating on Slade she glanced over at Justin and Lorren.

From what Skye had read, they'd been married around ten years, and it was plain to see they were still very much in love. Lorren practically glowed in Justin's presence, and certain things they did together seemed to come naturally, without much thought. The way they touched frequently, gazed at each other, and the smiles they exchanged. She thought about her own parents who'd been married five years before she'd come into the picture. The only time they came together was for family emergencies, such as when she'd found out about her adoption. Then they had been a united front against her and her decisions. Other than that it was all show. Oh, she believed that in their own way they loved her, but to them it was and always had been about dominating her life.

"So where are you staying while in town, Skye?"

She glanced up at the sound of Lorren's voice. "At the Caprice Hotel."

"That's a nice place, but we can't have you staying there," Lorren said, smiling. "You're welcome to stay here with us if you like."

Skye was taken aback by the invitation. "I can't possibly do that."

"Sure you can. We have plenty of room. And once you

meet Vincent you'll want to spend time with him, won't you?"

"Yes, but—"

"Then it's all settled. Slade can go back with you to town to help you with your things. You don't mind, do you, Slade?"

"No, not at all."

The sound of Slade's husky baritone, as well as the intensity of the gaze looking at Skye, sent shivers all through her.

Lorren smiled at everyone at the table. "Then it's all settled. Skye is officially our houseguest."

"Have you ever known such a bossy woman?" a grinning Slade asked Skye moments later while they finished off the rest of their lunch. Justin had a patient scheduled at one o'clock and had left for his office in the back, and Lorren had gone to pick their other two kids, Justina and Christopher, up from the bus stop. Justina was nine and Christopher was six.

Skye smiled as she glanced over at Slade. "Have you?"

Slade laughed. "Yes. As far as I'm concerned, all the women in the Madaris family are that way. What about your family?"

She shrugged. "I was my parents' only child. My mother didn't have any siblings, and since my father's only sister Aunt Karen's husband passed away before they had children, I didn't have cousins. But my family did have friends who had kids my age."

She didn't want to go into details of just how snooty those kids had been, so she had never fully developed friendship with any of them. She had practically gone through school being a recluse. Since her parents had selected her friends and she hadn't liked the ones they'd picked, she had basically done without.

"Must have been lonely for you growing up," Slade said, reaching out and tucking a twisted curl behind her ear.

She thought about what he said for a long moment or two, then said, "I didn't know it at the time, but now I can see that it was. But I did a lot to stay busy. I had my piano and ballet lessons. I also learned to speak French and Japanese, and then when I was old enough to do sports I had soccer."

He gave her a half smile. "For some reason I can't see you out on a field playing soccer. You seem too prissy for something like that."

She chuckled. "Trust me, my parents almost convinced me of that same thing, but luckily Aunt Karen came to my rescue. She got them to understand that every child needs some type of physical activity in their lives."

At that moment Slade's cell phone went off. After checking the caller ID he smiled over at her. "Excuse me a moment. It's my office calling."

"Sure."

Skye watched him walk off and suddenly images of Justin and Lorren Madaris filtered through her mind. It was so easy to see that they had a solid marriage; one that could handle anything that came their way. It was one built to last. That's what Skye wanted one day for herself: a marriage where she and her husband would enjoy growing old together—through the good times and the bad—a solid marriage where they would love each other forever.

She was convinced now more than ever that she would not have had that type of marriage with Wayne, so any misgivings she'd felt about his ending their engagement were not necessary. Whether Wayne or her parents realized it or not, he had done them both a favor. And for that she was eternally grateful.

She looked up when Slade returned. He glanced at his watch and then said, "Vincent should be here in an hour or so. I asked Justin before he left and he said there's no soccer practice today."

Skye set her glass of iced tea down on the table beside her when her hands began to tremble. Just thinking about meeting her brother for the first time had her feeling anxious. She took a deep breath to calm her nerves.

"You aren't getting all nervous on me, are you?" Slade came over to the table and sat down beside her and asked, flashing those sexy dimples of his.

She returned his smile. "Should I be?"

He shook his head. "What do I have to do to convince you that everything is going to be all right? We're Madarises and we're known for our warm southern hospitality. We plan to make you feel right at home."

Gosh, in a way she hoped not. But then Slade had no way of knowing just how her home life had been at times. Especially lately. Her father had somewhat mellowed, but her mother had not. She actually seemed resentful and hurt.

"I hear a car pulling up. It's probably Lorren returning with Justina and Christopher."

A few minutes later they could hear the front door open and then slam shut. A loud, masculine teenage voice then called out, "Mom. Dad. I'm home."

Skye's throat tightened and the hand at her side clenched. She knew the person who'd just walked in the door had to be Vincent. She met Slade's gaze, and he gave her an encouraging smile. "Remember what I told you," he whispered calmly as he stood. He then reached out, captured her hand, and pulled her up beside him.

She nodded. She not only wanted to remember everything he'd told her, but she wanted to believe it as well. She glanced toward the doorway when a teenage boy walked in. Her breath caught. At sixteen Vincent Madaris was already a very handsome young man. She could imagine how he would look ten more years from now. He was lanky as well as tall, but not as tall as Justin and Slade. However, Vincent had to be at least six feet already. He favored the younger pictures she'd viewed earlier in the photo album, and he was smiling.

"Hey, Slade, where is everyone?" he asked, coming into the room.

When Slade moved out of the way, Vincent noticed Skye when he walked closer into the room, and with manners that were lacking in a lot of teens his age, he offered her his hand, smiling. "Hello, I don't think we've met. I'm Vincent Madaris. Are you Slade's friend?"

At that moment Skye felt all kinds of turbulent emotions and fought the tears that wanted to form in her eyes when she stared into the face of her brother. She had to swallow the huge lump in her throat but couldn't do anything about the influx of feelings that suddenly filled her heart.

"And I'm Skye Barclay," she forced herself to answer in a calm voice that to her ears still sounded somewhat shaky. She glanced at Slade before smiling back at Vincent and saying, "And yes, I'm Slade's friend."

And deep in Skye's heart she believed that statement was true.

CHAPTER 4

"Vincent! Your dad and I didn't expect you home from school this early," a breathless Lorren said, quickly walking into the room with two kids on her heels. The little girl was a replica of her mother, while the little boy favored Justin.

"Hey, Mom," Vincent said, smiling. He then crossed the room to give Lorren a huge hug and kiss on the cheek. "With only one more week of school left before summer vacation begins, the teachers decided to end the school day an hour early for the rest of the week."

Lorren smiled. "You've met Skye, right?"

Vincent returned his mother's smile. "Yes. She's Slade's friend."

Lorren nodded before proceeding to introduce Skye to her other two kids.

"Are you Slade's girlfriend?" six-year-old Christopher asked, staring at Skye with wonder and curiosity in his eyes.

"He's never brought a girlfriend to our house before," nine-year-old Justina tacked on.

Skye shook her head, grinning. "No, I'm not Slade's girlfriend. We're just friends."

"Okay, that's enough questions, you guys. Skye will be staying with us for a few days, so all of you will get the chance to chat with her some more later. It's homework time."

Lorren glanced at Skye and Slade. "Excuse me for a minute. I need to get them settled in the study." She then said to Vincent, "Go let your dad know you're home."

"All right." Vincent quickly left the room to do as his mother instructed.

Lorren glanced over at Skye and gave her an assuring smile. "We'll talk with him after dinner. Now is probably a good time for Slade to help get your things from the hotel. By the time the two of you get back, dinner will be ready."

"All right, and thanks." Skye knew her voice sounded weak and shaky, but that couldn't be helped. At the moment every part of her felt the same way.

"This is everything?"

Skye nodded as Slade reached down to take the one piece of luggage from her. She smiled at the amazement in his voice and said, "I travel light."

The smile he returned had her toes tingling. "If you do, then you're the only woman I know who does."

Skye walked beside him out of the hotel to Justin's truck. They had left her rental car back at Lorren Oaks. A part of her still couldn't believe that Justin and Lorren had invited her to be their houseguest, which only proved what kind and thoughtful people they were.

And she appreciated the fact that instead of following her up to her hotel room, Slade had waited downstairs in the lobby while she packed, giving her privacy. The thought of them in a hotel room together did crazy things to her mind. Besides, the last thing she needed was for him to be standing around while she cleared the hotel's dresser drawers of her underthings, not that there was anything so spectacular about white cotton panties and bras. Like most women, she liked nice underthings, but the ones she wore tended to be of the traditional kind. When she and Wayne had begun sharing a bed, she'd tried changing her taste in lingerie for him, trying to appear sexy. Once Wayne had seen her in something she thought would turn the heat up in the bedroom, he'd said that wearing something like that, she reminded him of a floozy. So she had gone back to plain white cotton.

"You're quiet. You're not getting all nervous on me again, are you?"

Skye glanced up at Slade when they made it to the truck and he was opening the backseat to put her luggage inside. She wondered what he'd think if he knew her thoughts had been on her plain-Jane underwear. "No, I'm not getting nervous, although I'm wondering what's next."

Slade chuckled. "When we get back, we'll all sit at the table and eat the delicious meal that I know Lorren is preparing. But then it could be Justin who's doing the cooking, since that's a task they share. Afterward, you, Justin, and Lorren will break the news to Vincent as to who you really are."

Skye sighed. "You'll be there, too, won't you?"

He stared down at her before opening the truck door. Skye had just realized how close they were standing to each other. "If you want me there, then I'll be there."

"Yes. I want you there."

Slade nodded as he opened the door for her to get in. Earlier that day, when she had been looking at the photo albums, he hadn't asked if she had wanted him there or not; he'd just known that he had to stay. And then later the tears he'd seen in her eyes had done more to him than cause a tightness in the pit of his stomach. Her tears had touched him because he'd known they were sincere. Although he hadn't known her long, he truly believed there was nothing phony or counterfeit about Skye Barclay. What you saw was just what you got. And deep down he knew she would eventually be his downfall, because he wanted her.

That tightness in his stomach moved to his chest with that realization. He'd been told several times that men in the Madaris family knew the woman they wanted once they met her. Justin said it had been that way with Lorren the first time he'd seen her one night at a party. But then there were those, like Justin's brother Dex and Slade's uncle Jake, who'd recognized the women for them however, had tried like hell to fight it . . . only to eventually lose the battle.

Slade knew that he was not a man to do things on a whim. He usually thought through any and every decision he made. Not every woman captured his eye. Nor did he make the time to wine and dine each and every one he was attracted to. In other words, he was what Blade and Luke had referred to as a slow burn, which was a complete opposite from Blade, who in essence was a lit torch. Blade thought there wasn't a woman alive who could hold his interest for long, so it was Blade's goal to date as many as he could and have the most fun while doing so.

Slade saw himself as a man who'd rather take things slow. He wasn't one to act impulsive or make hasty decisions, especially when it came to a woman. But in one day Skye Barclay had tilted his world, and he was determined to find out more about the woman who'd done such an impossible feat.

"What type of work do your parents do?" he asked, getting in the truck and pulling the door shut behind him.

Skye glanced at him, wondering where that question came from. "My mother never worked outside the home and my father is an accountant, and has been for years."

Slade nodded before turning on the ignition to the truck. "Is that why you became an accountant, because your father was one?"

Skye shook her head. "No. I like working with numbers, and when I was growing up, Dad would take me to the office with him sometimes on the weekends while Mom spent her day at the hair and nail salon. I used to watch him work and eventually made the decision on my own."

She then asked Slade, "Did you always want to be an architect?"

Slade smiled. "Just about. The construction company that my brother and I own was started by my grandfather after he gave up teaching. There were seven Madaris brothers, and Grampa Milton is the oldest. The majority of them were educators, because at the time that was the most profitable profession, but somewhere along the way, after teaching for over ten years, Grampa decided he preferred being outdoors and working with his hands. It was then that he started the Madaris Construction Company."

Slade stopped talking long enough to look around, then proceeded to back out of the parking spot before he continued. "After Grampa retired my father ran the company for a number of years, and then after Blade and I expressed an interest in taking the company to a whole other level with all of today's advancements in computer technology, Dad decided to retire. He signed the entire business over to us."

"Boy, that was some kind of faith that he placed in you and your brother's abilities."

Slade nodded. "Yes, it was, but it only made us determined to succeed. I design the places we build, and Blade, with his engineering degree, is the one who makes sure my design is what the customer gets. We work well together."

"Is it just the two of you?"

"No, I have two younger brothers. Quantum is twenty-four and is in medical school at Howard University, and Jantzen, who is twenty-one, is a senior at Harvard and plans to stay there and work on his MBA for the next couple of years."

Skye found the information about Slade's family interesting and could tell just from how he interacted with Justin and Lorren that the Madaris family was a close one. She wondered how it would be to belong to such a close-knit family. Vincent certainly had been blessed to have Justin and Lorren in his life. She could tell they were positive role models and wonderful parents.

"So what do you think of Vincent?"

Skye stopped staring out the truck's window at the Texas sky and turned her attention across the seat to Slade. He had come to a stop sign and was looking at her. She immediately felt goose bumps skitter over her skin from that look. His eyes were so darn sexy. But then she thought everything about him was sexy and, on top of that, he was such a considerate person.

"Skye?"

"Umm?"

"What did you think of Vincent?"

She blinked. She couldn't believe she'd been sitting there staring at Slade like she'd lost it. "I think he's a clean-cut, all-around American kid who seems to enjoy life. I have to admit he has the manners that a lot of kids his age lack."

Slade laughed. "Trust me, all the members of the Madaris family have a part in that. We totally believe that it takes a village to raise a child, and we all try to do our part. While I was growing up, Justin and his brothers, Dex and Clayton, were Blade's, Luke's, and my mentors, our role models. We knew we could go to them when our parents didn't understand a thing that was going on in our lives. They were great. And then there was always Uncle Jake. He's just swell. Blade, Luke, and I are trying to do what Justin, Dex, and Clayton did for us. We make ourselves available to our younger cousins whenever we can."

Skye smiled. "I think that's wonderful."

Slade nodded. "We think so, too, and although some of those younger cousins are hardheaded and will eventually do what they want to do anyway, we try to give them good, sound advice and make them feel like they can talk to us about anything. Vincent and I are close mainly because I've always been close to Justin. I was in my last year of college when I got word of the adoption, and when I got a chance to meet Vincent I thought he was just what Justin and Lorren needed, and that he needed them as well. At the time he still had some medical problems because of the car accident and appeared somewhat shy and withdrawn. I've watched him grow, mature, and become more confident under his parents' love, and like I said, he's a good kid."

"Other than soccer, is there anything else he particularly likes?" she asked, wanting to know everything there was to know about her brother.

Slade chuckled. "Yes, girls. But he's not as bad as Blade was at his age, so I guess that's a good thing. Vincent is into noticing them, but he's not letting them take over his mind and interfere with his books. I know Justin and Lorren have talked to him, and I've talked to him as well. You have some pretty brazen young girls out there, and if a guy doesn't watch out, he can be a goner. Vincent is too young to get too caught up in the opposite sex now. In another year he'll be graduating from high school with his sights set on college."

"Any idea where he wants to go?"

"Yes. Justin's alma mater, Howard University. They have a very good architecture program."

"He wants to be an architect?"

"Yes, and he has the skill for it. He's helping me design Mama Nora's private quarters and has come up with some pretty good ideas."

They had left the city of Ennis and were heading toward the outskirts of town where Lorren Oaks was located. The small, quaint town of Ennis was a forty-five-minute drive from Dallas, and Skye had discovered upon arriving in town yesterday afternoon that there were more bluebonnets, the official state flower of Texas, around Ennis than anyplace else. And they were beautiful and enhanced the beauty of the roadways.

She sat back in the soft leather seat, appreciating this quiet time between her and Slade. She enjoyed talking with him but didn't want to wear him out. But there was so much she wanted to know about Vincent. And as if Slade read her mind, when the truck came to a four-way intersection he reached over and grabbed her hand and gently squeezed it.

"You won't find out everything you want about him in one day, Skye."

She tried to ignore the little sensuous chill that crept up

her spine from Slade touching her hand. "I know, but I can't believe all of this is happening."

Then, deciding to be honest with him about something, she said, "My parents and Wayne—my ex-fiancé—thought I was making a huge mistake by coming here. In fact, they were dead set against it."

Slade released her hand to resume driving, but she did notice the frown that formed around his lips. "Why were they against it?"

"They thought I would be intruding in the life Vincent had now, a life I had no part of. They felt I had no right to let him know of the mistake his mother had made at sixteen and were even more certain that Justin and Lorren would want to protect him from finding out—in fear of shattering his world."

Slade shook his head, chuckling. "Well, as you can see, things aren't like your parents and your ex-fiancé assumed."

Skye smiled over at him. "No, they aren't."

Skye's smile heated up Slade's insides, and at that moment he decided he just couldn't take it anymore. He had to finally do something, and he knew just what he wanted to do. He glanced around. They were less than a couple of miles from Lorren Oaks and he knew this stretch of highway was seldom used around this time of the day, since most people took the interstate. He pulled Justin's truck off to the shoulder of the road, under a bevy of oak trees. Slade's hands were shaking when he brought the truck to a stop, turned off the ignition, and unbuckled his seat belt.

Skye looked at him, confused. "Slade? Is something wrong?"

He leaned back in the seat and tilted his Stetson back from covering too much of his eyes while looking at her and said, "I'm not sure. I know we just met today and the only reason you showed up at Lorren Oaks was because of Vincent. The last thing you're probably interested in is an involvement with someone. Which is all well and good, but there's something I just got to do, Skye."

He could see the query in her eyes and knew she didn't have a clue what that "something" was. And her next question confirmed it. "What?"

Slade didn't hesitate in giving her an answer. "Kiss you. May I?"

CHAPTER 5

Skye went completely still.

The first thought that went through her mind was that she hadn't heard him correctly, but then all she had to do was look into the darkness of his eyes to see she hadn't imagined anything. He had asked to kiss her.

He had asked . . .

The next thought that immediately ran through her head was that Wayne never asked. Even on their first date he'd just assumed it was okay. After all, he was the most sought-after bachelor in Augusta, a well-known attorney who had a promising future. She should be grateful to be seen in his presence, so to his way of thinking a kiss was something he was entitled to.

But Slade had asked and he was waiting for her answer. She sighed deeply, knowing the only one she could give him. "Yes, you may."

The heat in his eyes should have warned her what she was in for, but when he leaned forward and she saw those sexy lips inching closer and closer toward hers, she was too caught up in the shivers that suddenly began running through her body. When he got close enough, instead of kissing her, he reached out and unsnapped her seat belt. Then he took those same hands and cupped her face, as if to study her features. His gaze was so intense that her heart began missing beats.

And then he was scooting closer and his hands dropped from her face to her shoulders, and then those lips were there, touching hers, moving over them with such tenderness that it almost brought tears to her eyes. When he deepened the kiss, still maintaining a certain degree of tenderness, she almost came out of her seat as sensations slowly began taking over all parts of her body. Never in her life had she experienced a kiss so heartfelt, deep, and passionate. She felt herself moving closer to those lips, and instinctively she wrapped her arms around Slade's broad, muscular shoulders.

She began kissing him back in a way she had never kissed Wayne, mainly because he'd never given her the chance. His belief had been that the art of kissing was male dominant. It was something a man started and a man finished, and usually Wayne's kisses were over before they had a chance to begin. He certainly had never taken the time to stir a blaze within her to the depth of what Slade was doing. And when the tip of his tongue began stroking the tip of hers, she moaned deep within her throat as liquid fire spread from the top of her head all the way to her toes.

How could something so gentle and sweet be filled with so much hunger and desire? And when he deepened the kiss to yet another level, every nerve within her sparked to life as she surrendered to the sensations hitting every part of her.

Moments later he pulled back slightly and began tracing the fullness of her lips, upper and lower, in a way that had intense desire flooding her body. Every cell within her was ignited, lit to an unknown power and sensitized to his touch and taste.

"I think we need to get back on the road," he said huskily while kissing the corners of her mouth.

"I think we need to get back on the road as well," were the only words she could get her mouth to say. It was a mouth he was still licking with the tip of his tongue.

A short while later he pulled back and leaned against his seat, taking a long, deep breath. He glanced over at her. "Thanks. I needed that."

She wasn't sure if it would be appropriate to respond by saying she needed that as well. Instead, she buckled her seat belt and tried to get her insides to stop quivering and her breathing back to normal.

Skye knew what had just happened between her and Slade was illogical, totally insane. It didn't make sense given the fact they'd just met that day. But when she glanced over at him and watched as he readjusted his Stetson on his head, buckled his seat belt, and started the truck's engine, she knew that as insane as it might seem, she had the hots for Slade Madaris and it appeared that he had the hots for her as well.

And at the moment, with her lips still tingling from where his had been, she didn't know just what to think about that.

During the rest of the ride to Lorren Oaks, Skye forced herself to think about it. What Slade had said earlier was true. The very last thing she was interested in was an involvement with someone. After going through all that emotional drama with Wayne, once he had broken the engagement it wouldn't have mattered to her if she'd never encountered a member of the opposite sex again.

But less than two weeks after their breakup she'd let another man kiss her and she had moaned with pleasure. If the truth were to be told, she was still feeling all kinds of tingling sensations through her body. She'd never known a kiss could have such lasting effects.

She glanced over at Slade. His eyes were on the road. They hadn't exchanged more than a few words since the kiss, and the tension in the air between them was so thick you could cut it with a knife.

Justin's truck was a stick shift, and each time Slade shifted gears and pressed down on the clutch, Skye saw how the denim material of his jeans pulled tight across muscular thighs. Where she came from men wore dress trousers more than jeans, but she had to admit that of all the times she'd seen a man in jeans, none had caught her attention in a pair like Slade had. He had to be, without a doubt, the sexiest man she'd ever met. And although it probably wasn't fair to compare him with Wayne, Slade made her ex-fiancé's kisses seem like a waste of good time.

"Do we need to talk about what happened back there, Skye?"

Slade's question in the quiet stillness of the truck's cab intruded into Skye's thoughts. *No, we don't need to talk about it,* she almost said, and then thought twice about it. Yes, they needed to talk about it. She had only one purpose in coming to Ennis, and she couldn't let him or anyone become a deterrent from her goal. She couldn't develop a relationship with her brother and work on building one with Slade at the same time. That would only complicate things. Getting to know Vincent was her priority, and anything else would defeat the purpose of her being here.

"I don't regret what happened back there, Slade," she heard herself saying softly. "But we can't let it happen again. It will only complicate things. The only reason I'm in Ennis is to get to know Vincent. I don't have time for anything else. Do you understand that?"

Slade nodded. Yes, he understood. No matter how attracted they were to each other, nothing could ever come of it. He saw her point, but he didn't have to like it. Whether she realized it or not, as far as he was concerned, something was going on between them that was just as poignant as her wanting to know her brother. And he wanted her to know it. The look of profound sensual pleasure on her face after their kiss had gotten a rise out of him—literally. He'd had to hold himself in check not to keep kissing her, tasting her, getting absorbed in everything about her.

"I think you are a nice person and all," he heard her tack on in a soft voice. "But the last thing I need in my life after breaking off my engagement a few weeks ago is to get involved with anyone else."

When the truck came to the turnoff to Lorren Oaks, he glanced over at her. "I know it's none of my business, but why did you and your ex split up?"

He was right, it wasn't any of his business, but she felt compelled to tell him anyway. At least the watered-down version of it. "Wayne and I didn't see eye to eye on a number of things."

"Like you coming here for instance?"

"Yes."

When he pulled into the driveway and turned off the truck, he sat and stared at her for several long moments before saying, "You're here on a mission, right?"

She'd never thought of it as that, but in a way she guessed she was. "Yes."

"And you prefer staying focused on that mission?"

She nodded, wondering where his line of questions was leading to. "Yes, that's right."

His sexy grin had her stomach tumbling. "Then I guess you can say that I'm on a mission as well, Skye Barclay," he said, slowly unbuckling the seat belt and adjusting his seat back. "And I'll be gracious enough to let you accomplish your mission first."

She swallowed hard. "And then?" she asked, forcing the words past her throat. A different kind of tension was surrounding them, making the palms of her hands feel wet and stirring some kind of indescribable ache inside of her.

Reaching up, he took his finger and smoothed the frown that had formed around her lips. "And then I get started with mine."

He smiled when he felt the shiver that passed through her body and then said, "Come on; I'm sure Lorren is ready to put dinner on the table."

Slade's words were still on Skye's mind as she unpacked her luggage and put her things away in the beautifully furnished guest room Lorren had given her to use. Thankfully, there hadn't been a mad rush to dinner when Skye and Slade had arrived. Instead, Lorren had shown her to her room and given her time to unpack and settle in. Dinner, Lorren said, would be in an hour, which was good timing for Skye.

Before leaving, Lorren had told Skye of her and Justin's planned strategy in telling Vincent about her. After dinner and once the other two Madaris children were put to bed, they would ask Vincent to meet with them in the study. And with Skye and Slade present, Vincent would be told everything. It was important to Lorren and Justin to be totally honest with their son.

Skye understood and appreciated that fact. A part of her wished her parents had been totally honest and up-front with her as well. It didn't bother her that she had been adopted and hadn't been told; what had bothered her more than anything was that once she'd discovered the truth, her parents' attitude about her wanting to find out anything about her birth mother had been almost hostile. They had taken it as a personal affront and had actually stopped speaking to her for a few weeks.

The social worker she had spoken with who had helped to steer her in the right direction in her search for her biological mother had indicated that most adoptive parents weren't that way. Most felt secure enough in their relationship with their child to not be concerned about that.

Skye sighed. Evidently her parents did not feel secure in their relationship with her. Even now she could recall that her mother always seemed distant, even when Skye had been a child. Her father's relationship with her had been different. When her mother hadn't been around he appeared to be more open and loving, which only puzzled Skye as she got older. For some reason she'd always felt that no matter what, secretly he would always be in her corner and if push came to shove, he would have her back. She had definitely been wrong about that. Her wanting to find out about her biological mother had bothered him just as much as it had her mother.

Skye then shifted her thoughts back to Slade and the comment he'd made in the truck about being on his own mission. Was he letting her know of his interest in her? Could that be possible when they'd just met that day? She thoughtfully nibbled on her lower lip as she remembered the look in his eyes just moments before he'd kissed her. The warmth and genuine interest as well the heated desire she'd seen in them had sent shivers through her body, had nearly pushed her over the edge.

But regardless of whether he was interested or not, she had to make sure things didn't go anywhere. Like she'd told him, she would have her hands full in getting to know Vincent. Even now she was wondering how she would manage to spend time with him when he lived here in Texas and she was in Maine. With summer coming up she wondered if he'd made plans for the summer. Would Justin and Lorren be open to letting Vincent come spend the summer with her in Maine? At the very thought of that happening she twirled around the room, thinking of all the places she would take him and all the fun things the two of them would do together.

She glanced over at the clock on the nightstand. The hour was almost over, and she didn't want to hold up dinner. Her stomach did a little flip at the thought of seeing Slade again, but she was determined to make sure he understood that the only thing the two of them could ever be was friends.

Skye glanced across the room at Vincent. He was sitting on the sofa smiling at something his mother was telling him. Although he appeared at ease, he had to be curious as to why he'd been invited to join the adults in his father's study.

Dinner had been a wonderful affair, and the food had been prepared by both Justin and Lorren. Lorren said the two of them enjoyed working together in the kitchen and that Justin was the real cook in the family, especially during those times her profession kept her extremely busy. She was a well-known author of children's stories, and the characters

she'd created for the books, the Kente Kids, were on a popular Saturday morning cartoon show. And if that wasn't
enough, she had begun writing books for preteens and teens,
something Lorren was excited about.

Skye switched her gaze from Vincent to Slade. He was
standing across the room talking to Justin. Then as if Slade
felt her watching him, he looked her way. There was something extremely intimate in the way their gazes connected,
and she couldn't help the warm sizzle that flowed through
her body. She tried dismissing the sensation but couldn't.
Nor could she break eye contact with him. The attraction
they shared seemed unreal, yet she sat there, caught in the
darkness of his eyes, unable to look away.

"Now that we're gathered together . . ."

Skye snatched her gaze away from Slade to place it on
Lorren when she spoke. A smile touched Lorren's lips when
she continued by saying, with her eyes on her son, "There's
a reason you're in here with us, Vincent."

Skye watched curiosity light his eyes. "You didn't call me
in here to tell me that my driving privileges had been re-
voked already, did you, Mom?" he said with a teasing glint
in his eyes.

Lorren laughed and said, "No, sweetheart, not unless you
know something your dad and I don't know."

He shook his head, grinning. "Not a thing." He glanced
over at Skye, smiling, and said, "My parents bought me a car
for my sixteenth birthday, but I'm only allowed to drive it to
school and back for now."

"Boy, you're lucky," Skye replied, returning his smile. "I
didn't get my first car until I was eighteen. Sounds like you
have wonderful parents."

"I do," he said quickly, smiling at Lorren and placing his
arms around her shoulders. He then glanced over at Justin.
"My parents are the best and I wouldn't trade them for the
world."

Skye believed him.

"Well, before things get too sappy in here for my taste," Slade said to Vincent, coming to stand beside the sofa where he was sitting, "I think I need to clarify a few things regarding my relationship with Skye."

Vincent started to laugh. "Let me guess. She's more than just a friend to you."

Slade lifted a brow. "What makes you think that?"

Vincent's smile deepened. "A number of reasons, but the main one is what Justina said. You've never invited a girl to our house before."

"And I didn't invite her," Slade replied. "In fact, Skye and I just met today when she came here to see your parents."

Vincent's eyes showed his surprise. "Really?"

"Yes, really," was Slade's grinning response.

"And the reason for Skye's visit is what your father and I want to talk to you about, Vincent," Lorren said.

Now he really looks puzzled, Skye thought. She watched as Justin pulled out a chair and sat in it, across from his son. And then he said, "Skye brought us some news we think you should know about. It concerns your biological mother."

"What about her?" Vincent asked anxiously. All amusement left his eyes and was replaced by concentrated interest.

It was Lorren who spoke. "Skye discovered that when your mother was sixteen she had a baby and that she gave the baby up for adoption."

It seemed to take a while for Lorren's words to sink in, and all the while Skye noticed that Vincent was staring at her. "My mother had a baby at sixteen that she gave up for adoption?" he asked, not sure he'd heard right. And he was asking the question of Skye.

Her throat tightened when she answered him. "Yes."

He nodded. "Did you know my mom?"

Skye shook her head and took a deep breath before responding, "No, I didn't know her."

"But you know for a fact that at sixteen she had a baby and that she gave it up for adoption?"

Vincent's tone did not indicate he didn't believe what Skye had said, but that he was having a hard time understanding how she would know such a thing. Skye understood why he would be confused. She glanced at Lorren, who nodded, giving Skye the okay to answer Vincent's question in the only way that she could.

"Yes, I know that she did because I hired a very good private detective to find out what he could about her. It was documented in the report he gave me. That's how I found out about you."

It was apparent Vincent was still somewhat confused. "But why would you want to find out anything about my mom?" he asked.

Skye swallowed before explaining things further. "Last year I found out I was adopted and after intense research I discovered the person who gave birth to me, my biological mother, was Kathy Claremont, who later became Kathy Lester."

She watched Vincent's face and knew the exact moment he figured out what she was saying. He leaned forward in his seat, stared at her for an intense moment and then said in a soft voice, smiling, "Hey, that's awesome and that's the reason I couldn't help but think how much you reminded me of her when I walked into the room earlier today when I got home from school. You look a lot like her. My memories of my mother get sketchier and sketchier the older I get, but today you reminded me of her because when I last saw her, she was about your age and, like you, she was very beautiful."

The way he was handling this, as well as his compliment, brought tears to Skye's eyes. "Thank you."

Skye watched as another realization lit Vincent's eyes, one he'd just been hit with. "That means you're my sister," he said in an astonished voice.

Skye nodded, quickly wiping away her tears. "Yes, that means I'm your sister." She knew the crack in her voice could probably be heard by everyone in the room, but at the moment she didn't care.

"Wow! That's cool!"

She then watched as the brother she hadn't known she had stood and crossed the room toward her, with a full grin on his face. She eased out of her chair on wobbling knees and took a deep breath as he got closer. When he closed the distance separating them, he reached out and pulled her into his arms and hugged her. All the fears, doubts, and apprehensions she'd been holding inside since leaving Maine came pouring out, and she clung to him. At this moment in time, he was the only sure thing in her life, and this was a pivotal moment for the both of them. Happiness squeezed her throat and she looked over Vincent's shoulder and saw Justin and Lorren. They were standing together, holding hands, and the smiles on their faces let her know they were pleased with how things had turned out, but hadn't been surprised. They had known their son.

Skye then glanced over at Slade. Their gazes held for the longest time, and then he winked at her and that wink meant everything to her, because in his own way he was letting her know how happy he was for her.

Then Vincent pulled back slightly and grinned up at her. "I'm going to enjoy having an older sister. Thanks for finding me, Skye Barclay. And welcome into my life."

CHAPTER 6

Skye woke up the next morning in the best of moods and immediately reflected on what had happened last night.

Vincent had accepted her as his sister.

She was so elated she wanted to call her parents and Wayne to tell them how wrong they'd been about Vincent and the Madaris family. Vincent's adoptive parents had been kind and had not seen her as a threat, and Vincent had not rejected her. But still, she had a feeling her parents and Wayne wouldn't want to hear what she had to say. They were probably still stewing that she had made the trip and wouldn't want her to call and tell them they had been wrong.

She fluffed her pillow and sat up, thinking how Justin, Lorren, and Slade had given her and Vincent time alone last night to talk. He'd had a million questions for her, and of course she hadn't been able to answer all of them. He wanted her to tell him about adoptive parents and how she'd felt knowing she'd been adopted. He had also been concerned that she was angry with their biological mother for giving her up.

She had assured him she hadn't been and that she could understand why a sixteen-year-old would make such a decision. She told him about her job as an accountant, and he'd told her of his plans to become an architect like Slade. She could tell from the way Vincent talked that he admired his older cousin.

And she had promised Vincent she would be there when he got out of school today. He'd been fearful she would be catching the next plane back to Maine, but she'd assured him that wouldn't be happening and that thanks to Lorren's invitation, she would be their houseguest for the rest of the week.

A giggle bubbled up in her throat when she recalled how he had talked her into a game of soccer to be played when he came home from school today. He tried baiting her by saying he wanted to see if she was any good. She smiled, thinking that she would have to prove to him just how good she was.

Last night she had the best sleep she'd gotten in a long time. After going to bed actually smiling about how Vincent had accepted her, she had later dreamed about Slade. She hadn't intended to, but it seemed so natural for him to invade her dreams. And in her dreams he had kissed her several more times, each hungrier than the last, and she had awakened at some point during the night filled with a kind of ache in the lower part of her body that she'd never experienced before.

Thinking she had lain in bed long enough and the least she could do was check to see if Lorren needed her for anything this morning, she got up and slipped on her robe. She was about to cross the room to go into the adjoining bathroom when a sound from below caught her attention.

She padded in her bare feet to the balcony. The ranch house was huge and elegant, and its air of openness and warmth was breathtaking. Nearly every bedroom overlooked a large enclosed patio, which had a one-of-a-kind swimming pool. Other than at a gym, Skye doubted she'd ever seen a pool so large. Before going to bed she had stood in this very spot and glanced down at the pool with its zigzag shape that had been enhanced with some sort of special lightings. It had been simply beautiful, and to her way of thinking it was stunning now as well, because the man who had filled her dreams full of fantasies last night was there, standing on the diving board, about ready to plunge in.

He was looking so incredibly sexy wearing only a pair of

swimming trunks that showed just what a great physique he had. He actually looked like an Adonis come to life, she thought, giving him a thorough once-over as her gaze moved from the top of his head all the way to his toes before he lunged into the water. The man was perfect. Even his dive into the water was perfect.

Drawing in a deep breath, she stepped back before she was seen and ambled back toward the bed to drop down on it. Jeez. No man had a right to have a body that looked like that. She wondered if what was wrong with her—why she was so attracted to Slade—was the result of neglected hormones. She and Wayne had stopped making love a long time ago. He claimed he was too busy with important court cases. She hadn't doubted him, since he was a man who was obsessed with winning.

Getting up, she decided she couldn't hide out in her room forever. There were certain things that she had to be strong enough to resist, and at the moment Slade Madaris topped the list.

Slade levered himself on the edge of the pool while watching Skye come down the stairs. His gaze took in her every graceful step. Today she looked younger than her twenty-six years, wearing a pair of khaki shorts and a pullover pink blouse and her hair pulled back in a ponytail. He thought that she could pass for a girl of twenty easily.

He had decided to get out of the pool because the heated water was turning cold, but after seeing Skye a cold swim might not be a bad idea. Especially after the dream he'd had of them together last night. As much as he'd tried not thinking about the kiss they'd shared, he had. In fact, his dreams had gone a little further and they had indulged in other things besides kissing. He had awakened that morning expecting to find his sheets scorched.

"Good morning, Slade."

His chest tightened at the sound of her voice. He watched as she made her way around the rattan furniture. "Good morning, Skye. Did you sleep well?"

"Yes, thanks for asking. And I want to thank you for last night."

Surprise sparkled in his eyes. He wondered if perhaps they had shared the same dream, then quickly decided there was no way they could have. "What are you thanking me for?"

"Being here when I met with Vincent. I think your presence helped immensely."

He regarded her closely as he thought about what she had said. "Why do you think that?"

"Because he looks up to you. I can tell. You're a good influence on him, a wonderful role model and that's good."

"Thanks."

"You're welcome."

He began drying off with a huge towel. He glanced up to find Skye watching him. "Is anything wrong?"

Skye didn't trust her voice to speak until she could get her breathing under control. "No, nothing's wrong."

She glanced around, trying to look at anything but him. "Is Lorren back from taking the kids to school?" Lorren had mentioned she would be doing that this morning. And Justin would be going into town. He volunteered his services at the hospital at least one day a week.

"Yes, she's back," Slade responded. "But now she's locked in her office trying to finish this book she's writing. She told me to convey her apologies and that she'll be joining us for lunch. I'm to keep you entertained until then."

"Oh."

He chuckled as he slipped into a pair of shorts and pulled a T-shirt over his head. "You don't sound too happy about it."

Skye managed a tight smile as she sat down at the table. To be honest, she wasn't all that happy about it. Everything about the man, from the sexiness of his voice to those "make you drool" dimples, made Slade temptation at its finest, and she needed to stay focused.

"So what would you like for breakfast? Rubena, their housekeeper, is on vacation, and I was instructed to prepare breakfast for you—whatever it was you wanted."

"No, absolutely not," Skye said, not imagining someone doing such a thing for her. Her parents had a housekeeper, too, but no one had waited on her since she'd moved out of their home. "I don't need you to prepare breakfast for me. A glass of juice is all I need."

"That might be all you want, but it's definitely not all you need. Do you not normally eat a well-balanced meal?"

"Not normally."

"Then I guess today will be your lucky day, because that's one thing I'm good at."

"What?"

"Preparing a well-balanced meal," he said with a smug look on his face. "And if you're afraid I don't know what I'm doing, you're free to join me in the kitchen to watch."

She thought about his invitation but a second, then chuckled and said, "Slade Madaris, you're on."

She did more than watch. Under his encouragement she ended up pitching in. Of course, after explaining her cooking skills lacked any serious anointing, she did some relatively simple things like scrambling the eggs and buttering the toast. And after she convinced him her coffee would probably taste like mud, he had kept her away from the coffeepot. He'd said good coffee to a Texan was just as important as a good horse for him to ride. And when she'd let it slip out that she didn't know the first thing about riding a horse, either, Slade seemed totally shocked.

"There's no way I can let you get back on a plane for Maine without at least introducing you to Basic Horse Riding 101," he said, grinning as they sat down at the table.

"Whatever," she said, grinning, pulling her plate close. "Umm, everything looks delicious. You surprised me. You really do know your way around in the kitchen."

He chuckled. "That's a trait of all Madaris men. We learn early how to fend for ourselves so we won't become helpless at the hands of any of the overzealous ladies."

Skye lifted an eye. "Overzealous ladies?"

"Yes, those who think one way to capture a man's heart is through his stomach."

She grinned as she bit into a slice of bacon. After savoring it and then swallowing, she said, seemingly aghast, "You mean there are women who actually think that?"

"Oh, you would be surprised."

No, she probably wouldn't. When it came to a man like Slade, she could just imagine a woman doing just about anything to gain his attention. It was a good thing she wasn't in the running, because she couldn't cook worth a damn. She wondered what it would take to attract a man like him. Oh, she knew he was attracted to her, but the way she saw it, attraction to the opposite sex for most men came natural. No biggie. Men had a tendency to always think below the belt anyway.

"So, who taught you how to cook?" she decided to ask.

"My great-grandmother, Laverne Madaris. She's in her late eighties and is still one feisty gal. When you've reached a certain age, you begin taking her cooking classes. Vincent will have to enroll in them pretty soon. It wouldn't surprise me if she has gotten something set up for him this summer."

Skye hoped not, especially when she intended to ask Justin and Lorren if Vincent could spend the summer with her in Maine. "Well, your great-grandmother did a wonderful job."

"Thank you."

"Tell me some more about your family. They sound really interesting."

Skye and Slade spent the next half hour finishing their meal and sipping coffee. She liked listening to the sound of his voice when he told her about all the cousins he was close to and admired. He shared fond memories with her about the escapades of his twin, Blade, and his cousin Luke. She could tell from the sound of Slade's voice that they were close and there was nothing one wouldn't do for the other.

After she listened to him, her life seemed so mundane in comparison. She couldn't mention anything that happened during her lifetime that had been earth-shattering, unless you counted the time she caught the wrong bus home from school and got lost for a few hours. She'd been ten at the time and had gotten tired of waiting for the private car her parents would always send for her and decided to do like the other kids and take the bus. That had been a big mistake. Even Congressman Baines, who'd been her father's top client at the time, had gotten all involved. All it had taken was a phone call from him to the Augusta Police Department and they had turned the city upside down looking for her. When she'd been found, it had to have been one of the most embarrassing moments of her life.

"A penny for your thoughts."

She glanced up into Slade's smiling eyes. "Oh, I was just thinking about my one moment of defiance. Happened when I was ten."

"Tell me about it."

"All right."

She told him the story, and telling it to him made her realize just how serious her actions had been at the time. Anything could have happened to her.

"The congressman must have thought a lot of your father to get involved the way he did."

Skye nodded. "My father worked for him for years as his private accountant, and we consider him a close friend of the family."

Slade poured another cup of coffee and said, "Congressman Baines' son is making a name for himself as a very popular and well-liked senator."

"Yes. I don't know Senator Ryan Baines all that well, but I do know he's very popular with a lot of the voters in Maine."

A few moments later and they were finishing up with breakfast. "Now for that riding lesson," Slade said, leaning back in his chair.

Skye lifted a brow. "You're serious, aren't you?"

"Yes." He checked his watch. "It shouldn't take us any time clearing off the table and loading the dishwasher. Then let's agree to meet back down here in about thirty minutes."

Skye smiled. The thought of learning something new appealed to her. "I might as well warn you that I don't pick up on things easy."

Slade leaned in close across the table and whispered, "I'll be patient."

Her heart thudded in her chest and she felt goose bumps form on her arms. How was she supposed to get through a riding lesson with him? It had been murder on her senses just getting through breakfast.

She met his gaze. "Are you sure about this?"

"Yes, I'm absolutely positive."

CHAPTER 7

"Hey, you're not doing too badly for a greenhorn."

Skye chuckled as she glanced down at Slade. She was actually sitting atop a horse, and Slade was holding the reins, slowly leading the animal around the wide-open space of the backyard. Her first challenge had been finding the courage to get up on the huge animal's back, and the next had been not holding on too tight.

Slade, good to his word, was patient. He had explained every part of the saddle, the different types of horses there were, and why he had selected the one that she was sitting on. "Jessie is a right friendly gelding and is the horse that Justin used to teach Vincent to ride."

"Vincent? This horse is that old?"

Slade chuckled as he led the horse toward another area of the ranch. "Yes. The expected life span of a horse is approximately twenty to thirty years," he explained. "So there's a good chance Jess might be around for Vincent's kids."

He brought the horse to a stop. "Now back to your lessons. These," he said, pointing to the horse's ears, "are good indicators of what's going through a horse's mind, so keep an eye on them whenever you're in the saddle. Ears that are laid back against his neck mean the horse is unhappy or annoyed about something. When the ears are pricked up and facing forward—like they are now—that means the horse is happy and interested. Flickering ears mean the horse is listening and attentive, and lowered ears mean the animal is somewhat bored."

Skye nodded, taking it all in. "You certainly know a lot about horses."

Slade began walking the horse again and glanced up at her and wished he hadn't. The backdrop of the morning sun placed a glow on her face. His gaze zeroed in on her lips and he thought they looked full and inviting and the sight of them teased him with all kinds of possibilities. "I've been around horses all my life," he forced himself to say, slowing his steps.

They had come to an area of Lorren Oaks that was basically secluded. He hadn't intentionally brought her here, but it seemed like a good place to stop and rest a bit. After all, she'd been riding, but he'd been the one doing all the walking.

"Where are we?" Skye asked, glancing around. "The scenery is simply beautiful."

He had to agree with her on that. This was his favorite part of Lorren Oaks. "We're still on Madaris land, but we're not far from the original boundaries. Justin purchased the adjoining lands a few years ago, so it's still somewhat inhabited and untamed, and he plans to keep it that way."

Slade reached up to help her off the horse. "Come take a look around."

When he lifted her off the horse's back, before her feet could touch the ground he drew her close. "Umm, you smell good."

She clutched tight to his shoulders and leaned back to look at him. The darkness of his eyes made her breath catch, and instinctively she wrapped her arms around his neck. For some reason she felt totally relaxed and the thought of being in his arms made her tingle all the way to her toes.

"Look at me, Skye."

She didn't want to look at him, but did so and met his

eyes. The tender smile on his lips made a tightness settle in her chest. "I know what you said yesterday," he said huskily. "About not wanting me to kiss you again, so if you're totally against it, I won't do it. But if there's any possible way that we can share another kiss, can we?"

Skye groaned inwardly. His question had her heart pounding hard against her ribs, and a wave of anticipation almost made her dizzy. The look in his eyes was breaking down each and every defense she had erected, and she suddenly felt overwhelmed.

Reaching up, she cupped his chin with her hand—dimples and all—and smiled. "Umm, yes, we can."

And then she did something she had never done before. She took the initiative by leaning up and covering his mouth with hers. Never in her entire existence had she wanted or needed to taste a man more.

She felt her feet touch the ground when his arm moved around her waist to pull her even closer to the fit of him, letting her have her way with his mouth. She wasn't sure just what the heck she was doing with it, but she knew she had to sample as much of him as she could.

It came as a total surprise when she heard him moan from deep within his throat, which indicated whatever she was doing to his mouth she was doing at least partly right.

Incredible.

A part of her wanted to remember her prim and proper New England upbringing, but at that moment the only thing she could think about was how she felt in Slade's arms and how her tongue had swept inside his mouth, tasting, teasing, and exploring one side to another.

How long they stood there kissing was anybody's guess, but when breathing became a task they could no longer ignore, she pulled her mouth from his and dropped her head onto his chest. He gave her time to get her breathing under control while he did likewise with his.

Then he reached out and lifted her face to his and gently

brushed her cheek with the back of his hand. He smiled and said in a deep, throaty voice, "That was some kiss, Skye."

She returned his smile and surprised herself by saying, "And you have one heck of a taste, Slade."

Slade laughed, and the sound echoed loudly through the trees, pastures, and meadows. She was something else, he thought, and an innate urge within him pushed him to kiss her again. He pulled her into his arms for another kiss, surging into the heat of her mouth like a greedy man yet always remaining gentle. And he knew at that moment that Skye Barclay was getting into his system and there wasn't a thing he could do about it.

A short while later, back in the guest room, Skye lay across the bed trying to make the move to call her parents. Regardless of whether they had wanted her to come or not, they deserved to know she had arrived safely and was all right. And if they were to ask how things were going, she would tell them. But she wouldn't mention anything if they didn't care enough to inquire.

She pulled out her cell phone and a few moments later she was holding her breath while the phone rang at her parents' home. Because of the time difference, it was breakfast time in Maine and chances were her father hadn't left for work. He had hired an assistant a few months ago, and on most days rarely went into the office before ten.

Pretty soon an older feminine voice came on the line. "Yes?"

Skye breathed in deeply. "Mom, this is Skye. I called to let you and Dad know I'm all right."

There was a long pause and then her mother said, "Did you accomplish what you went there to do? Did you meet *him*?"

Skye knew her mother was referring to Vincent. "Yes, I met him. He's a nice person, and so are his adoptive parents. He knows the truth now and is fine with it. He's not placing judgment on what his mother did when she was sixteen, and neither am I."

"Well, I still think you were wrong to tell him. Whatever image he had of his mother before has now been tainted by you."

Skye shook her head. "No, Mom, that's not true. Why do you want to believe that?"

Without answering, Edith Barclay said, "Your father hasn't left for work yet. He's here and wants to talk to you."

Skye could hear her mother passing her father the phone. "Skye?"

"Yes, Dad."

"Are you okay?"

Skye closed her eyes. Some days she didn't know what to make of her father. This was one of those times. There were times she felt he was there for her, but lately, more times than not, he had sided with her mother against her on matters that were important to her. "Yes, Dad, I'm fine, and I've met Vincent."

"Did he ask you a lot of questions regarding his mother?"

Skye thought her father's question rather odd. "No, he knows I didn't know her and that she gave me up, so there's nothing he can ask me about her."

"I thought perhaps he wanted to know what you found out about her from your investigative reports."

"Oh. No, he didn't ask anything. He's a good kid, Dad. A clean-cut, all-around American kid. The Madarises did a great job in raising him."

"And the Madarises? They don't have a problem with you being there?"

"No, in fact, they invited me to stay in their home instead of the hotel, so that's where I am."

"That was very kind of them."

"Yes, they are kind people." When there was a lag in the conversation, Skye said, "Look, Dad, I'm going to let you go since I know you have to go into the office. Tell Mom that I—"

"When are you coming home, Skye?"

"Probably on Sunday. I want to spend as much time with Vincent as I can, to get to know him." She decided now was not a good time to mention that she intended to ask the Madarises about Vincent spending part of his summer with her in Maine.

"Wayne came by yesterday," her father said. "He asked about you."

Wayne was the last person she wanted to discuss with either of her parents. "I don't know why he would. The last time we talked he made it pretty clear that if I came to Texas our engagement was off."

"I think he regrets saying that."

"Well, that's too bad, Dad. I no longer have plans to marry him. Calling off the wedding was really a blessing and the best thing for the both of us."

"That young man is going places, Skye. He's a good match for you."

Skye sighed. Her parents had been able to convince her of that a few years ago, but not now. Especially after spending time with Slade. He and Wayne were as different as day and night. Wayne had an arrogant air about him, while Slade was the epitome of a perfect gentleman. Even when he had kissed her, he had maintained a decorum of honor and respect.

"I no longer think he's a good match for me, Dad, so let's leave it at that."

"We'll talk some more about it when you get back to Maine, young lady."

Skye exhaled. When would either of her parents accept the fact that she was no longer a child? It was as if her father had turned a deaf ear to her words. If the issue involved Wayne, they had nothing to talk about.

"Good-bye, Dad."

"Good-bye, Skye. We hope to see you at the end of the week. Taking all this time off your job can't be good."

"It's fine, Dad. I got a lot of vacation built up that I haven't taken. Mr. Wells was really understanding about it. Good-bye, Dad."

She then hung up the phone wishing there was something she could say to her parents to convince them that finding out about her biological parents was not a threat to them. In spite of their somewhat shaky relationship in recent years, she loved them as the only parents she'd ever known.

She got off the bed and headed for the bathroom to take a shower. She would be joining Lorren and Slade for lunch. Memories of her kiss with Slade ran through her mind, sending shivers through her body. She couldn't dismiss the way he held her in his arms while kissing her. Totally. Unhurriedly. She smiled thinking about just how much she'd liked it.

She had liked it a lot. Maybe a little too much.

"Justin, have you and Lorren lost your minds?"

Justin rolled his eyes at the sound of his brother's booming voice coming in through his cell phone. He was en route back to the ranch to see one of his patients on an emergency basis—although he had to admit any time old man Smith saw him it was considered an emergency. He had answered his cell phone thinking it was Lorren.

"Good morning to you, too, Clayton. How's Syneda and Remington?"

"Never mind us. Lorren called Syneda this morning and told her about this woman showing up claiming to be Vincent's sister."

Justin shook his head, certain those were not the words Lorren had used in her conversation with Syneda. "She isn't claiming to be his sister. She *is* his sister."

"And how do you know that for sure? Did you ask for any proof? What about identification? Did you ask to see any of this documentation she claims she has? What about that investigator's report?"

"Clayton, stop being so suspicious of everyone. I respect that as an attorney you've probably seen or heard it all, but trust me and Lorren to know when to protect our son and when not to."

"And you believe this woman's story?"

"There's no reason not to believe it."

"Well, let me give you one. Have you forgotten what Vincent stands to gain when he turns twenty-one?"

No, Justin hadn't forgotten. His parents' wealth at the time of their deaths had been held in trust for Vincent—minus what the State of Texas had deducted for restitution for the two years he'd been a ward of the state. Because his mother's parents had been fairly wealthy and Vincent was the lone survivor, he would inherit quite a sum. A few million, to be exact.

"Don't you think it's odd that this woman would show up now?" Clayton asked.

"No, I don't think it's odd if she only recently discovered she had a brother. Besides, Clayton, it's not like Vincent will be turning twenty-one anytime soon. He has five years to go."

"Yes, but how do you know she's not going to make a claim against any of Vincent's trust? If what she says is true, then Kathy Lester was her mother as well, and she might feel she's entitled to some of it."

Justin sighed. "And if what you say is true, knowing Vincent, he won't have any problems sharing it with her if that's what he wants to do."

"I'm just trying to help protect my nephew's interest."

No, you're sticking your nose where it doesn't belong like you've always done, Justin thought. For as long as he could remember, Clayton was the brother who thought he knew what was best for everybody. And because he was an attorney, he was also the brother who enjoyed a good argument.

But Justin had no desire to accommodate him today. "I appreciate that, Clayton, but Lorren and I know what we're doing, and once you meet Skye, then—"

"Skye? What kind of name is that?"

Justin chuckled. "You can fix your mouth to ask that when you're married to a woman named *Syneda*?"

"Yeah, well, Syneda's name means something," he said defensively.

"And I'm sure the name Skye means something as well. Besides, I wouldn't cause problems with her if I were you. I have a feeling she's more than piqued Slade's interest. She's pretty."

"So what of it? He's a Madaris. I'm sure it won't be the first time a pretty face has caught his attention. But Slade has a history of not letting a pretty face get to him."

"That might be true," Justin said, smiling, thinking of the way Slade had kept looking at Skye across the dinner table last night. "But I have a strong feeling she might be the one exception."

CHAPTER 8

Slade tried studying the sketches he had made a few days ago and discovered his concentration level was at an all-time low.

Pulling off his sunglasses, he propped them on top of his head and leaned against the side of the house while glancing at the area where the addition would be. There was enough land on Lorren Oaks to build another huge ranch house if Justin wanted to. But what he wanted was a place adjoining his where the woman who'd raised Lorren could live the rest of her life worry free and surrounded by those she considered family.

It would be single-story to accommodate Mama Nora's arthritis. The elderly woman couldn't climb stairs like she used to, and it would be roomy enough to have its own kitchen, bath, and sitting area to give her the privacy she needed.

When Justin had approached him about it a few months ago he had been backed up in work. The Madaris Construction Company had projects lined up through next year, and they were constantly sending out bids for more. Currently they had a huge bid in with the city of Houston to build a $10 million mini sports arena that would be used for all of the high schools' sports activities as well as the annual commencement events. Their major competitor, Collins Construction, was trying to say that he and Blade had an edge in the bidding process because of the Madaris name. But that wasn't true. It was because of the Madaris name that most companies that solicited their bids seemed to make them work harder to prove their worth. That didn't bother them because they were confident in their abilities and in the end they always completed a quality product, down to the buyers' specifications.

Slade heard a sound and turned in the direction of it and saw Skye, strolling down the walkway. Her head was bowed down as if she had a lot on her mind. She hadn't glanced his way, and with the trees serving as a buffer, chances were she hadn't seen him. Her hair was still in the ponytail that it had been in earlier when he had given her her first lesson in riding a horse.

He suddenly wondered how it would feel to let her hair loose around her shoulders at his whim, to twine his fingers through the twisted tresses, bury his face in them, before moving his mouth to taste her lips. He shifted slightly when he felt the fierce attraction he'd felt for her since day one. And those kisses they'd shared hadn't helped matters, not to mention the way her body had a tendency to automatically press tight against his whenever they kissed.

With the bidding war between Madaris and Collins Construction coming up in the next few weeks, he needed to keep his mind focused. At present it was focused all right. Focused right on Skye. At first it had only been his intent to be friendly toward her, mainly because he could tell when she'd first arrived that she was extremely nervous. But somewhere along the line, in a short space of time, his interest had changed. Hell, he'd practically even told her he had his own agenda where she was concerned.

His jaw tightened and the hand holding the clipboard clenched. He'd never been on a mission for a woman before. He dated when it suited him, and when it didn't he was just as happy staying at home with a cold can of beer and watching whatever sci-fi flick was on the tube. Women had never been a necessity to him like they were to Blade. His brother loved women. In fact, everyone claimed Blade was their cousin

Clayton reincarnated, since Clayton, in his pre-Syneda days, had been Houston's bad boy who went for anything in a skirt. He'd even kept a huge case of condoms in his closet, which he'd proudly passed on to Blade.

Slade shook his head, grinning, thinking of how his brother was putting those damn things to good use. When it came to safe sex Blade knew the score and would never let a pretty face blow his mind.

Like Slade was doing if he didn't get a grip.

Personally, he didn't need an involvement in his life right now, and according to Skye, neither did she. So why was it hard to fight the attraction? Why was he making it into such a big deal? And why did he care so much about when something bothered her—like it was evidently doing.

This morning when he'd taken her out on Jessie, she had been in the best of moods, excited about meeting Vincent yesterday and his acceptance of her last night. From the way she was walking now, oblivious to her surroundings, like she had a lot on her mind, Slade wondered what had upset her, and he could tell by the slump in her shoulders that something had.

He continued to watch her, and then, as if she felt his eyes on her, she slowly lifted her head and turned. Their gazes connected. Locked. For the longest time they stood staring at each other, across a distance of over thirty feet, and then, as if on instinct, he put aside his clipboard and reached out his hand to her.

He watched as she breathed in deeply and took a step. Then she was moving toward him. He watched her come to him and he knew whatever was causing her misery, he wanted to take it away, slay whatever dragons were causing the worry lines on her forehead.

When she got close enough for them to touch, she took his outstretched hand and he tugged her closer. Without wasting any time or thinking twice about what he was doing, he leaned down and touched his lips to hers and began kissing her with a longing he didn't know he was capable of exemplifying. And from the way she was kissing him back, it seemed she needed the kiss as much as he did. What was there about her that made it so easy to share himself, his feelings, his desires?

He continued to kiss her, slow and deep, building passion like he'd never taken the time to build before with a woman. What he was doing was confusing the hell out of him, and when she wrapped her arms around his waist and leaned in closer, getting more into their kiss, while he felt her soft breasts press against his chest, he was driven by an instinctive urge to devour her mouth completely. Automatically he splayed his hands across her bottom and pulled her closer, her hips flush against his. And he felt her heat, even through the material of his jeans. And then he moved his hands to her hair and did what he'd thought of doing earlier. He let it loose, ran his fingers through the twisted tresses while he continued to kiss her.

Remembering where they both were and what they were doing, he slowly pulled back on the kiss, drawing in a ragged breath while savoring the taste of her. He pulled her closer into his arms and gave her the hug he felt she needed.

"You okay, Skye?" he asked huskily against her ear.

She nodded her head against his chest and mumbled, "Yes, I'm okay."

He wasn't convinced. He pulled back a little and took his finger and lifted her chin so their eyes could meet. The smile she tried giving him was weak at best. Something *was* bothering her. She wasn't okay. But he wouldn't press the issue. If she wanted him to know what had her upset, she would tell him.

In the meantime . . .

"Come on," he said, holding her hand and leading her toward a wooded path.

She straightened her bent shoulders and gazed at him, asking softly, "Where are we going?"

"To take a walk."

She smiled. "Another walk?"

"Yes. I've always discovered when I have a lot on my mind, walking helps."

She glanced down at the clipboard he had placed on a nearby table. "But I don't want to take you away from your work."

A fine tremor settled in the hand holding hers. How could he explain to her that at that moment his work didn't matter, when his work had always mattered? "Don't worry about it. Everybody needs to take a break from work every once in a while."

For the next twenty minutes they walked quietly while he held her hand. To him they seemed like old friends and not two people who had just met yesterday. In retrospect, that in itself made no sense at all. It just felt right.

They came to the end of the path, which connected to a natural stream. Skye thought it was a beautiful parcel of land that Justin and his family used often, as indicated by the picnic tables and benches as well as a tree house in one of the huge oak trees. In fact, there were two tree houses.

Skye glanced up and studied both. Each was situated in a large oak tree, and they were about twenty feet from each other. One had definitely been built for a girl. There were frilly pink curtains in the windows, and instead of having to use your physical skill to climb up the tree, there was something akin to a spiral staircase leading to it. Skye shook her head. She had never seen such a thing before.

Slade followed the direction of her gaze and smiled. "Justin and I built that for Justina for her fourth birthday. Those stairs were my idea. In fact, I designed the entire thing." He chuckled. "I guess you can say it was my first project as an architect."

"Wow! That was some playhouse for a four-year-old."

"Yes, I have to admit it was at the time, but it was designed to grow with her, and from what I understand, she still gets a lot of use out of it. She's at the age where she likes her privacy, away from her nagging brothers. Although she adores the both of them, they can get on Justina's last nerve at times, with her being the only girl."

Not for the first time Skye felt a tinge of envy for anyone who had not been an only child. She used to beg her parents for other children, and they had flatly refused, saying she was all they intended to have. Now she wondered why she had been adopted in the first place. That had never been shared with her. She could only assume that one of her parents could not conceive a child. Then that would explain why they had been so adamant about not giving her a sibling. It wasn't that they hadn't wanted to but that they couldn't.

"Ready to head back?"

Slade's words intruded on her thoughts. "Yes, and you're right; walking helps clear a lot off your mind."

"I hope you're not worried about Vincent. I think last night proved he wants you to be a part of his life."

Skye smiled. "No, that's not it."

"Oh."

Feeling she probably owed him an explanation, especially since he'd taken so much time with her today, she said, "I talked to my parents, and I just can't figure them out at times. I know they were upset about me coming here, but I would think since I've told them how receptive both the Madarises and Vincent are, they would be happy for me."

"But you think they aren't?"

"Yes, I more than got that feeling after talking to them a short while ago."

Slade tried looking at it from her parents' point of view and said, "Don't be so hard on them, Skye. Maybe they're afraid they will lose you. They'd had you all your life, and now you're embarking on another life that doesn't include them."

"But it can include them, Slade, if they let it. They have

no reason to think my finding Vincent will mean my not wanting them anymore. I think they would understand, considering I'm just meeting Vincent, that quite naturally I'd want to spend time with him, and get to know him. That has nothing to do with how I feel about them. They are my parents and I love them."

She didn't add that at times through the years they had been hard to love, especially her mom. Whenever she would do something not in keeping with her mother's wishes, she would get the silent treatment until she would bend to Edith Barclay's will. Her decision to marry Wayne had been one of those times. Skye could now admit she never loved him and had only agreed to marry him to satisfy her parents.

"Well, take it from someone who knows, parents can be a real trip sometimes, but when push comes to shove, they have our best interests at heart and we wouldn't trade them for the world."

A part of Skye knew what Slade said was true. Although the Barclays hadn't been the warmest and most loving of parents, she believed they loved her in their own way. And as far as having her best interests at heart, she assumed that was the reason they'd been adamant about her marrying Wayne. Where she was from, some parents still practiced the art of arranging marriages for their kids, especially if they thought it would be a good match financially.

"Skye?"

"Yes?"

Instead of answering her, Slade blew out a deep breath and then rubbed his hand down his face. "You know what's happening between us is crazy, don't you?"

Her eyes darted nervously from Slade to the tree house's staircase. She thought of pretending as if she didn't know what he was talking about. But she did know. "Yes, and I thought we had decided it wouldn't work. At least for me it won't."

"Then why do you let me keep kissing you?"

Now that was a good question, one she didn't have an answer for. The only one she had, which she wouldn't dare share with him, was that she enjoyed his kisses. Almost too much.

"Skye?"

She returned her gaze to his and decided to be truthful . . . a little bit. "I feel comfortable with you, Slade. I have from the first. And maybe it's wrong to let you take such liberties, but . . ."

"But what?" He leaned against the trunk of a smaller oak tree and she watched as his lips tipped into a sexy smile. "Go ahead and tell me. But what?"

She shrugged. "I don't know. I hope you don't think bad things about me because I have let you kiss me a few times."

Three times, to be exact, he thought. And yes, he was counting and dying to take the fourth. "No, I don't think that way at all. Friends can kiss."

But would they do so with the same intensity? Skye couldn't help asking herself. "So, that could be a good reason. The reason I let you kiss me is because we're friends."

"Kissing friends?"

She studied the look in his eyes. She could see blatant desire in them and knew the truth had nothing to do with friendship, but she wasn't ready for either of them to admit it. "Yes, kissing friends. That's a lot safer than being kissing cousins, don't you think?"

He smiled. "Umm, now that's a thought. Since you're Vincent's sister and I consider him my cousin, does that mean you're my cousin as well?" His gaze then dropped to her mouth.

She'd seen the movement of his gaze, and his focus on her lips sent a spiraling sensation through her midsection. "Technically, we aren't cousins. Biologically, we aren't, either. But if you want to think of me as your cousin, I don't have a problem with it."

He shook his head as he eased away from the tree to take

a closer step toward her. "No, I don't want to think of you as a cousin. I like thinking of you as a friend better. A very special friend."

"One you like to kiss?"

"Yes, one I like to kiss."

And with that said, he lowered his head and glided his tongue across her lips before staking his claim on her mouth by devouring her lips for a fourth time. The first thought that came to his mind was that each time he kissed her was better than the last. The second thing was that he could spend the entire day kissing her and would never get tired. Their mouths fit perfectly. Their tongues mingled completely. And each time he mated his mouth with hers he was getting detailed knowledge of her mouth. He knew just what to do to hear that little catch in her voice, that certain sexy moan, and what to do to make her tongue grab hold to his like it was something she had to have and anything else . . . anyone else, for that matter . . . was unacceptable.

Finally, he slowly pulled his mouth back and watched as she took her tongue, that same irresistible tongue he had feasted on, and licked her lips. Watching her made him lick his own. "Had enough?" he asked, clearing his throat.

She laughed a little self-consciously. "Do you want the truth?"

"Always."

"No."

That answer satisfied him. He pulled her back into his arms as raw need shot through him. Consumed him. He thrust his tongue into her mouth when she parted her lips on a sigh, and began tasting her all over again. And this time he wouldn't let up until they both had enough. Which could very well be a long time from now.

CHAPTER 9

Slade sat at the dinner table, hearing what Vincent, Justina, and Christopher were saying as they filled everyone in on the happenings at school that day.

Slade was hearing but not listening.

His attention was focused on Skye who was sitting across the table from him. He thought about their walk earlier that day, trying to remember every little detail, especially the kisses they had shared. He would need those memories to sustain him when he was back in Houston working on all those projects that were lined up for him to do.

"So what do you think, Slade?"

He blinked, realizing Justin had asked him a question. "Excuse me?"

Justin shot a knowing grin his way. "I asked what you thought of Vincent going to Maine for a few weeks this summer to visit with Skye? That would mean him altering the plans the two of you have made."

Slade glanced around the table and saw that Justina and Christopher had left, probably to do their homework. He hadn't realized they were gone. Everyone was staring at him. Damn, what had he missed?

"I'm sorry, my mind was elsewhere for a moment," he offered as an excuse. He glanced across the table at Skye and Vincent. "You want Vincent to visit with you this summer in Maine?" he asked.

Skye nodded, smiling. "Yes, but Lorren mentioned he's

supposed to work for you and your brother at Madaris Construction this summer as a student intern."

Slade leaned back in his chair. "Yes, that's our plan." He glanced at Vincent. "Which do you prefer doing?"

Vincent smiled excitedly. "Both. I've been looking forward to spending the summer in Houston with Gramma and Grampa and everyone, and especially working for you and Blade since I want to be an architect one day. But I want to spend time with Skye as well."

Slade nodded. "We could possibly split the time and instead of you being in Houston the entire summer, you could be there for the first two months and then go to Maine for the last."

Vincent's eyes lit up. "Could that be arranged?"

Slade shrugged. "It will depend on whether your school agrees to it." He turned his attention back to Skye to explain. "Vincent attends a college preparatory school where he gets college credit if he does something that relates to the field of study he intends to pursue at a college. Usually, it requires him to fulfill so many hands-on hours."

He gazed back at Vincent. "I suggest that you check with the guidance department at your school tomorrow."

Vincent nodded eagerly. "I will."

"And if that doesn't work," Skye said to everyone at the table, "I have another idea that just might."

"And what idea is that?" Justin asked, smiling after taking a sip of his coffee.

"I could take a leave of absence from my job and come spend the summer in Houston."

Lorren lifted a surprised brow. "Can you just take off like that?"

"Yes. My employer is real flexible. I've worked with them for a long time, ever since college, and I've put in a lot of extra hours over the years and have rarely taken time off. Besides, I had planned to take a three-month block of time off after my wedding anyway, and—"

"You're getting married?" Vincent asked, surprised.

Skye glanced at him. "I was but not anymore." And not wanting to go into any further details about her canceled wedding plans, she said, "I really don't think taking the extra time off will be a problem. And although I would love for Vincent to see Maine, I don't have a problem spending time in Houston. I've never been there before and hear it's a nice place."

"It is," Justin said, proud of the city where he was born. "And you're willing to take a leave from your job this summer?"

Skye smiled. "Yes, if it means getting to spend some time with Vincent. I have enough money saved where I can do it without it hurting me financially."

"If you get bored we could always use help at Madaris Construction," Slade spoke up and said. "In fact, Sherri, our present accountant, will be going out on maternity leave next month, and I haven't had time to contact a temporary agency about getting her a replacement."

Skye lifted a surprised brow. "Are you offering me a job for the summer?"

Slade chuckled as he shook his head. It seemed that he was. What had he been thinking of just now, doing such a thing? But the offer was out there and he couldn't withdraw it. If she accepted it he would try like hell to find a way not to kiss her every chance he got. He would keep their relationship in the office strictly business.

He inhaled deeply before saying, "Yes, I am."

"Boy, that's cool!" Vincent exclaimed. "Now we'll both be working for Madaris Construction Company."

Skye didn't want to get Vincent's hopes up regarding that. "I appreciate you making the offer, but I'll have to think about it, Slade," she said in a voice that to his way of thinking sounded kind of breathless. Was she, too, wondering how they would keep their attraction under control if they were to work together?

"It was just a suggestion. If Vincent's school goes along

with letting him work for us for only two months, then you won't have to come to Houston at all," Slade said.

At that moment something hot spread all through him. The thought of her being in Houston, even for a short while, was almost too much to think about.

Later that night Lorren snuggled close to her husband. Everyone had gone to bed hours ago, and she had worked on the last chapter of her book while Justin had read an article in one of his medical journals.

Now that she had his full attention, she asked, "Wasn't that a wonderful gesture that Skye made to offer to spend time with Vincent this summer in Houston if he can't get away to visit her in Maine?"

Justin wrapped his arms around his wife. "Yes, it was."

"And after that soccer game Vincent and Skye played after dinner, she approached me, worried about how the other family members would feel. She doesn't want to take away any time they plan to spend with him this summer while he's in Houston. I told her not to worry about it and that the Madaris family isn't that way. His grandparents, aunts, uncles, and cousins will be glad to share him with her." Lorren chuckled. "I think Vincent has called everyone and told them about her and they're looking forward to meeting her. I managed to convince her there's enough love in the Madaris family to go around, but she'll see for herself once she meets the rest of the family."

Justin agreed, "Yes, she will."

"So, what do you think is happening between Slade and Skye?" Lorren rose up a little in bed to ask.

Justin chuckled. "You've picked up on it, too, have you?"

Lorren's lips eased into a smile as she settled back down beside him, in his arms again. "How could I not, Justin? The sexual tension surrounding them is so thick you could actually cut it with a knife. Reminds me of how things were between us in the beginning."

Justin nodded. "Skye's a very pretty girl and you know the Madaris men. They do have eyes for beauty."

"Yes, and at least it's Slade and not Blade. If it was Blade, then I'd be worried."

Justin lifted a brow. "Why's that?" he asked, although he already knew the answer.

Lorren rolled her eyes. "Come on now, Justin; you know Blade. He's going through his bad-boy Clayton Madaris stage where every pretty face captures his attention, but not for long. He's earning the reputation of being a heart-breaker. I always figured Slade would be more like you. Once he meets the woman he wants, he will pursue her with diligence."

"So you think his offer of summer employment to Skye is his way to do that?"

"Yes, but I don't think he realizes it yet. Although he might be planning to pursue her, it won't hit him as to why he's doing it until much later. When it comes to matters of the heart, the men in your family have a tendency to be rather slow."

Justin chuckled. "You think you have the men in my family figured out, don't you?"

She smiled up at him. "Yes, I think so."

Justin pulled her closer into his arms. He thought she had the men in his family figured out pretty much as well. He then remembered his conversation with Clayton that day. "I talked to Clayton earlier today. He's concerned," he said softly.

"Yes, I know. Syneda's told me. She doesn't agree with his take on things, and neither do I. I truly believe everything about Skye is what we see and she doesn't have an ulterior motive for seeking Vincent out. Once Clayton meets her and sees the kind of person she is and how much her relationship with Vincent truly means to her, he'll see how wrong he is in thinking such a thing."

"And I agree. But you know Clayton."

She chuckled. "Yes, I do know Clayton, but I'm convinced in this case he's wrong. I saw the look in Skye's eyes the moment Vincent accepted her as his sister. She was truly touched. I don't know what type of family life she's had with her adoptive parents or the reason behind her canceled marriage plans, but for some reason I get the feeling she's a person who's been virtually alone all of her life and now she just wants to belong to someone."

Justin had gotten that same impression as well, and if he had things figured out right, Vincent wouldn't be the only person Skye would eventually belong to. He had a strong feeling that before things were over, she would belong to Slade as well.

As Justin pulled Lorren into his arms for the kind of kiss he'd waited practically all day to get, he thought that this summer should be a rather interesting one.

It was close to midnight and Skye was still up and pacing the confines of the bedroom she'd been given to use. She stopped and pulled in a deep breath. What could she have been thinking about making an offer to spend the summer with Vincent in Houston?

But deep down she'd known why she had done it. Now that she had found her brother, she didn't want to lose him. She wanted to spend as much time as possible with him, getting to know him and him getting to know her. It hadn't dawned on her at the time that being in Houston around Vincent also meant being around Slade. A part of her hoped that Vincent's school would let him spend the last month of summer with her; then she would have no reason to spend the summer in Houston. No reason to be around Slade. No reason to consider his job offer.

Her parents would literally go bonkers at the thought of her putting in a leave of absence from her job. They wouldn't

understand and would think she'd taken leave of her senses.
But what she'd told the Madarises at dinner was true. Now
that her wedding was officially off, she still had the money
tucked away that she'd saved, so taking off work for the summer wouldn't put her in a financial bind. And if she took the
job Slade offered, that meant she would be around Vincent
even more.

Again, she reminded herself that it would also mean being
around Slade. She inhaled deeply, thinking of the situation
that would place her in. Already her body had established just
how responsive it was to his kisses, his touch, his very presence. She should be distancing herself from temptation and
not placing herself right smack in the middle of it.

When she finally got tired of pacing the floor, she took
off her robe and slipped back into bed. First things first. First
she would have to deal with her parents if she decided to
spend the summer in Houston, and then she would deal with
the situation with Slade.

As she snuggled under the covers, she remembered the
ride she'd taken on horseback and later the walk she'd
shared, both with Slade. She also remembered their kisses.
Each time Slade's lips had moved over hers with such tenderness, it not only nearly brought tears to her eyes, but it
also had increased a hunger in her midsection—one she
only experienced when kissing him. For some reason, whenever she was in his arms, she felt exclusively his. Never had
she felt she belonged to any man exclusively. Not even
Wayne.

Slade, whether he intended to or not, had definitely made
her feel that way. She released a slow breath as she gazed up
at the ceiling. An image of Slade smiling down at her with
those sexy dimples seemed to appear there. She blinked.
Sheese. She was definitely losing it.

She tossed on her side and closed her eyes. Moments
later a hum of pleasure stirred from her lips when she again
thought of all the kisses the two of them had shared. Those

thoughts were still on her mind when she finally drifted off to sleep a short while later.

"Alex, you're awake?"

Alexander Maxwell glanced over at the clock on his nightstand before glancing over at his wife, who'd been sleeping beside him. The phone had awakened the both of them. "I am now, Clayton. What do you want?"

"Sorry to call so late, but I wanted to wait until Syneda was asleep. I need you to run a background check on someone."

Alex, a former FBI agent who owned a private investigation company, raised a dark brow. "Who?"

"A woman by the name of Skye Barclay."

Alex pulled himself up in bed. "Isn't that Vincent's new sister?"

"So you've heard?"

"Who hasn't? Vincent has called just about everyone. He's excited about it."

"Well, I want to make sure that excitement doesn't backfire on him."

Alex frowned. "Why would that happen?"

"Justin and Lorren are taking this woman's word about everything. I want to make sure she's really who she says she is and that she doesn't have an ulterior motive for seeking Vincent out."

Alex raised his eyes toward the ceiling. "Why are you so suspicious of everyone, Clayton?"

"Hell, I've learned my lesson. I wasn't suspicious of you when I should have been. Had I known you had the hots for my sister, I would have—"

"Done nothing, so get over it." A smile touched the corners of Alex's lips when he gazed down into the sparkling brown eyes of his wife. She had that *just-made-love-to* look on her face, mainly because he had finished making love to her less than an hour ago and they had dozed off to sleep. And now, thanks to Clayton, they were awake again.

"I got Christy just where I want her," he said. "I'll do what you've asked and check out Ms. Barclay, but I think your suspicions are unfounded. I'm only hearing good things about her."

"And they're all coming from Justin, Lorren, Slade, and Vincent, no doubt. I want to make doubly sure their assessment is correct. You know how I feel about unwanted surprises. Someone has to protect the family from them. Good night, Alex."

"Good night, Clayton." Alex sighed as he leaned over and hung up the phone.

"I gather my brother is sticking his nose where it doesn't belong as usual."

Alex gave a warm smile down at his wife. "I guess you can say that. He doesn't trust Vincent's new sister."

Christy laughed. "He hasn't even met her, and from what I hear she's a nice person. Clayton is just getting downright cynical in his old age."

"Maybe. But to put his fears to rest, I'll check her out . . . tomorrow." His voice trailed off somewhat when he felt Christy's hand touch his thigh.

"Yes, tomorrow," she said softly.

He reached out and brushed a lock of her reddish brown hair away from her face. They had been married almost two years, and each day he fell deeper and deeper in love with her. "When do you plan to tell the family our good news?" Earlier that night a pregnancy test had confirmed what they'd suspected. They were having a baby and were both thrilled to death about it.

Christy smiled up at him. "At the retirement party Uncle Jake is giving Senator Lansing in a few weeks." She snuggled closer into his arms. "I want it to be our secret for a while."

Alex returned her smile. It wouldn't be the first secret they had managed to keep from the family. "I want it to be our secret for a while, too."

When he felt her hand move on his thigh again, he said, "This might sound like I'm one greedy bastard, considering what we just did less than an hour ago, but I want to make love to you again." His voice was low and intimate.

She placed her finger to his lips to silence him and said, "If you're greedy, then I'm greedier, because I want to make love to you again as well, Alexander the Great. And I love you."

He smiled against her finger before catching it in his hand and kissing it. "And I love you, too, and I intend to give you everything you want, Christy Madaris Maxwell."

And then he lowered his head to settle his mouth over hers.

CHAPTER 10

"Good morning, Slade."

Slade stood when Skye walked out on the patio. With the sun in the sky as a backdrop, Skye looked wide-awake, refreshed, and utterly beautiful. He'd had a rough time getting to sleep last night. She had dominated his thoughts and his dreams.

As if operating on autopilot he took a step and walked around the table and moved toward her. His gaze slowly raked over her, liking what he saw. She was wearing a pair of jeans and a western shirt. Lorren had probably loaned her the outfit, because for some reason he couldn't imagine the outfit being something she owned. She had a little makeup and the shade of the lipstick on her mouth would give any red-blooded male plenty of ideas of just what he would love doing to her lips. It definitely gave him plenty.

He came to a stop directly in front of her, mere inches separating them. "First you eat; then it's riding lesson number two."

She smiled, nodding. "Okay." She glanced around. "Have Justin and Lorren left for Dallas already?"

Justin and Lorren were spending the day visiting friends, John and Juanita Graham. John was a Texas Ranger and he and Justin had been close friends for years. "Yes, they've gone, and the kids have all left for school. You know what that means, don't you?"

Shaking her head, she had a feeling he was about to tell her. "No, what does it mean?"

He took a step closer. "It means unless Rubena picks today to return from her vacation, we're all alone and will have the entire place to ourselves."

The huskiness of his voice as well as his close proximity to her, not to mention the sexy grin on his face, sent a heated sensation shooting to all parts of her body. She swallowed hard before asking, "Will we?"

"Yes, and do you know the first thing I want to do this morning?"

She shook her head again and hoped the twisted curls on her head hid her smile. "No, I'm clueless as to what's the first thing you want to do this morning."

"Take a guess."

She glanced up at him, and his promising smile pretty much spelled things out for her. They needed to talk regardless of whether talking would do any good. It seems when it came to this sexual attraction they shared, they preferred kissing instead of talking. A part of her wondered what would happen when they discovered kissing was not enough.

Before she could get her mind to think any further about that question, he took a step even closer, getting all into her personal space. She met his gaze, and automatically her mouth tilted upward to his. He smiled as he placed his arms around her shoulders and pulled her closer to him.

"This," he said in a husky tone, "is the first thing I want to do this morning." And then he lowered his lips to hers.

The moment their mouths touched, Skye released a deep moan. And when he intensified the kiss and at the same time shifted one of his hands upward, moving her twisted curls aside to lightly stroke the satiny skin at her neck, another moan, this one coming from deep in her throat, rumbled in her chest. Something warm and inviting began spreading to all corners of her body.

She returned the kiss in the ways he'd taught her to do over the past couple of days, and she mated with his tongue as if her life depended on it.

A need she didn't quite understand seemed to suddenly fill every pore of her being as he continued to kiss her, sending sensational shivers all through her body.

The clearing of a deep, husky throat immediately caught their attention, and she pulled away from Slade so abruptly, she almost lost her balance. His hand snaked out and captured her around the waist to keep her from falling. She turned, relieved Justin and Lorren hadn't returned unexpectedly. What she saw was two men—two tall men—leaning against the brick wall staring at her and Slade with something akin to amusement lurking at the corners of their lips.

Her attention was snagged by Slade's deep voice when he asked in an annoyed tone, "What are the two of you doing here?"

She watched a mischievous smile play over the lips of one of the men. He was the one who had dimples just like Slade. "Luke and I were curious as to what was keeping you here, so we decided to come and check things out for ourselves." His smile widened before he added, "And now that we see the reason, we understand completely. Sorry for the interruption."

Both men then turned and walked away.

Slade studied Skye's features, trying to gauge her reaction to his brother and cousin's untimely interruption. He could tell she was uncomfortable with the situation by the way she was looking everywhere but at him.

He reached out and ran a finger along her chin, then tilted it upward so their gazes could connect. "If you want me to regret kissing you just now, I won't."

"But your brother and cousin—"

"Have lousy timing and are probably pea green with envy

right now. Don't get all nervous on me, Skye. Relax. For them to see me kiss you isn't a big deal."

Skye took a deep breath and then she took two steps back. "It might not be a big deal to you, but it is to me. I care about what people think about my character."

"And you don't think I care about mine? And what does kissing me have to do with your character?"

Skye inhaled deeply. "I don't want your family thinking the wrong thing about me. About us."

He dug his hands into the pockets of his jeans. "And what's the wrong thing they can think, Skye?"

She nervously rubbed her hands together. "The misconception that there's something going on between us."

His deep chuckle caused a shiver to pass through her body. "Sweetheart, whether you want to admit it or not, there *is* something going on between us. How many kisses will it take for you to accept it? Did you not admit just yesterday that we're special friends who enjoy kissing?"

"Yes," she answered honestly. "But—"

"But what?"

Her chest rose and fell as she took another deep breath. "But what's everyone going to think if you and I are painting this picture of two people who are doing something?"

She stood there looking so damn proper, even in her jeans and shirt, he wanted to reach out and kiss that proper look right off her lips. "What exactly are they supposed to think we're doing?"

She looked at him with an exasperated expression on her face. "More than just kissing, Slade."

His eyes held her captive when he leaned closer and whispered huskily, "Don't put any ideas in my head, Skye."

His words made her pulse rate increase, had visions dancing in her head. Her heart began to pound against her ribs. "You aren't taking any of this seriously, are you?"

Smiling, he reached out and draped his arms around her neck. "I'm taking *you* seriously, Skye. Never doubt that.

I don't want you to think we did anything wrong because we were caught kissing. People kiss. Friends kiss. I thought we cleared that up yesterday."

They had, but she hadn't expected for them to put on a show for anyone today. "I might be making a big deal out of this, Slade, but I was raised by parents who felt respecting yourself and others respecting you is the most important thing."

"And you think that I don't respect you?"

"I don't want you to think that I make a habit of letting men kiss me."

"Again, I thought we cleared all this up yesterday. I don't think that. In fact, I feel damn special that I'm the one kissing you."

"Do you?"

"Yes."

"Th-thank you," she whispered, and Slade could actually see relief in her expression. He wondered why she was so hung up on what others thought of her. Granted he wished more women cared, but for her it seemed to be an obsession with protocol.

"You don't have to thank me, Skye. You're very unique. I knew that the moment I opened the door to you a few days ago. I don't know the last time I've been this attracted to a woman, and it doesn't come as a surprise that the woman is you, mainly because in just the two days I've gotten to know you, I've come to accept that you *are* special. And don't worry about Blade and Luke. After you meet them, you'll see they're great guys."

He then smiled teasingly and added, "Even if they do have lousy timing."

He then pulled her into his arms. Instead of giving her the kiss he wanted to give her, he just stood there and held her in his arms.

Skye grinned across the table at Slade's twin. Slade had been right. Blade and Luke were two great guys.

It had only taken a few seconds to size Blade Madaris up as a player and Luke as a loner. Both men were extremely handsome and had great personalities. And with Slade in the mix, she could imagine the trouble the three of them could get into when they were together. And it wasn't hard to tell they were related. There seemed to be several similarities with all the Madaris men she had met.

Rubena, Justin and Lorren's housekeeper, had come back to work from a weeklong vacation and had set the table to serve breakfast on the patio.

"So when will you know if you're coming to work for me and Slade this summer?" Blade asked Skye.

She raised a brow and glanced across the table at Slade. He threw up his hands, laughing. "Hey, don't look at me; I didn't say a word to anyone. One thing you're going to discover about the Madaris family is that news travels fast, so if you want something kept a secret, you'd better keep it to yourself."

"And no matter what you do," Luke added after taking a sip of his coffee, "don't tell Traci or Kattie. That's like publishing it in the newspapers."

Skye smiled. "Who're Traci and Kattie?"

"Two of Justin's sisters, and they pass information through the family like wildfire."

"But how would they know of my plans for the summer?"

"Vincent," Blade said, chuckling. "He probably was so excited at the thought that the two of you would spend the summer together in Houston that he called everyone. Well, not exactly everyone, but he talked to the people who like keeping the family informed about things."

Skye had to smile at that. She liked the thought that Vincent was excited about their spending time together. "You said Traci and Kattie are two of Justin's sisters. He has more?"

Slade nodded. "Just one more. Christy is the baby girl who's about your age. She married Alex Maxwell two years ago. And Alex's brother, Trask, is married to our cousin Felicia."

"Oh." Skye sighed. This was getting rather confusing. Earlier they had mentioned that Lorren's best friend, Syneda, was married to Justin's brother Clayton.

Blade smiled. "Are we confusing you, Skye?"

"No," she insisted, chuckling, not about to admit anything to him. "It's just that your family seems to get bigger and bigger every time someone talks about them."

"It's probably even larger than you can imagine. There were seven Madaris brothers. All are still living except for Uncle Robert. He got killed in the Vietnam War. That was Felicia's daddy," Luke explained.

Skye nodded. "Who're Justin's parents?"

"Uncle Jonathan and Aunt Marilyn," Slade replied. "They had six kids. Justin is the oldest; then there's Dex and Clayton. Then came the girls, Traci, Kattie, and Christy."

"Don't try to learn about everyone now," Luke warned. "There are too many of us. Besides, if you decide to spend the summer in Houston, you'll get to meet everyone at the Madaris family reunion in July."

She looked surprised. "I will?"

"Yes. I'm sure Great-Gramma Laverne has heard about you by now. She'll want to check you out."

Skye lifted a brow. "Check me out for what?"

She saw Blade and Luke exchange amused glances. Slade, she noticed, had suddenly grown an interest in the contents in his coffee cup and was gazing down into it.

It was Blade who finally spoke, and the smile on his face reminded her so much of Slade. "To see which of her great-grandsons she can match you up with."

Skye blinked, pretty sure she had not heard him correctly. Before she could ask Blade to repeat himself, Luke said, smiling, "But don't worry about it. We'll make sure she knows you already belong to Slade."

You already belong to Slade.

A few hours later Luke's statement still bothered her. That

was the kind of nonsense she didn't want anyone to start assuming. And although she and Slade had tried convincing the two men they were nothing more than friends, she had a feeling Luke and Blade hadn't believed them. But then how convincing could you be when you'd been caught kissing?

After breakfast Slade had given her another riding lesson while Blade and Luke had gotten settled in the guest rooms Rubena had given them to use. When Skye and Slade had returned to the ranch Rubena had a message from Vincent. He had called from the guidance counselor's office at school. In order to get full credit for the student internship, he would have to work for the Madaris Construction Company the full three months. There could be no exceptions.

After Rubena had delivered the message and walked off, Slade glanced over at Skye. "Does that mean you'll be spending your summer in Houston?"

Skye inhaled deeply. She'd been hoping it wouldn't have to come to that. "It looks that way, because I really want to spend time with Vincent. But I don't want to disrupt any plans he's made with your family."

Slade smiled. "You won't be. He has cousins his age that he hangs out with whenever he comes to town, but all of us are so glad to see him whenever he visits Houston, we have him rotating all over the place. But he mostly stays with his grandparents Uncle Jonathan and Aunt Marilyn."

Skye nodded. "I think it's just wonderful how all of you just embraced him into the Madaris family although you knew he was adopted."

"It didn't matter. Once Justin and Lorren claimed him as their son, that pretty much settled it. He automatically became one of us, and you'll find when it comes to family, the Madarises protect their own. It's just that simple."

Skye wished it would have been just that simple in her world. Her aunt Karen had always been kind to her while she'd been growing up, but when her mother had seen the relationship getting too close, she had stepped in and had stopped

Skye from going over her aunt's house on the weekends to visit with her. Skye had never understood why her mother had done that. Skye assumed that since her mother and aunt didn't get along most of the time that had had a lot to do with it, but now she wondered if her adoption was the reason. Since she'd found out she was adopted from overhearing the conversation between her aunt and her parents had her mother been fearful that Karen would let something slip around her? Had that fear led Edith to end Skye and her aunt's close relationship?

Skye shook her head. Little did Edith know that her close relationship with her aunt didn't end. Oh, there had been years they hadn't been able to talk like they used to, but once she left home for college to live on campus, she and her aunt met each week for tea at one of the café houses on campus. Those days had been the high points in her life. Her aunt had always been there giving her support when things got rough with her parents. And her aunt had given Skye her blessings when she'd told her of her decision to find Vincent. In fact, her aunt had been the only supportive one.

"Skye?"

She blinked upon realizing Slade had been talking to her. "Yes?"

"I asked what are your plans?"

She shrugged. "I really haven't made any. Other than knowing for certain I'll be spending time this summer in Houston." Which was only a couple of weeks away. This was the last week of school for Vincent, and according to Lorren he was supposed to report to work for Slade the second week of June.

"I guess I need to return home and set everything in motion," she said, which she knew also meant breaking the news to her parents. That would be the hardest part because she knew there was no way they would understand her reason for what she had to do.

"I'll need to put in the paperwork to my employer, which won't be a problem. Then I'll check on a place for me to stay in Houston and—"

"You can stay with me."

She glanced up at Slade. "Excuse me?"

He smiled. "I said you can stay with me. Our construction company built some pretty nice condos for millionaire land developer Mitch Farrell. As part of our compensation package, Blade and I are owners of several of them that we lease out. Both Blade and I live there."

"And you want me to live with you?"

His smile widened. "I think that would be a rather nice arrangement."

Well, she didn't. She was having a hard time trying to figure out how they would share office space if she took him up on his job offer. She didn't want to think how things would be if they were to share personal space as well. Besides, her moving in with him would definitely send out a wrong message to his family. They'd probably think there was more between them than friendship. It was obvious his brother and cousin already thought so.

"Thanks, but no thanks, Slade. I don't think us living together, even for three months, would be a good idea. I'll just check the Houston rental sections to see what I can find."

"Don't bother. If you don't want to share quarters with me, then there's a vacant condo I often use as a model, so it's completely furnished. You're welcome to use it."

"I couldn't possibly do that."

"Sure you can. Consider it as a favor from a friend. You're going to like it and it's within minutes from the Madaris Office Park."

Sky raised a brow. "The Madarises own an office park?"

Slade chuckled. "Justin and his brothers, along with Uncle Jake, are the owners. They commissioned me and Blade to build it, and thanks to Mitch Farrell, the Madaris Building went from being a four-story office building in downtown Houston to an exclusive fifteen-story building that's surrounded by a cluster of upscale shops, restaurants, and a beautiful park with a huge man-made pond. All of it is erected on a huge parcel of land on the outskirts of town. The condos are right across from the pond."

The place sounded beautiful and the chance to live in one of the condos was tempting. But . . .

"Can I think about it, Slade?"

"Yes. I'm sure living arrangements while you're in Houston are just one of many things you'll have to think about. But the offer is out there. If you want to fly to Houston to take a look at it, then let me know. I'll be returning to the city on Sunday."

She nodded. She would be leaving to return to Maine on Sunday as well. That meant she had only two more days to spend with Vincent before leaving.

And only two more days to spend with Slade.

She hung her head for a moment. Why did the thought of not seeing him for two weeks bother her?

"Skye?"

She lifted her head up and met his gaze. "Yes?"

"Whatever it is that's bothering you, let it go. Things are going to work out just fine. You have to believe it."

At that moment, a tremble ran through Skye's body. Slade Madaris had to be the most positive man she knew. From the moment she had first met him, all he'd done was offer her encouragement. And something else he'd done was introduce her to passion. The man had more passion in his little finger than Wayne had had in his entire body. She had never met a man such as Slade and doubted she ever would again. He had a way of making her feel feminine and attractive without really trying. It was the way he would look at her, smile at her, talk to her in that throaty and sexy voice of his.

"So now I have two offers out there on the table," he said. "One is for you to come to work for me this summer, and the other is a place for you to stay. The decision, Skye Barclay, is yours."

CHAPTER 11

Almost a week later after returning to Maine, Skye still hadn't made a decision regarding Slade's offers. She had, however, gotten an approval from her employer for a leave of absence for the entire summer. Now the only thing remaining was telling her parents what she planned to do.

As she sat at the desk in her office she glanced out the window. She had a beautiful view of the city's skyline as well as the Kennebec River.

She'd always thought that Augusta was a world-class city where its citizens were able to pursue lifelong learning while attending first-class schools, patronizing libraries and historic and cultural facilities. Downtown, where her office was located, was considered the heart of the city, and a lot of buildings were situated along Water Street and throughout the Capitol complex.

As she sat there, she couldn't help but recall the last two days she had spent in Ennis with the Madaris family. It had shown her that a normal family life did exist for some people. Everyone had been simply wonderful, and she had hated when Sunday had come around and it was time to leave.

She had quickly made friends with Slade's brother Blade and his cousin Luke, and Justin and Lorren's hospitality still had Skye in awe of their love, not only for each other, but for their children as well. Because of them, her brother had grown up to be a very special young man with outstanding respect for others and values.

And then there was Slade.

Her heart caught every time she thought about him. After he had made those offers to her, there was never a time the two of them were alone. They spent time with Blade and Luke as they shared more and more tidbits about the Madaris family as well as some of their escapades while growing up. It was easy to see the three weren't just relatives by blood but were also close friends who wouldn't hesitate to do what they could for one another.

She couldn't help but smile each and every time she recalled something she and Slade had done together. Thanks to him she'd had her first horse-riding experience, and she now appreciated the value of taking walks whenever she had a lot on her mind. Even without trying he had made her feel special, not only as Vincent's sister but as a woman as well.

She couldn't forget the kisses they had shared, and in the final days when, thanks to Blade and Luke, he couldn't seem to get her alone, she couldn't help but remember the flirtatious glances and heated looks he had sent her way. Those memories only made the decision of whether to take him up on his offers that much harder.

She jumped when the intercom buzzed on her desk. She glanced at her watch and saw it was almost lunchtime already. She had called her parents asking to meet with them later today. It would be then that she would tell them of her plans, and no matter what, she would not change them.

When the intercom buzzer sounded again she quickly reacted by hitting the speaker button to respond to her secretary. "Yes, Ida?"

"Wayne Bigelow is here. He says he's taking you to lunch."

Skye frowned. Just showing up out of the clear blue sky and thinking she was supposed to drop her plans just for him was typical Wayne. They didn't have lunch plans. In fact, as far as she was concerned, there was no need for them to see each other at all. He had said what he had to say to her, had told her exactly how he felt, before she'd left for Texas.

"Do you want me to send him in, Ms. Barclay?"

She could hear the annoyance in Ida's voice. Evidently, as usual, Wayne was out in the reception area being a nuisance. For some reason he thought whenever he walked into a room, everyone was supposed to stop whatever they were doing and give him their full attention. He truly didn't like being ignored. He'd probably heard she had returned to town and was a little ticked off that she hadn't called him. Maybe it was time to let him know they really had nothing else to say to each other. He needed to get on with his life like she planned on getting on with hers.

"Yes, Ida, please send him in."

Within minutes he strode into her office. She glanced up at him. He was handsome; she would have to give him that. But an acknowledgment of his good looks was all she would give him. The man was so full of himself it was a shame. In her opinion his attitude only diminished those good looks. And he'd always had a *better than thou* attitude about him. Spending time with Slade and seeing how a true gentleman carried himself made Wayne's offensive behavior that much more obvious.

"Get your purse, Skye. I'm here to take you to lunch."

She shook her head. And of course he expected her to obey his orders since he had walked into her office barking them out. He hadn't taken the time to do something courteous like give her a proper greeting, ask how she was doing or how her trip was. Doing any of that would have meant it was all about her, but Wayne intended for it to be all about him. She wondered how she had remained engaged to him for the time that she had.

"Hello, Wayne. We didn't have a lunch date and at the moment I'm too busy to drop whatever I'm doing to go anywhere with you." She flipped open a file that was on her desk for good measure.

"Besides," she decided to add, "why would we go out to lunch? It's not as if we're still seeing each other. If I recall, you called off our wedding before I left for Texas. I'd think you would be getting on with your life like I'm trying to do with mine."

He pulled out the chair across from her desk and sat in it, waving her words away with his hand. "Your stubbornness got me pretty upset and I said some things I should not have. But I'm over that now. I've decided the wedding is back on, and have called the planner to let her know it as well."

That bit of news angered Skye. The audacity of the man! She threw down the file she held in her hand. "You should not have done that, Wayne, because the wedding is not back on."

"Sure it is. Same date. Same time. And," he said in a low voice that was meant to really capture her attention with its supposed sexiness, "I've called that place in Hawaii to let them know the honeymoon is back on as well."

She had heard enough. "If you're counting on me marrying you, then you will be left standing at the altar alone, because I have no intentions of showing up. I know what you said to me that night and—"

"Like I said, you made me angry, Skye. How was I supposed to act?"

Like a true gentleman and not an ass, she wanted to say. Instead she said, "Like someone who cared about my feelings. But you didn't."

He stood angrily. "You had made up your mind to travel miles away to meet someone you didn't know based on some investigator's report. Someone who didn't know you and could probably care less that you existed."

"That's right and what you should have been was supportive."

"Supportive while my future wife made a fool of herself? Get real, Skye. What purpose did it serve, finding this so-called brother of yours? Okay, according to your parents, you were treated decently, but what's to come of it? Is he willing to leave the parents who raised him to start a life with you?"

"That wasn't my purpose in going, Wayne. I just wanted to meet him and get to know him."

"Fine, and I hope you've done both, because now you're back and I intend for us to move forward in our wedding plans."

Now it was Skye who stood. "There won't be any wedding plans because there won't be a wedding. That's the last thing I plan to say on the matter. Now I would appreciate it if you left."

He looked surprised, almost shocked. "You're asking me to leave?"

"Yes."

He frowned. "Okay, I can see that you're still upset, but we can talk about this at another time. I'll drop by your place later," he said, heading for the door.

"You aren't welcome at my place any longer, Wayne."

He didn't turn back around, nor did he stop walking. He merely tossed over his shoulder, "Sure I am. You'll have cooled off by tonight. I'll make plans for dinner." And then he opened the door and left.

For the longest moment she was too stunned to speak. In essence Wayne hadn't heard anything she'd said, and if he had heard it, he hadn't been listening. Well, she would have to show him. She would make sure the security guard who manned her apartment building knew that Wayne was no longer welcome.

She was about to sit back down when the intercom on her desk sounded again. She reached out and pushed the button. "Yes, Ida?"

"Your aunt Karen is on the line."

A smile touched Skye's lips. She had returned to town only to discover her aunt had taken a trip to Boston with friends. "Please put her on through."

A few minutes later her aunt's cheerful voice sounded. "Skye, how are you?"

"I'm fine, Aunt Karen; how was your trip to Boston?"

She heard her aunt's quick laugh. "Oh, as usual it was wonderful. I have to tell you all about it."

She leaned back in her chair and made a quick decision. "How about now? What are your plans for lunch?"

"I don't have any. Would you like for us to meet somewhere, let's say in half an hour?"

"I'd love to. There's so much I want to tell you," Skye said excitedly.

A few minutes later, she hung up the phone. At least there was one person who was interested in knowing how she'd spent her time in Texas.

Wayne Bigelow waited until he had gotten into his car and snapped on his seat belt before making what he considered an important call on his cell phone. As soon as the voice he wanted to hear came on the line, he said, "She's trying to be difficult."

There was a brief pause before the party he'd called said, "Then it's up to you to make sure she doesn't become a problem. You're a man with incredible charm, and I suggest you use it. You should never have broken off your engagement to her."

"I thought doing so would make her come around."

"Well, evidently you were wrong. The success of your future depends on you being able to control her. Under no circumstances is she to find out the identity of her biological father."

Wayne rolled his eyes. "I really don't think that matters to her. She hired a private investigator to find out the identity of her mother. And right now she's so caught up in this brother she's found."

"Maybe. But then I don't believe in taking chances, and

I'm depending on you to make sure she doesn't take her search any further."

Then without saying anything more, the person ended the call.

Slade stood at his office window on the fifteenth floor of the Madaris Building with his hands dug deep into the pockets of his trousers. He had been working on a project all morning and decided to take a break since it was nearing lunchtime. Instead of going out, he'd asked his secretary to order a sandwich and soda from the café on the ground floor.

Below, he could see a number of people eating lunch on the benches by the pond, while others used their lunchtime to take a brisk walk. It was a beautiful day and the first week in June. He, Blade, and Luke had returned to Houston the same day Skye had left to return to Maine, and he'd tried to keep busy ever since to keep her off his mind.

But he found it wasn't working.

He thought about her every waking moment, and last night he had gone so far as to contact Lorren for her phone number, so he could give her a call to see how she was doing and to ask if she had thought any more about his offers. But something had held him back from calling her.

This morning when he'd awakened he had considered sending her flowers, since it seemed every floral arrangement he looked at reminded him of her freshness and beauty. And he couldn't let go of the memories of all the kisses they had shared. He had not only been taken by her; she had also shaken his world and left him mesmerized.

He turned around when the buzzer on his desk sounded. Crossing the room, he pressed the button to respond to his secretary. "My lunch has arrived already, Claire?"

"No, sir. You have a visitor. Your uncle Jake Madaris is here to see you."

A smile spread across Slade's lips, corner to corner. "Please send him in."

It didn't take Slade long to wait for his grand-uncle to open the door and walk in. In Slade's opinion, his grandfather's youngest brother was the epitome of a Texan man from the top of the Stetson he wore on his head all the way down to the expensive leather boots he wore on his feet. A man in his late forties, he was tall at six-seven, and as far as Slade was concerned, he was the best uncle anyone could ever have. Slade loved and respected all his uncles, but Jake Madaris would always have a special place in all of his nieces' and nephews' hearts, because even with his extremely busy schedule of running one of the biggest and most productive ranches on a stretch of land not far from Houston, he'd always made time for them while they'd been growing up.

"What brings you off the Whispering Pines ranch, Uncle Jake?" Slade asked, crossing the room to give his uncle a huge bear hug.

"I'm meeting Nedwyn for lunch to discuss plans for the retirement party that Diamond and I are giving him in a few weeks."

Slade nodded. Senator Nedwyn Lansing and his uncle Jake had been good friends for years. Senator Lansing had first been Jake's deceased brother Robert's best friend, and after Robert Madaris had died in the Vietnam War, the senator and Jake had forged a strong friendship. The senator had retired last month after serving in the United States Senate for over twenty years.

"How is the family doing? Diamond, Granite, and Amethyst?" His uncle was married to former movie star Diamond Swain. Years ago she had traded in the bright lights of Hollywood to be a stay-at-home mom and rancher's wife. On occasion, she could be pulled out of retirement to do a movie or two, and that was only when her and Jake's good friend Sterling Hamilton sat in the director's chair.

Jake smiled as he always did with the mention of the wife and children he loved and adored. "Everyone is doing fine. Since I was in town I thought I'd start from the bottom floor of this building and work my way up to the top before meeting Nedwyn at a restaurant across the way. I've seen Dex, Christy, and Alex, and Clayton and Syneda. And everyone seems to be doing fine. Blade and Luke came out to the ranch and spent a few days last week and I talked to Justin on the phone last night. He shared Vincent's good news. I understand you got a chance to meet his sister while you were in Ennis a week ago."

"Yes, and she's a real nice person. I'm glad she and Vincent found each other."

At that moment the buzzer on his desk sounded again. "Excuse me, Uncle Jake," Slade said, right before hitting the speaker button to respond to his secretary's summons. "Yes, Claire?"

"Your lunch is here, sir."

"Thanks."

"Well, let me be going," Jake said, walking with Slade toward the door. "I don't want to keep Nedwyn waiting."

"How long will you be in Houston?"

"For the rest of the day. I'm going to try to get by to see everyone, and Mom wants to talk to me. It seems she's been dreaming about fish again."

Slade lifted a brow. "And she thinks it's Diamond?"

Jake laughed. "No, I think she wants to hear it directly from me that it's not Kimara."

Slade laughed. Kimara was married to Jake's good friend Kyle Garwood, and already the couple had seven children, all under the age of ten, which included two sets of twins. "I thought Kyle and Kimara have decided not to have any more children," he said.

Jake grinned. "They have but I guess Mom doesn't want to leave any stone unturned."

"Personally, I think it's Syneda," Slade said, knowing what kind of reaction he would get from his uncle.

Slade watched Jake stop dead in his tracks, and in a serious tone Jake said, "Please, Slade. Don't scare us like that."

Slade laughed. Everyone knew just what a handful Remington was. But then the little girl was Clayton and Syneda's child, so her antics at times really weren't surprising. She was a chip off both of her parents' blocks.

"You will be coming to Nedwyn's retirement party at the ranch later this month, right?" Jake asked.

Slade nodded. "Yes, I plan on being there."

"Good, and bring a date. You need to get out and meet someone before Blade corners the entire Houston market."

"I have met someone," Slade said, immediately thinking of Skye.

"Glad to hear it, and I'm looking forward to meeting her."

Slade smiled when he responded by saying, "And I'm looking forward to you meeting her as well, Uncle Jake."

CHAPTER 12

Skye always enjoyed having lunch with her aunt, and this time she had a lot to tell her. She told her all about Justin and Lorren Madaris and how kind they had been to her. And she mentioned Slade briefly, only to say he had been visiting the Madaris family and had been kind to her as well. She wasn't ready to share just what good friends they had become to anyone just yet. She spent most of the time talking about Vincent and what a wonderful brother he was and how mature and well adjusted he was for his age.

And then after their meal, she decided to tell her aunt of her decision to spend the summer in Houston. Not surprisingly, her aunt thought it was a wonderful idea but quickly reminded her that her parents would not think so.

Skye thought of her aunt's words as she took a sip of her tea. She then glanced up at her aunt. "Please help me to understand something, Aunt Karen; just why are my parents so opposed to me establishing a relationship with Vincent?"

Karen shook her head. "I really don't know, just like I don't understand why they were so against you ever knowing you were adopted. Even now Edith blames me for your finding out since you overheard my conversation with them. People adopt kids all the time and I always assumed they would tell you, and when they hadn't, I merely asked them about it that day."

Skye nodded. "What do you remember about my adoption?" she asked.

"Not a whole lot," Karen said. "At the time I was married to your uncle Larry. He was a Foreign Service diplomat and we were living in Japan. I came back home to discover Tom and Edith had gotten you as a newborn through a private adoption. I had known for years that Edith couldn't have any children because of a childhood illness, but I'd always thought that she and Tom had pretty much decided to go through life childless, so I was surprised that they had adopted you. I was surprised yet pleased."

Skye nodded again. She also knew that her aunt had always intended to have children herself, but after her husband had died at an early age of colon cancer, she never remarried. "Well, I'm telling them about my plans tonight, and regardless of how they feel about it, I plan to establish a relationship with Vincent and will spend the summer in Houston."

At that moment Skye's cell phone went off. She pulled it from her purse hoping it wasn't Wayne. She glanced at the identification of the caller and didn't recognize the number. Curious, she made an excuse to her aunt and flipped her phone open to answer it. "Yes?"

"Skye, how are you?"

Skye closed her eyes for a moment at the sound of the ultrasexy voice. And to make matters worse, visions of his handsome face flooded her mind. When she reopened her eyes she found her aunt looking at her curiously. "Slade?" she asked, although she knew it was him.

"Yes. I had you on my mind and thought I would give you a call. I got your number from Lorren. I hope you don't mind."

She shook her head. "No, I don't mind, and to answer your other question, I'm doing fine. I'm having lunch with my aunt at the moment, though."

"Sorry to interrupt."

"No, that's okay. It's good hearing from you. How are Luke and Blade?"

She could hear him chuckle. "They're fine, just trying to stay out of trouble."

She smiled thinking of the pair and knowing staying out of trouble for those two would be a rather difficult task. "I'm still thinking of your offers but haven't made a decision about either yet," she decided to say, wondering if that was the reason he had called.

"Take your time; the offers aren't going anywhere. I just don't want you to worry about a thing while you're here in Houston. I'm looking forward to your visit. Well, let me let you get back to enjoying lunch with your aunt. It was nice talking to you, Skye."

"It was nice of you to call. I'm looking forward to my visit as well."

"Okay, and you take care. Good-bye."

"Good-bye, Slade."

Skye's stomach did a funny little flip when he ended the call and returned her phone to her purse. When her aunt cleared her throat Skye glanced across the table and looked into her aunt's smiling face.

"Why is it I get the feeling that you didn't tell me everything there is to know about Slade Madaris?"

Skye couldn't help the smile that touched her lips. "Mainly because the man is too good to be true; at least compared to Wayne he is. He is everything Wayne is not."

"Then I'm impressed."

Skye chuckled at her aunt's comment. Karen had never liked Wayne. Skye started to tell her aunt of Wayne's visit to her office and changed her mind. She hoped she had made herself clear to him, and if he did show up at her place later that day, thinking he could just waltz his way up the elevator to her apartment, he would be in for a big surprise.

"Thanks for this guest list, Nedwyn," Jake Madaris said, standing and tucking the piece of paper into the pocket of his jacket. "Diamond is excited about planning the party in your honor."

Senator Lansing smiled. "And I appreciate the both of you doing it. My secretary said the list is pretty complete."

Jake nodded as he sat back now. "What do you plan to do with yourself now that your days in the Senate are over?"

"Rest and relax. The person elected as my successor will do an excellent job, and I had no problems turning everything over to him. I plan to enjoy life." He got quiet for a moment before adding, "I also planned to do something else that I've put off for years, but I want to talk to you about it first."

Jake lifted a brow. "Sounds serious. What is it?"

Nedwyn smiled. "Maybe you should ask *who is it* instead."

Jake grinned. "I think I already have an idea. It's Diana, isn't it?"

When a huge smile spread across Nedwyn's face, Jake knew he had given the right answer. Nedwyn had confided in him years ago that he had fallen in love with Jake's deceased brother's wife. The reason Nedwyn had never tried pursuing a relationship with Diana was because he hadn't been sure how she would feel about it—she had been widowed for many years and hadn't thought of remarrying. Besides, Nedwyn had been one of Robert's best friends.

"Yes, it's Diana. For the past year, with me spending more time in Houston and less in the nation's capital, we've been seeing each other quite a bit and she's been my date at a couple of social functions. I think she feels comfortable in that role and has no idea I've been in love with her for years."

Jake leaned back in his chair. "Now is the time to let her know how you feel, Nedwyn, don't you think? I never understood why you held back before. After meeting and falling in love with Diamond, I wish every man had a special woman in his life. Robert and Diana had a good marriage, and I know losing him in 'Nam was hard on her." He remembered that time like it was yesterday. His niece Felicia had been barely two years old when they got the word that Robert had lost his life while serving his country.

"Diana tried devoting her time to raising Felicia," Jake said. "But as you know, she shared that task with her husband's six brothers, which I'm sure wasn't easy for her. That's why we all think so much of her. She didn't move away with Felicia to start another life someplace else. She stayed right here, enmeshed in the Madaris family. She is and always will be a beautiful and special lady to all of us."

Nedwyn absorbed what Jake had said. He thought she was a beautiful and special lady as well. He also considered her a good friend. He had realized that he had fallen in love with her a few years ago but didn't make a move because he hadn't wanted her under the media's scrutiny as someone he was interested in, especially when that person was the widowed wife of the man who had been a very close friend. Only two people knew how he felt about her: Jake, and one of Nedwyn's other best friends, Syntel Remington, millionaire oil magnate.

"I figured I'm not getting any younger, Jake, and I want to settle down and spend the rest of my life with someone I care about, so I intend to start letting Diana know just how I feel," he said softly, with a firm conviction in his tone.

Jake took a sip of his wine, smiled, and said, "All I have to say to that is it's about time."

"Clayton, this is Alex. Can you talk?"

Clayton Madaris leaned back in the chair at his desk. "Yes. I don't have to worry about Syneda popping in. She's downstairs having lunch with Caitlin," he said of his brother Dex's wife. "What did you find out?"

"Nothing, really. The woman is who she says she is. In fact, she's led a pretty sheltered life. Her adoptive parents are pretty well-off, and over the years they have given her the best of everything. She went to private schools all her life and has pretty much had servants at her beck and call. I don't see her looking Vincent up just to get money out of him when she's had plenty of money of her own over the years.

And I don't see where she's ever been wasteful with it. In fact, she gives a lot of it away to a number of charities."

Clayton nodded. "What type of work do her parents do?"

"Her mother has never worked outside the home, and her father is an accountant."

Clayton lifted a brow. "And the man can afford servants and private schools on an accountant salary?"

"It seems both her parents came from wealthy families and received trust funds when they reached a certain age. They are considered part of Augusta's elite class. And speaking of trust funds, Skye is set to receive one on her thirtieth birthday. And it's a pretty hefty sum, so trust me when I say she really doesn't need any of Vincent's money. You can drop the notion that she's a gold digger, because she's not."

"Hearing you say that makes me feel better."

Alex chuckled. "I figured it would. So, I'm closing my file on her, unless there's something else you want me to check out."

"No. It sounds like you did a thorough job as usual. I appreciate it, and remember, it's between the two of us."

"I might as well warn you that Christy knows. She was awake that night you called me."

"Then just tell her to keep her lips zipped. She'll do what you say."

Alex chuckled. "Oh, like Syneda always does what *you* say."

Clayton frowned. "Don't be a smart-ass. Just keep your wife quiet. Good-bye, Alex."

Skye entered her parents' home with the weight of doom on her shoulders with what she had to tell them. She had opened the door and made it to the foyer when she heard a sound. She turned and saw Helen, the forty-two-year-old woman who'd been her mother's personal assistant for the past eight years, coming down the stairs.

Skye had discovered when she was in her last year of high school that Helen Stone was not only her mother's personal assistant but her personal spy as well. Unbeknownst to Skye, Helen had kept a log of every boy who'd called her to pass on to her mother. Not only that, although Skye could never actually prove it, she had a feeling that Helen was the one who'd told her mother she was seriously considering attending a college in another town after the woman had eavesdropped on a conversation Skye had with the college admitting office. Since then, she had never trusted the woman.

"Miss Skye, I didn't know you were back."

Skye didn't have to wonder how the woman had known she'd gone anywhere. "Yes, I'm back, Helen. Where are my parents?"

The smile the woman plastered on her face was phony as a three-dollar bill. "They just finished dinner and are in the study drinking their evening wine. Should I let them know you're here?"

"No, that's not necessary. I can do that myself." Skye walked off feeling the heat of the woman's stare on her back. There was no doubt about it: Helen was definitely loyal to Edith Barclay.

Skye entered the room and the first thing she noticed was that her parents were huddled together on the sofa discussing something important, as well as private, since they were whispering. For them to be whispering seemed rather strange. Why would they be talking secretly in their own home? Especially since the only other person around to listen was Skye's mother's trusted servant. Or maybe they had learned their lesson from the last time when Skye had arrived unexpectedly and overheard one of their "private" conversations.

"Hello, Mom and Dad."

She watched how they nearly jumped apart, surprised to see her standing in the doorway. "I hope I'm not interrupting anything," she said.

Her father immediately stood and walked toward her with a smile on his face. It was sad to think that she could no longer tell if it was real or fake. "Skye, it's so good having you back. When did you return?"

"Sunday, like I said I would."

Her mother frowned at her after taking a sip of wine. "And you're just getting around to visiting with us now?"

Skye's father quickly glanced back over his shoulder after giving her a hug. "Come on, Edith; I'm sure Skye had a lot to do after she returned."

"Thanks, Dad, and I did," she said, smiling, appreciating her father coming to her defense.

"Now that that's all been cleared up, have you seen or talked to Wayne?" her father asked, taking her hand and leading her toward an empty chair in the room.

Skye frowned as she sat down. She had an idea as to why her father was asking. "Yes, but only briefly. He stopped by the office today to invite me to lunch."

That news pleased her mother immensely, if her huge smile was anything to go by. "And over lunch did the two of you work things out?"

Skye shook her head. "No. In fact, I didn't go to lunch with him since I was busy and there's nothing for us to work out, Mom. I'm not marrying Wayne."

"Skye, stop being unreasonable," her father said, and, to Skye's way of thinking, rather harshly. "The man wants to marry you."

"Does it matter to anyone that I don't want to marry him?" she asked in a bitter tone. She had told her parents her feelings on the matter. Why were they still trying to shove Wayne Bigelow down her throat?

"Is there a reason you're so against the idea?" her father asked, pouring another glass of wine like he really needed it. He seemed nervous about something.

Skye decided to take his odd behavior in to think about later. "Yes, there are plenty of reasons, and I stated them before. Wayne broke our engagement, but it was for the best. A marriage between us would have never worked."

"Could you tell us why you feel so strongly about that?" her father tried asking in a calm tone as he went back to sit beside her mother on the sofa.

Skye looked at both her parents and said, "I don't love him."

She watched her mother roll her eyes and wave her ringed hand when she said, "Skye, women of good breeding learn to love the men they marry."

"Well, good breeding or not, I doubt if I'll ever learn to love Wayne."

"How do you know if you don't try?" her mother all but snapped. "Why are you being so difficult?"

"And why are the two of you ignoring how I feel and shoving Wayne at me? It's like the two of you stand to gain something if I marry him."

She watched the wineglass almost drop from her father's hand, sloshing wine over his trousers. Had what she said hit some sort of nerve?

"Of course we stand to gain something with your marriage to Wayne," her mother said quickly, handing her husband a linen napkin. "We'll have the assurance of knowing that you will be taken care of. Your father and I aren't getting any younger, Skye, and your well-being is important to us."

Skye wished she could believe that, but for some reason she felt her well-being had nothing to do with it. It was more of her parents' grasping at the opportunity to continue to control her life through Wayne. "Well, I appreciate your concern, but I'm a big girl. I can handle myself and make my own decisions about what I want to do."

She inhaled deeply before she said, "In fact, I've made a decision that I want to tell you about."

"And what decision is that?" her father asked gruffly. She could tell he was not finished with their discussion of Wayne.

"After meeting Vincent, I want to spend more time with him this summer. I can't very well do that with me living here, so I've decided to spend the entire summer in Texas."

"What!" her parents exclaimed simultaneously, with shocked looks on their faces.

Before they could recover, she quickly said, "I'm taking a leave of absence from my job and plan to spend three months in Houston, where Vincent will be working as a student intern for two of his cousins' company. That way we can get to see each other more."

Her father stood after setting his wineglass on the table with a loud thump. She was surprised he hadn't broken it. A type of rage that Skye had never seen before was on his face. What was wrong with him? She had grown up used to her mother's dramatics, but never her father's. "I forbid you to do such a thing," he all but roared.

Then her mother stood beside her husband, presenting a united front. "I agree with your father. We forbid it."

Skye studied her parents for a moment. She'd known they wouldn't like her decision, but she never figured it would have them this angry and upset. A part of her was tempted to give in to them as she usually did. But when she saw them look at her expectantly, she knew that was just what they expected her to do.

But not this time.

Now that she had spent time with the Madarises, she had seen how a normal family could be, one where dictatorship wasn't practiced, where a person's wants and desires were respected. It saddened her to know all that she'd missed while growing up in this household.

Skye shook her head as she stood, tightening her hand on the purse she held. "I'm sorry my news has upset the two of you, but I won't cancel my plans because of you. Spending the summer in Houston is important to me and it's something that I want to do. It's something that I *will* do, whether I have your support or not."

"And you will turn your back on us?" her father asked angrily.

"Dad, it's not turning my back on you and Mom; it's finding myself, doing something that I want for a change, something that will make me happy. Why can't you and Mom understand that? Why can't you see that I deserve to have some happiness in my life?"

Her father snorted derisively. "All we see is how ungrateful you are for what we've given you. And until you come to your senses, we'd rather that you not visit us."

Skye knew she was probably standing there looking as if someone had slapped her or had even gone so far as to throw an ice-cold bucket of water in her face. "You are cutting off our relationship because I won't bend to your will?" she asked, getting angry at the very thought that yes, that's what they were doing.

"If that's the way you see it, then I guess that's what it is," her father responded while her mother stood by his side nodding her head in agreement. "We want you to remain here and start planning your wedding to Wayne again. And until you do that, we prefer not to see you."

Skye inhaled deeply as she stared at her parents. "Remember, this was your decision and not mine."

She turned and walked out of the room and, moments later, out of the house. And she didn't look back.

Wayne removed the phone from so close to his ear when the loud voice nearly yelled right into it. After a few seconds, he returned it to his ear.

"When you think about it," he said when he was able to get a word in, "her spending time in Houston might not be a bad thing. Skye is all caught up with this brother she's found. The last thing she'll think about is finding out the identity of her father. In that case, you don't have anything to worry about."

"I want to be certain of that," the party on the other line

snapped. "Did you ever see a copy of the report from the private investigator that she hired?"

"No."

"I want a copy of it and I don't care how you get it. I want to make sure there's nothing in it that will make her start wondering about anything."

"Okay, I'll get a copy."

"And I think while she's in Texas you should visit her a few times. Perhaps if she believes that you care about her building a relationship with her brother and are supportive, she will soften up toward you some."

"Maybe," he said stubbornly, not really caring if Skye softened up toward him or not. He glanced over at the naked woman sleeping beside him. Sex between them had been good as usual, but then he wasn't a person who let good sex rule his mind. Nor was he a person who liked being taken for granted. He had no intentions of sitting around and waiting for Skye to come to her senses. He'd gotten pretty pissed earlier that night when he had arrived at her place and the security guard had outright refused to grant him entrance up to her apartment.

"There's no maybe about it. I want it done. You have a lot to gain if things go down as planned. I wouldn't screw up now if I were you. Do you understand?"

Wayne frowned. "Yes, I understand. Completely."

CHAPTER 13

Slade stood, almost incapable of breathing, while watching Skye come down the escalator to the baggage claims area. As soon as her feet hit the floor she saw him and smiled and began moving in his direction. Emotions filled his chest as he began walking forward to meet her.

He had been surprised at the phone call he'd received from her a little less than a week ago. He hadn't asked any questions; he'd just listened. She wanted to take him up on both offers, and after he assured her there wouldn't be any problems with it, she had quickly ended the call. Since that night he had wondered what had driven her to make the decisions she had. He had heard the gloom in her voice and wondered the reason for it. But when he saw her in the flesh, the reason didn't matter. She was here now and he would make sure he kept that smile in her eyes.

Over the past couple of weeks he had thought of her often and had refused to try to figure out the why of it. The important thing was that he had thought of her. And just like she felt she needed time to spend with Vincent, Slade felt that he needed time to spend with her. Time to sort out all these emotions he was feeling and why the closer he got to her the more his chest felt like it was about to burst.

She was wearing a pair of jeans and a pretty red top and she looked good, sexy in a prissy sort of way. And the twisted curls on her head had a copper glow that seemed to highlight the beauty of her face. The more he saw her in jeans, the more he liked it. By the end of the summer he would have converted her into a full-fledged cowgirl, leather boots and all.

She was only a few feet away and a shiver ran down his spine. He ignored all the other people walking quickly by, either going to catch their flights or there to meet their loved ones. His mind was concentrated on one person, one particular woman.

The moment he was able to reach out and touch her, he wrapped both his arms around her and lifted her off her feet. "Hello, Slade," she said, smiling down at him.

At that moment he wasn't able to force his mouth to work for a response. The only thing he was compelled to do with his mouth was join it with hers in a kiss. The first thought that ran through his mind the moment their lips touched was that he needed this. He needed to hold her in his arms this way, semi-suspended in air, while his mouth devoured hers. And the way her tongue latched onto his quickened his pulse.

When he became aware of a few whistles and catcalls, he thought it was time they ended things. Besides, they both needed to breathe in much-needed air. "That was some welcome, Slade," she said, smiling up at him, when he had placed her back on her feet.

He smiled. "You liked it?"

She chuckled. "Yes, I liked it."

"Good." As he took her hand in his they moved toward the area where her luggage was located.

"I have three bags," she turned to him to say.

He lifted a teasing brow. "I thought you traveled light."

She grinned. "I'm going to be here all summer, Slade."

He nodded as he pulled the three bags that she pointed out to him off the carousel. She didn't have to remind him about how long she would be staying. He was looking forward to every day she would be there. "There're a lot of activities planned for you beginning this weekend. Vincent is anxious for everyone to meet you, so Justin's brother Dex and his wife, Caitlin, have a dinner party planned tomorrow night in your honor in their home."

"That's very kind of them."

He winked at her. "Hey, haven't you figured out by now that the Madarises are kind people? And before you ask about Vincent, he'll be arriving tomorrow. Justin and Lorren are flying him in," he said, leading her out of the terminal toward the parking lot.

She nodded, recalling that Justin and his brothers shared ownership of a private plane, a Cessna.

"You know what that means, don't you?"

Slade's question recaptured her attention. She glanced over at him. "No, what does it mean?"

He smiled at her before leaning forward and placing a kiss on her forehead. "It means, Skye Barclay, that I'll have you all to myself for an entire day and a half. What do you think of that?"

At that moment Skye felt her pressure spike up sky-high and she really couldn't think at all.

"Slade, this place is beautiful," Skye said. And she really meant it. The condo he had offered her to use was more than she had imagined. Fully furnished, the place was huge and located on the twenty-fifth floor. The building appeared like a tower that overlooked a beautiful park with a spectacular view of a pond that connected to the Madaris Office Park. He'd said he and Blade had named the park Laverne Square in honor of their great-grandmother.

The view outside the window was incredible, and looking out of it, Skye could see the fifteen-story office structure—the Madaris Building. Below it stood a smaller tower surrounded by numerous shops, restaurants, banks, boutiques, and several other professional offices, as well as a movie theater. Everything she saw had been designed and built by Slade and Blade, the owners and CEOs of the Madaris Construction

Company. If this was a testimony of their work, then the two men should be proud of their accomplishments.

She turned around to look at Slade. He hadn't moved from leaning against the closed door. On the ride from the airport he had kept the conversation light, occasionally pointing out various landmarks and places of interest they'd passed.

Even during the ride up to the condo in the elevator she had tried to keep her breathing normal, especially whenever he planted those dark eyes on her. From the moment she'd first seen him at the airport, her heart hadn't acted normal. He had been easy to spot in the mass crowds of people. He had stood out, tall, lean, and unbearably handsome, wearing a pair of jeans, a dark jacket that emphasized the muscular breadth of his shoulders, and a pair of leather boots.

She hadn't forgotten how good he looked; she just hadn't expected the shock of seeing him, as gorgeous as he wanted to be, too brutal to her senses, so raw to her nerves. But what had almost made her drool when she'd seen him was the way he always looked wearing a Stetson on his head. Totally magnificent. Completely Texan. Provocatively male. That was how he looked now.

She was so glad he had kissed her when he'd seen her. A part of her would have been disappointed if he hadn't. When it came to kissing, they seemed to enjoy it immensely when they were doing it to each other.

She watched as he eased away from the door and began walking toward her, removing his Stetson and tossing it on a nearby table. No man, she thought, other than Slade Madaris, could look this good just walking. There was something about his confident stride that could totally block out her senses. There was nothing arrogant and conceited about him. What you saw was what you got, and what she was seeing, the closer he got, sent a frisson of heat down her spine, playing havoc on her peace of mind and staggering her senses.

She scrambled like heck to restore her brain cells, the ones that had literally gotten fried when she'd seen him at the airport, but found that she couldn't. And when he came to a stop directly in front of her, she saw how his nostrils were flaring as if he had picked up her scent.

"We're alone, Skye," he said huskily. The rich baritone of his voice caused heat to form between her legs, and she didn't have to figure out why. There was something about Slade that connected to her, reached out to her, and started her entire body to react on all levels. She was attuned to him like she'd never been to another man, and his proximity had tingles invading her entire body.

She swallowed. "Yes, we're alone," she agreed.

He leaned down to kiss her, immediately invading her mouth with his tongue, and she was right on it, quick and eager to take everything he was offering. She participated, sucked on his tongue like it was something she had missed doing the past couple of weeks. And it had been. Each time she remembered their kisses, this was the part she remembered the most—all the tongue play they had shared. But she had a feeling they were about to share something else. And it was something she needed and so badly wanted.

"You taste good," he whispered, pulling back slightly, dotting the side of her face with his kisses. "It's even better than I remembered." And then he was staring at her, holding her gaze with his seductive one as if he was determined for her to read what was in his eyes. She knew he wanted for her to see only assurances. No doubts.

And what she saw took her breath away. There was an overwhelming sense of longing in his gaze. She had never encountered this level of desire, a height filled with such intensity. The air surrounding them was becoming too intimate, too cozy, too downright tension-filled. She wanted to look away, break his hold on her captured gaze, but she found herself incapable of doing so. She was too sexually attracted to him.

Then he slowly reached out and ran his fingers through her hair while still holding her gaze. He pulled on her hair and gently tugged her mouth to his. He didn't kiss her again; instead he whispered words against her moist lips. "I want to make love to you, Skye."

His voice was raw with desire and need. She heard it, felt it, could actually taste it against her lips. Awareness stirred within her and she could barely stand the heat escalating up her body from it. Goose bumps covered her skin from top to bottom, and at that moment she knew she wanted the same thing Slade wanted.

She didn't bother questioning why this was happening to her. How Slade had the ability to do this to her, make a perfectly rational person act totally irrational. If she was drunk, then she wasn't ready to sober up yet. And if this was insane, then you could just call her stone crazy.

She reached out and wrapped her arms around his neck, brought her body closer to his, felt the intensity of his need for her in the lower part of her body as she looked deep into the darkness of his eyes. "And I want to make love to you, too, Slade," she whispered against his lips.

As if her consent was just what he'd been waiting for, he bent his head again, captured her mouth with his, and wrapped his arms around her waist to draw her even closer.

As if he wasn't about to be hurried, as if he had all night and then some time to make love to her, he savored her mouth once more. Each stroke of his tongue was gentle, greedy, yet as close to perfection as a kiss could get. And she shivered in his arms under the onslaught of what he was doing to her.

Moments later Slade broke off the kiss and took a step back to remove his jacket. Then he reached out to unbutton her top. He was glad there were just a few buttons. Only four of them, in fact, and each one he set free showed more and more of the colorful lace bra she wore underneath. And when he removed her blouse and tossed it aside, he saw how the fullness of her breasts was pressed against lace. He reached out and used the tip of his finger to trace the outline of her breasts, stroking the tips of her nipples through the material in the process, and heard her breath catch more than once.

Deciding he wanted to finish undressing her in the bedroom, he swept her off her feet and into his arms. Quickly moving around furniture, he made his way across the living room and down the hall to one of the bedrooms. This particular condo was perfect for her, and he'd known it the moment he had made the offer, not to mention it was conveniently right across the hall from his—something she wasn't aware of yet.

The only other condo on this floor was owned by a man who spent most of his time traveling abroad, so from the time Slade had lived here, it was as if he'd had the entire floor to himself. Now he had no qualms about sharing it with Skye.

Skye released her arms from around Slade's neck the moment he placed her on the huge bed. She glanced around. The bedroom was simply beautiful, and she could immediately tell it had a designer's touch. Slade had said this condo was used as a model to show others interested in purchasing other condos in the building. The furnishings and the design had been meticulously well thought out to capture the opulent taste of anyone who truly liked nice things. Skye could just imagine how much a place like this cost, considering the view you got from your living room window every morning.

The feel of Slade's hand tracing a path down her jean leg captured her attention. "It's time for these to come off, don't you think?" he asked in a deep, husky voice.

Skye really didn't know what to think. Whenever Slade touched her it was as if she was launched into a state of being where she was incapable of thinking at all. She could only feel. From the first, he had awakened feelings and emotions deep inside of her that she hadn't known existed.

Thanks to him, she wanted to feel; she wanted to experience the wonders of life between a man and a woman. It was an opportunity she had been fully denied until now. When she thought of what she and Wayne had shared, she knew it wouldn't be anything compared to this. All she had to do was stare into the darkness of Slade's eyes to know that he would be the most considerate of lovers. It would matter to him how she felt and what she thought. There was no doubt in her mind that in his arms she would be receiving many wondrous lessons. A frisson of heat zinged through her body at the thought of all the things he could teach her.

"Skye?"

She smiled as he continued to hold her gaze. "Yes, I agree. It's time for them to come off."

She swallowed hard when his hand reached out and went to her waist to unsnap her jeans. The moment his fingers brushed against her stomach, she sucked in a deep breath.

The sound had him glancing up at her after he'd removed her shoes. "You okay?"

"Yes, I'm okay."

He nodded. "Lift your hips so I can pull them down your legs."

She did what he asked, glad of two things. First, that they weren't skintight and he didn't have to struggle to peel them off her, and second, that she had decided to get rid of the plain Jane white panties and bras and purchase some colorful matching ones. According to the salesclerk, the color of the panties and bra Skye was wearing was an exotic lime. She'd liked the sexy sound of that, and she had liked even more how the color seemed to bring out the complexion of her skin.

She watched Slade toss her jeans aside, and then he reached out his hand to her. On her knees she crossed the mattress' short distances to him, and he pulled her into his arms, held her gently. "I like what you're wearing," he whispered hotly against her ear. "But I have a feeling I will like you even better not wearing anything at all."

Before she could even try to think of anything to say to that, he released her and took a step back, and Skye knew that he was about to remove his own clothes. A part of her was curious, fascinated. She had never seen a man undress before, not even Wayne. He'd claimed that wasn't the way things were done. He had enjoyed seeing her undress for him but had never undressed for her, and never had he made an attempt to undress her.

Her attention came to full alert when she saw Slade's hand go to the belt buckle of his jeans. The movement was as easy and smooth as anything she'd ever seen. There was nothing mechanical, staged, or planned in anything he was doing. Being sexy came natural for him.

"Do you prefer that I take my shirt off first?"

His question had her looking up, meeting his gaze. It was her opinion that it didn't matter what came off first, as long as something came off. Shaking her head, she said what she knew he would probably say to her if she had been the one asking the question. "Do whatever makes you comfortable. The decision is yours."

She then decided to add just so that he would know, "I've never seen a man undress while I watched before."

"Not even the man you were to marry?" he asked, and she could tell from the sound of his voice and the expression on his face that he was clearly shocked.

"Yes, not even the man I was supposed to marry. He had a different view on sex than most people."

"Doesn't sound like it was a good one. That's really sad."

Skye agreed. But until now she never thought about just how sad it was. She had gotten used to Wayne's habits, his unusual take on things. Now she was glad she didn't have to deal with them . . . *or him* . . . again.

"So, Slade Madaris, what's your view on sex?"

The promising grin he sent her was slowly building fire in her body. "It's hard to explain. Besides, I'd rather show you."

And she wanted him to show her. From the moment he

had opened the door to Justin and Lorren's home a few weeks ago, his presence had affected her, and when she had returned home, she'd had a gut feeling as to why. And today seeing him again only reconfirmed it.

She loved him.

She was not one who would normally believe in love at first sight. Skye Barclay, daughter of Tom and Edith Barclay, was too no-nonsense to even consider something like that happening.

But deep down, Skye knew that it had. With a tenderness she had found endearing and a sense of caring she had discovered was such an ingrained part of his character, without even trying, Slade had captured a huge chunk of her heart. To be totally honest, he had ensnared all of it. He had shown her that all men weren't cut from the same cloth. And that in itself said a lot.

Her attention was drawn back to Slade's hand movement. Evidently he'd made a decision to remove his shirt first, and she watched as he went about performing the task.

"I might as well warn you," he said softly as he removed the shirt from his body and tossed it aside.

"What?" she breathed out, but just barely. Shirtless, he was a fantasy come to life. There was no other way to describe him with his flat chest, muscled shoulders, lean and strong-looking body.

"I've been thinking of making love to you for some time. You, Skye Barclay, have invaded my dreams quite a lot."

She decided to be honest with him as well. "It can't be any more often than you've invaded mine," she said softly.

He smiled at her admission and she watched his hand return to his belt. "Then the rest of the day should be interesting."

There was no doubt in her mind that it would be. He pulled the belt through the loops and then went for the zipper of his jeans. He paused to bend over to remove his socks and boots and toss them aside. When he straightened back up, he gave her a smile that had her entire body drumming with both tension and desire.

Then her heartbeat began hammering in her chest when he started easing the jeans down his muscular thighs and strong legs, exposing the sexy pair of black briefs he wore, briefs that could barely cover the evidence of the rigid, hard length of his aroused body. Not that it mattered. The heat in his eyes was another clear indication of just how sexually stimulated he was.

"Now we need to remove the last of our clothing, don't we?" he asked.

"Yes." She couldn't think of a time she'd even wanted to get out of her clothes more.

Wordlessly he crossed the room back to the bed, holding her gaze with every step he took. When he was close to her, he leaned his hip against the bed frame and reached out and unhooked the front of her bra. The firm and full breasts jutted forward, the darkened tips of her nipples protruding proudly. Taking his finger, he began caressing each tip. And when her breathing escalated to an almost unbearable height and the low whimpers started, he took his full hand and cupped her breasts and began massaging them gently before taking his fingers to caress the nipples all over again.

"Slade." She said his name in a shaky breath.

"Yes, Skye?"

"Stop torturing me."

He smiled. "Is that what I'm doing?"

"Yes."

He gave her a lopsided grin. "There're several degrees of torture, you know."

And to prove his point, he dipped his head down and let the tip of his tongue replace his finger. The moment he closed his mouth over her breast she moaned deep in her throat as he vigorously began licking the hardened bud, which seemed to grow even harder, making it more distended in his mouth.

Moments later he transferred his mouth to the other breast and provided it with his same brand and degree of torture.

The sexy moans and groans she was making were sending him over the top, pushing him over the edge. He lifted his head and whispered in her ear, "Tell me when you've had enough."

She didn't hesitate in saying, "I've had enough."

"Umm, that's too soon." He then eased her back on the bed. "We haven't even gotten started good yet." He then reached out and slid her panties down her legs.

When she lay naked before him, Slade had to grip the edge of the bed to keep the rumble of desire that was spreading rapidly through his body from overtaking his control. Never had he wanted to make love to anyone like he wanted to make love to Skye. He reached and gently rubbed a hand over her bare belly, feeling the shiver that passed through her beneath his hand.

He then trailed his fingers across her stomach, as if to brand the letter *S* into her skin. His fingers then moved lower until they reached the area between her legs, and then he eased his finger into the moistness of her womanhood.

"Now you've really done it," she warned breathlessly.

He smiled. "Trust me, baby. I haven't done anything yet." And with that said, he began gently stroking her in a way no man had stroked her before.

Another shiver ran down Skye's spine with Slade's intimate caress, and she dug her hands into the bedspread to keep her sanity. The logical side of her brain tried to convince her that making love wasn't supposed to be like this. It was supposed to be over before these sorts of feelings could overtake your mind.

But not with Slade. He was slow, exceedingly thorough, and painstakingly torturous in his dealings with her.

"Earlier you asked what was my view on sex." He leaned down and placed a kiss on her bare belly. "This," he said, cupping her feminine mound, "is the best view I've ever seen."

He placed kisses along her inner thigh before pulling back to remove the last of his clothing. Afterward, he stood before her naked and aroused as he retrieved his wallet out of his jeans and pulled out a condom packet and then proceeded to sheathe himself.

He walked back over to the bed and eased his body onto it. The first thing he went for was her lips. His tongue slid between them in an invitation that she readily accepted, devouring her mouth with a need that he felt all through to his bones.

Now that he was getting satisfied with the taste of her, he wanted to go further and get inside of her. He eased his body in position over hers. He wanted her to feel his need and began rubbing the hardness of his aroused member against the apex of her thighs and could feel her shudder in his mouth. And then she was taking over the kiss, sucking and stroking his tongue like her life depended on doing so, and helplessly he groaned deep within his throat.

Not being able to handle any more, he tore his mouth from hers and breathed in deeply. He stared down at her. "What are you trying to do to me?" he asked huskily, fighting to get the words out.

"Torture you like you're torturing me."

His face was an aroused mask. "The torture ends. Are you ready?"

She smiled back up at him. "Yes, I'm ready." She lifted her hips automatically to receive him.

He remained still above her, holding himself in check, for one short second before sliding into her slowly, holding her gaze while he did so and watching the display of pleasure reflected in her features the deeper he went. She felt stretched and full and he felt hard and was getting even harder.

Instinctively she wrapped her legs around his hips when Slade began moving, thrusting into her once, twice, over and over, getting lost in the pleasure of being inside of her to a degree he had never before done with any other woman. He threw his head back and a deep guttural moan forced its way through his clenched teeth. It was as if this was where he belonged and where he always wanted to be, in a place that was uniquely hers and was quickly becoming exclusively his. His heart pounded ferociously against his ribs at the very thought.

He leaned down and recaptured her lips, taking her mouth with a hunger that sent shivers through him and at the same time drugged his mind with what they were sharing. Delicious sensations overtook him at the slow, rhythmic pace he set while showing her how to move her body in sync with his. Each thrust seemed to stroke and tease, and she arched her hips to mate with his own. He released her mouth to begin whispering intimate words into her ear and described in detail just how she made him feel.

When he felt her entire body shudder, indicating she was drowning in sheer ecstasy, he quickened the pace and locked his legs around her and held tight. His release came as a powerful orgasm rammed into him.

He called out her name the same time she cried out his; the sensations that were tearing into him were so intense, his body seemed to go into a super-shock mode as waves and waves of pleasure washed over him, seemingly non-stop.

By the time the last spasm shook her body as well as his own, he knew what they had shared was one of those incredible experiences that he wanted to share with her for an entire lifetime.

CHAPTER 14

Skye woke up hours later to find she was naked and in the bed alone. She hadn't remembered Slade getting out of the bed, but she did recall every little detail of their making love. And they had done so more than once. At least three times before she had finally drifted off to sleep.

She couldn't help but wonder where she had gotten so much energy. She had never looked forward to sleeping with Wayne and had never gotten the amount of pleasure from the experience as she had with Slade. She hated to keep comparing, but the two men were so vastly different it was simply astounding. She couldn't discount the possibility that the fact that she was in love with Slade probably had a lot to do with it.

She knew she needed to get up, take a shower, and start unpacking. This would be her home for the next three months, and already she was looking forward to spending her time here. She didn't want to think about how her parents had literally turned their backs on her because she'd refused to bend to their will and how Wayne had called, giving her one last warning, the same day she had left for the airport. He wanted her to know that he wouldn't be waiting around for her forever. Before hanging up the phone she had tried to explain that he didn't have to wait for her at all because they were not getting back together. For some reason, he wanted to believe their wedding was back on and they would have a Christmas wedding like they'd originally planned. He might be having a Christmas wedding, but she had no intentions of being the bride.

"You're awake."

Skye turned her body toward the sound of the sexy, masculine voice to find Slade standing in the bedroom doorway with a tray in his hand. "I thought I would whip us up something to eat since it's past dinnertime," he said, walking into the room.

She pulled herself up in bed, conscious of the state of her undress. He had slipped back into his jeans and he came and sat on the edge of the bed while placing the tray on the nightstand. He had made a couple of turkey sandwiches, had grabbed bags of potato chips and two cans of iced tea.

"You didn't have to do that," she said, but was glad he did, at the sound of her growling stomach.

"No problem. I have to make sure you keep your strength up."

She couldn't help but smile when he handed her a moist wipe for her hands. "So in other words, you have an ulterior motive for being so nice to me."

He chuckled. "Yeah, you can say something like that."

She knew she needed to say a number of things to him. First she had to thank him for giving her one of the most wonderful experiences of her life. "Thank you, Slade."

"I told you that you didn't have to thank me for—"

"I'm not talking about the food any longer. I want to thank you for sharing what you did with me. Like I told you, Wayne had a different view on sex, and since he was the first and only other person I've slept with, I didn't know there was any other way. Today you showed me differently."

Slade went about uncovering their sandwiches and said curtly, "The more and more I hear about this guy, the more I don't like him."

"To be completely honest, I never liked him myself."

Slade lifted his head and met her gaze. "Yet you were going to marry him?"

Skye inhaled deeply, knowing she needed to explain. She owed Slade that. "In Maine things are done differently between wealthy families. It's not uncommon for the parents to match their children up for marriages. Although my father is an accountant, he came from a well-off family. So did my mother. And their parents arranged their marriage when they were still in their teens. If my father never worked a day in his life it wouldn't matter, because he'd have money coming in from the trust funds his family established for him."

Slade nodded. He knew about trust funds. His uncle Jake, the one in the family with a head for investments, had established trust funds for all the younger Madarises when they turned sixteen that were to be paid out starting on their thirtieth birthdays. The smart ones had turned the money back over to Jake when they'd reached that mark so he could reinvest it for them. Everyone in the family knew that when it came to ways to make your wealth grow, Jake was the man. Even now, at a mere thirty-two, Slade considered himself pretty well-off, and thanks to Uncle Jake, his money was growing daily.

"So your marriage to him was being arranged by the two sets of parents?"

"Yes, and Wayne and I agreed to what they wanted so our parents wouldn't yank our trust funds away. At least Wayne was doing it for that reason, since he stands to lose half of his if we don't marry. I have no such stipulation on mine, thanks to the person who set it up for me."

Slade lifted a brow as he watched her bite into her sandwich. "Your parents didn't set it up?"

She shook her head. "No, someone else did. I believe it was an older aunt or somebody. I never asked, but I do know my parents can't deny me access to it when I turn thirty. Trust me, as angry as they are with me for coming here this summer, they would have done anything they could have to stop me."

He nodded, not really surprised that her parents hadn't

given her their blessings to spend the summer in Houston, but she had come anyway. He would love to think he had something to do with it, but he knew the reason. The only reason she was here was to spend time with Vincent.

"So, how does your ex-fiancé feel about the possibility of getting denied some of his trust fund because the two of you won't be getting married?"

Skye met Slade's gaze. "That's what's so strange, Slade. I've told Wayne countless times that we won't be getting back together, but he acts like he doesn't want to believe me. Even earlier today he called before I left for the airport and I had to break it down to him again that we would not be getting married on Christmas Day."

"Christmas Day?"

She nodded again. "Yes. All Bigelows get married on Christmas Day. It's a tradition that got started by his family generations ago."

"How old is this guy?"

"Twenty-nine. He'll turn thirty in April, but he has to be married to me by then."

Slade shook his head. Now that was an arranged marriage if he'd ever heard of one. What if the couple weren't compatible? What if they didn't love each other and were in love with other people? He guessed those things didn't matter. People who established those types of stipulated trust funds used money as an enticement for people to marry the person they felt was right for them, regardless of how the individuals felt about it.

He got the impression that Skye didn't want to discuss her ex-fiancé any longer when she asked, "The kitchen is stocked? Is that how you were able to fix these delicious sandwiches?"

He smiled. "No, your cupboards are bare. I went to my place and used the stuff I had in my kitchen to fix them."

She took a sip of her tea. "I know you said you have a condo in this same building; what floor is it on?"

"This one."

He knew his words caught her attention when she stopped sipping her tea. "You're also on the twenty-fifth floor?"

He tried not looking at her when he said, "Yes."

Evidently, she began suspecting something, because then she asked, "How close is it?"

He glanced up at her, trying not to smile under her quizzical stare. "It's right across the hall."

She didn't say anything as his words sank in. Then as if for clarification purposes, she asked, "Your condo is right across the hall?"

"Yes." He decided not to go into any details about their having the entire floor to themselves for the time being.

"Don't you think us living so close is a little too close for comfort?"

He couldn't help the smile that touched his lips. "Sweetheart, after what we shared earlier, it might not be close enough for me."

Skye began nibbling nervously on her bottom lip. She hoped she hadn't sent out the wrong message to Slade by sleeping with him. Although she loved him—something he didn't know and she didn't intend to tell him—her purpose for coming here hadn't changed. She wanted to spend time with Vincent, and she didn't want his family getting the wrong idea about her and Slade. But then, she wondered what idea they could get now that wasn't true, especially after she and Slade had shared a bed today. So technically, they were lovers. But still, she had to get him to understand.

"Slade, you do know why I'm here, don't you?" she asked.

He met her gaze and the dimples in his smile were getting her body hot all over again. "Because you missed me."

She had done that, but that wasn't the reason. "I'm here to spend time with Vincent. I don't want you to think that—"

He placed a finger to her lips. "Hey, don't get nervous and uptight on me. No sweat. I know what brought you to

Houston, Skye. But then I also know something else that maybe you need to know as well."

"What?"

"I can act as discreet toward you as I can, but my family knows me and it won't take long for them to figure out just how much I'm interested in you. I can't and won't pretend you aren't important to me, so please don't ask me to take anything we share lightly, because I can't and I won't. But I will promise not to dominate your time. I just want you to know that I'm here, right across the hall, whenever you need me."

Skye didn't know how to respond to that. He was being extremely gracious about things, but then she had discovered from the first that Slade was a very generous and gracious man. "Thank you, Slade."

"You're welcome. But there's something I think I ought to tell you up front."

"What?"

"I want you something awful and it's going to be hard to keep my hands off you when we're around others, but I will. But once we're alone, Skye, do you know what will happen?"

She smiled. "I think I do, but tell me anyway."

He decided to show her, and moving the tray aside, he lowered his mouth to hers.

Slade went to his own apartment to get dressed for dinner, and after he'd left, Skye took a shower and dressed in a pair of black slacks and a light pink blouse. Her body was still tingling over the lovemaking they had shared.

And now they were going out to dinner together. Their official first date, although she didn't want to think of it as such. But then how could she not when she loved him the way she did? However, she would keep her love for him to herself. It was a secret she would share with no one, because nothing could ever come of it. The last thing she needed was to dream about things that couldn't happen. She was a realist. She didn't believe in dreams. How many times had she dreamed that her mother would start being kind or that they would have a normal family life, something that never happened?

But then there were dreams worth holding on to. Like the ones she'd had of Slade when she had returned to Maine. She had dreamed of him holding her in his arms, kissing her passionately, constantly, non-stop, and then there were those of when he would make love to her. He had made the real thing so much better than the dreams, and she'd thought the dreams she'd had were pretty heavy. There had been nothing lightweight about them at all.

The sound of the doorbell caused her to jump. She smiled, knowing it was probably Slade, and headed for the door. She opened it and found him standing there, leaning one broad shoulder against the door frame. He was wearing a pair of dark gray pleated trousers and a white shirt, and he looked the epitome of everything male.

The dark eyes that looked her up and down, from head to toe, were turning her stomach to jelly, and then when she remembered all the intimate things they had done together earlier, she knew a tint had to be showing in her features.

"You're beautiful."

His words had her shaking her head yet smiling nonetheless. The man definitely knew how to dish out compliments, and he was very generous with them. "Thanks, and I think you're beautiful, too."

Now it was he who shook his head. "Men aren't beautiful."

"Then I guess you're an exception, Slade Madaris, because in my eyes, you are beautiful."

Instead of standing there arguing with her, he leaned over and gently kissed her lips. "You're having a delirious moment. I think it's time I fed you more than chips and a sandwich. I'm going to take you to a place that serves big juicy steaks, Texas size, with all the trimmings that go with them."

"Sounds delicious."

"I think you'll be pleased. Are you ready to go?"

"Yes. I just need to grab my purse." She took a step back inside the condo. He pushed away from the door frame and followed her inside, closing the door behind him.

She picked up her purse off the breakfast bar separating the living room from the dining room area, and spinning back around, she almost collided with Slade, who was standing directly behind her. "Oops, I didn't know you were standing so close."

He reached out and placed his arms around her waist and pulled her closer to the fit of him. Then he leaned forward and those so-desirable lips of his moved over hers with such tenderness that something warm and cozy began to spread all through her.

Moments later he pulled back and whispered in a raspy voice, "Thank you for such a wonderful afternoon, Skye."

He was thanking her when she figured she should be thanking him. She had done more than share a bed with him this afternoon, more than made love with him. She had shared an experience with him that even now still had her body tingling from head to toe. There was no way what they'd shared hadn't had an impact on her life. For the first time ever, she knew how it felt to be wanted by a man, desired by him, and taken to a level of lovemaking with him that could set your soul, as well as your entire body, on fire. She felt moisture form in her eyes at just how special their afternoon had been together. For the first time ever, she had felt she'd been special to someone. Truly special.

She stared at him, wanting to say the words to make him understand. She opened her mouth to speak, but no words came out. Instead she focused on his lips and thought she could show him better than she could tell him.

She leaned up and kissed his cheek. She then slid her lips to taste the area along his firm jawline. Moments later the tip of her tongue tasted the corners of his mouth, and then with a deliberate purpose, she placed her mouth over his.

On a deep sigh he parted his lips, and she invaded his

mouth with hers, tasting him as hungrily as he'd ever tasted her. She felt his hands tighten around her waist as he pulled her closer to the fit of him, letting her feel how aroused he was.

She continued kissing him, stroking her tongue with his, while her heartbeat hammered relentlessly in her chest. And when she couldn't take any more, she pulled her mouth back and inhaled a deep breath.

He reached out and tipped her chin toward him and met her gaze. The eyes holding hers were dark, hot, mesmerizing. "You are so unlike anyone I've ever known. So utterly different in a good way," he whispered hoarsely as his lips quirked into a smile. "But you like playing with fire, don't you?"

She grinned at the incredulity in his voice. "I don't mind as long as I can count on you to be my fireman who's willing to put out the flame if it gets out of hand."

He chuckled. "Well, in that case, I think we need to leave before we end up burning this place down," he said softly with meaning as he took her hand in his.

As he led her to the door, she whispered over at him, "I think you're right."

By the time they had arrived at Fleming's Prime Steakhouse & Wine Bar, Skye's heart had stopped hammering in her chest. And when she was seated at the table she and Slade had been given, she was ready to relax and feed her stomach as the delicious scent of food filled her head.

She glanced around, liking the décor of low ceilings, dark wood, paneled walls, leather upholstery, and soft lighting, which gave the interior an upscale feel. After they had been served water and handed menus, she took a sip and glanced over at Slade. "I'm sure you've been here before, so what do you suggest?"

He smiled at her from across the table. "For me it will be their classic prime-rib-that's-grilled-to-perfection steak, but I know in your neck of the woods, seafood is the name of the game, so if you prefer to go that route, then I suggest either their lobster tails, steamed crab legs, or wild Alaskan salmon that you can complement with various side dishes that include a baked potato and macaroni and cheese."

Skye's eyes lit up. "Oooh, I love macaroni and cheese."

"Then I'm going to have to prepare dinner for you one night and include it on my menu."

She lifted a dubious brow. "You can cook good macaroni and cheese?"

He leaned back in his chair and chuckled. "Not only is it good; it's mean. And if you're a person who likes cheese, then it's the dish for you. I use my great-grandmother Laverne's own recipe. We all do. It's been passed down the Madaris line for years and is one we can share freely. Now the Madaris prized tea is another matter."

She smiled over at him. "What about the tea?"

"It's a secret. The only persons who know what goes into the making of it are the males in the family, but only when they reach the age of thirty-five. So I don't know the ingredients yet, and in a way I don't want to know."

Skye raised her brows. "Why?"

"Because there are certain female members of the family who think they have a right to know and are trying to find out, and I don't want to be placed in a position where I'm cornered by any of them." He chuckled. "They can be ruthless in the pursuit of finding out things they have no business knowing."

Skye grinned. She knew he was just teasing about the women being ruthless, and she enjoyed listening to anything he had to say about his family. She had heard enough to know they were a tight-knit group who might fuss among themselves, but she had a feeling when it came to the real deal, they backed up their own.

She and Slade ended up ordering a huge steak for the both of them, along with seasoned rice and macaroni and cheese. The wine list had been massive, and they had selected one that the manager on duty had suggested. And the highlight of the evening had been the molten chocolate cake that had nearly melted in their mouths.

"So what do you think of a Texas-size steak?" Slade asked, wiping his mouth with the napkin.

"It was wonderful. Everything was wonderful. Thank you for bringing me here."

"You're welcome." He glanced at his watch. "It's still kind of early. How about me taking you over to the Madaris Building and showing you around?"

She smiled. "I'd like that."

The building was empty. Not surprising for a Friday night. Everyone had probably left on time to begin their weekend. The entire office park occupied a landmass of over fifty acres, and the goal was to provide a self-contained community where persons could work, play, and live. Expansion of the site to include several tennis courts and two more condo buildings was to take place beginning the first of the year.

Slade had explained that there were fifteen floors, with a total of twenty-one occupants. Several rather large companies, such as Madaris Explorations, which was owned by his cousin Dex, took up an entire floor due to laboratory space and the number of employees. The exterior structure was made of both stone and brick to enhance the landscape, and the entrance was a beautiful glass atrium. There were several restaurants, boutiques, and a day care on the ground floor. One of Justin's sisters, the one named Kattie, also owned a bookstore located on the ground floor. And the Madaris Publishing Company that was responsible for the printing and distribution of Lorren's books, was also on the ground floor.

Slade's cousin Clayton and his wife, Syneda, both attorneys, had their law office on the fifth floor; his uncle Jake had an office also on the fifth floor, which he seldom used, since he rarely left the ranch. And Alex Maxwell, who was married to Slade's cousin Christy, who was Justin's youngest sister, had an office on the tenth floor. To Skye it sounded like one huge family affair.

Slade used his master key to let him and Skye in, and in no time they had caught the elevator up to the fifteenth floor. Like Madaris Explorations, the Madaris Construction Company took up the entire floor, letting Skye know it was not a small operation by any means.

The setup of Slade and Blade's company was professional, the furniture practical and ergonomically correct. Slade showed her Blade's office, which in her opinion fit him perfectly. Being the natural predator he seemed to be, he had a lot of glass in his office, almost wall-to-wall, that would provide on any given day a view of his surroundings without giving him the feel of being caged.

There was also an office where the accountant worked, as well as a licensing department that handled all the permits that had to be applied for and pulled with the city before work could begin on any project. Slade showed her all the state-of-the-art equipment they used to assure the soundness and sturdiness of any building they erected, as well as the drafting room, which he used exclusively to design any given project.

Last, he showed her his office. Unlike Blade's, there was only one huge window in the room, but the view at night was breathtaking. Skye crossed the room to stand in front of it to admire the landscaping and how after dark the lights lit up the pond and nearby lake. Across the distance she recognized the building that housed the condo where she was staying.

"You and Blade have to be proud of your accomplishments, Slade. The view from up here is simply beautiful."

"Thanks, and we *are* proud of everything we do. But we're also blessed with a family who believed in us and gave us a chance. When we started out on this venture we had just celebrated our twenty-fifth birthday. A lot of people said my father, grandfather, and uncle Jake were taking a chance on us, and that Mitch Farrell was just plain loco. But we proved them all wrong. Now, we basically get to pick and choose the projects we want. But I have to admit there are some that don't come easy, due to our family name. They think we get the jobs we acquire because of connections."

Skye heard the tremor in his voice and knew he was bothered by anyone thinking that way. Again, she couldn't help but note the difference between him and Wayne. Her ex-fiancé thrived on connections. In fact, he felt it was his God-given right to have them.

"You know I thought of this often," Slade said, easing up behind her. His arms came around her, bringing her back against him to rest her frame intimately against his.

She rested the back of her head on his chest. Contented. "You thought of what?" she asked softly.

"You, here in my office with me. You and me standing at the window looking out at night, seeing all the lights, the moon, the stars . . ."

"Umm, you sound like a romantic."

He rested his chin on the top of her head. "In that case, I guess I am. But only with you. I never envisioned standing here at this window with anyone but you."

The logical part of her brain told her to take what he said as a sweet comment and not make a big deal out of it. But the part of her that loved him did make a big deal out of it. One thing she knew about Slade was that he didn't say things just to say them.

"You also know what else I thought of a lot?"

"No, Slade, what else did you think of a lot?"

He turned her into his arms. "Standing here in this room, this very spot kissing you." A devilish smile crinkled the corners of his lips when he said, "Granted that's not all I thought about doing in this spot with you, but for now kissing will do."

He leaned down and slipped his tongue between her lips and moaned the moment it settled in her mouth. He moaned again, loving the taste of this woman and thinking it was one he would never get tired of. Each time they kissed made him want to kiss her that much more. And then the heated tips of her breasts that were pressing against his chest weren't helping matters.

He pulled back slightly and whispered against her lips, "Spend the night with me. In my condo. In my bed. Between my sheets."

He heard her breath quicken and went on to say, "Tomorrow Vincent will arrive and the time we have to spend together will decrease. Tonight is all we'll have for a while, and I want to use it to the fullest. Will you let us do that?"

Skye didn't have to debate with herself whether to take him up on his offer. She wanted this night with him as well. After that, her time and attention would be devoted to Vincent. Slade understood that.

But there was tonight.

"Yes," she said, smiling up at him. "Tonight is all we have, so let's take full advantage of it."

CHAPTER 15

"I'll never take you up on another offer, Slade Madaris," Skye said in an exhausted voice as she uncurled her legs from beneath his muscular body when he shifted off her. She had no energy left. All she wanted to do was sleep.

Slade let out a long breath as he reached out and pulled her close into his arms. He felt as exhausted as she sounded. But then they *had* said they wanted to take full advantage of tonight.

With the little energy she still had, she turned to him. "We are normal people, aren't we?"

He nodded, smiling. "Yes, we're normal."

"Just making sure."

He chuckled. "I gather you and Mr. No Brains didn't do this often."

She knew who he was talking about. "Umm, like I said, Wayne had a different view on sex. Besides, are there really many people who'd do it this often?"

He glanced at her, surprised she'd ask. "Sure. Most people that I know would."

She looked up at him. "Must be super-humans."

He laughed. "No, just regular people with healthy sexual appetites."

"Don't tell me; let me guess. It runs in your family."

He pulled her even closer into his arms and placed a kiss on her forehead. "Yes, such appetites run in my family."

She recalled observing Justin and Lorren and how

touchy-feely they were. They loved each other and had no problems showing it. Skye thought of her own parents and wondered how differently things could have been for them if they had married other people instead of being forced into a marriage with each other. She couldn't recall ever seeing them display any type of love and affection. In the past she never paid much attention to it, assuming that's how it was for most couples. Meeting members of Slade's family had opened her eyes and made her realize the home life she'd assumed was healthy really hadn't been.

"Ready to take a nap?"

She raised a brow. "A nap? It's way after midnight. Most people are fully asleep by now."

"But we aren't most people, are we? We're a couple whose time together will be limited, and we've decided to take advantage of it."

Skye closed her eyes, too sluggish to argue. Besides, she'd seen it happen before when she would think there was no way she could possibly go another round with Slade and she would end up doing just that. There was something about the way he could touch her, taste her, talk all kinds of sweet stuff in her ear, whisper words and phrases she'd never heard before. Words guaranteed to turn her on. She had definitely lived a sheltered life.

But then a part of her was acutely grateful for the passion he had introduced her to. Passion she doubted she would have had in her life with Wayne. When she returned to Maine, at least she would have that: memories of the passion.

"We will be taking just a nap, Skye. I plan to wake you up in an hour or two."

Her eyes remained closed, but her lips curved in a smile. "I'm going to have to do something about that healthy appetite of yours."

"Want me to give you some ideas?" And then she felt it. His tongue on her breast, hungrily sucking the nipple into his mouth.

She still refused to open her eyes, although heat was beginning to generate between her legs again. "I thought we were going to take a nap."

"I changed my mind. I decided I want to taste you in a place I haven't tasted you yet."

Skye's eyes flew open. What on earth was he talking about!

And then she felt him place a kiss on her stomach, one of those kisses that trailed his wet tongue around her navel. A helpless groan escaped her lips. She knew he heard it but chose to ignore it and continued to lick all over her skin.

"Slade?"

"Umm?"

"What arc you doing?"

"Tasting you."

And then he showed her just what he meant when he moved away from her tummy to start on the smooth skin of her inner thigh.

"Slade. Don't."

The request, weak at best, came too late. He shifted his mouth, and his lips latched on to her womanly core. He used his tongue to taste her like she was a treat he just had to devour. She quivered. She moaned. She whispered his name over and over.

Finally she said, "Slade. Please *don't* stop."

He didn't. He kept it up, insistently kissing her that intimate way, tasting her again and again until her body came apart, rocking, rolling, reeling, and shuddering in one breathtaking pleasurable climax.

She half-sighed, half-laughed. "You don't play fair."

He pulled back up in bed and tenderly kissed her lips. "Sweetheart, when it comes to making love to you, I don't play at all."

He pulled her closer into his arms and entwined his legs with hers. "Now you can take a nap."

Skye closed her eyes and a smile curved her lips. And the

only thing she could think of before drifting off to sleep was that the man holding her in his arms was simply amazing.

"I feel guilty for keeping you out so late, Diana," Senator Nedwyn Lansing said, opening the car door for the beautiful woman at his side. "It's way past midnight."

She smiled as she slipped into the leather seat of his Infiniti. "We're too old to have a curfew, Ned, so please don't worry about it. The play was magnificent, and if they had a second show, I would have been tempted to stay and watch it again."

He gave her a smile before closing the door, and as he walked around the front of the car to get into the driver's side, she whooshed out a long, deep breath. It was getting harder and harder to be around Nedwyn and not let her feelings for him show. What was wrong with her? What had been wrong with her for a few years now? Ever since she'd discovered she saw him as more than the man who had been best friend to her late husband and whom she considered her best friend now. Over the years, he'd always been there, even while being the public servant in the nation's capital. She'd always known he'd been just a phone call away and if she'd ever needed him, he would drop whatever it was he was doing and come to her. She had known it, although she'd never taken him up on it. To her daughter, Felicia, he'd always been her godfather, and he had always been there, fulfilling the promise he'd made to his best friend.

Diana studied Nedwyn's expression for a brief moment when he opened the car door and got in. She'd always thought he was a very handsome man and had been surprised over the years when, although he had dated, he'd never seemed to give thought to settling down and marrying. Whenever Diana would ask him about his life as a bachelor, he would tease her and say he was already married to the Senate, and fulfilling the role of Senator Nedwyn Lansing

and doing a good job for the people he represented was all
he needed.

"You buckled in?" he asked, glancing over at her.

She smiled. "Yes, now it's your time."

He chuckled, his voice rich and deep in the interior of the
car. She thought that at fifty-nine he was an extremely handsome man who wore his age well. He was in excellent physical shape, no doubt due to their weekly games of tennis and
golfing. He stood tall, over six feet, and had such a stately
stature. He had a light brown complexion, with the most gorgeous hazel eyes she'd ever seen. And when he smiled, there
appeared the cutest little cleft in his chin.

She knew that over the years he had captured a lot of
women's interest, but so far he hadn't reciprocated the interest to any one of them. For a while Diana had thought he
would eventually marry this one woman he had dated steadily
for a couple of years, a law professor at Howard University.
Diana had thought the woman very attractive and, at the
time, possibly what Nedwyn needed. After their breakup,
he later confided that she had been too demanding for his
taste and when she had given him an ultimatum to set a
wedding date, he had refused and she had walked. The one
thing Diana did know about Nedwyn was that he was not a
man who would be forced into any situation he didn't want
to be in. That was one of the reasons she had kept her feelings for him to herself. If she couldn't have his love, then
his devoted friendship was the next best thing and she was
satisfied.

"How's the grands, Diana?"

He asked the question while pulling out of the parking lot.
It was a beautiful night, and she was glad he'd asked her to accompany him to the play. Since he had been spending more
and more time in Houston due to his retirement, they were
spending a lot more time together, but she never considered it
dating. In her mind they were too old and too close as friends
for that. She had dated occasionally, since at fifty-seven she

still enjoyed going places and doing fun things. But lately it seemed that the men were becoming too aggressive. The rules of dating as well as the expectations were changing, and she had decided a year ago that she wanted no part of it. She now preferred group activities with friends or, like tonight, she would keep herself busy until Nedwyn called. And she had to admit that lately he had been calling a lot.

"The grandkids are simply wonderful," she said, smiling over at him. "I talked to Austin earlier today, and he had a lot to tell me about school. Madaris tried telling me something, too, but at two she's still forming her words. However, I did get the gist of what she was saying." Diana chuckled. "She's going through the potty-training stage and she wanted to let me know she did good today."

The senator laughed. "They are precious, aren't they?"

Diana smiled. "Yes, they are, and Robert would have adored them, wouldn't he?" she said of her late husband.

Nedwyn returned her smile as fond memories flashed through his mind. "Yes, Robert would have adored them, just like he adored you and Felicia. And speaking of Felicia, how are things going with her lingerie shop? I understand that she's thinking about expanding again."

"Yes, she is. And this time on a national level. She's received calls interested in a possible franchise. If she went that route, then that would free up her time to travel more with Trask, especially during football season while he works as a sports commentator for the NFL."

Trask Maxwell, Felicia's husband and childhood friend—or childhood enemy, whichever way the stories could be told—had grown up to become a football legend. He'd played professionally for years, until a knee injury at the age of thirty-four brought an end to his football career.

"I ran into Felicia and Trask the other night at the shopping mall," Senator Nedwyn said. "They looked so happy together, and a part of me actually envied what they had.

Then I thought of all the wasted years when I could have had someone special in my life."

His words surprised Diana. This was the first time he had ever mentioned regretting not sharing a serious relationship with a woman. Would he contemplate doing that now? Was she about to lose her best friend? A lot of women wouldn't understand or accept the type of relationship the two of them shared. There had even been rumors of their being lovers, which was so far from the truth, since other than a peck to the cheek, Nedwyn had never even tried to kiss her.

"At least your building is well lit," Nedwyn interrupted her thoughts by saying. They had arrived at her condo.

"Yes, and well secured. I love staying here." She had taken her nephews Blade and Slade up on purchasing a condo in this building even before it was completed. Her house had gotten too big for her, as well as too lonely. She had wanted to buy a condo with everything modern and all the amenities of condo living. She hadn't regretted it. And it felt good to know that a few family members were close by, since both Blade and Slade also lived in the building.

"So, are we still on for our game of tennis tomorrow?" Nedwyn asked, bringing the car to a stop in front of her building.

"Yes, we are," she said. "Same time."

"All right. And what are you doing on Sunday?" he then asked.

She shrugged. "The usual. Church and then dinner at Felicia's. Why?"

"I thought it would be nice if we had dinner together. At my place. With the both of us doing the cooking. What do you think?"

For a quick moment, she didn't know what to think, but she quickly recovered and smiled over at him. "I think that would be nice."

"Then I'll leave it to you to plan the menu and we can go

shopping for everything at the grocery store tomorrow. Is that all right with you?"

She nodded. "Yes."

"Good."

He then opened the door to come around on her side of the car to open the door for her. She sat there stunned. Nedwyn wanted to spend more time with her, and she really didn't know what to make of it. She truly didn't want to get her hopes up.

She smiled when he opened the door and offered her his hand. Moments later, he walked her inside, nodding a hello to the security doorman on the ground floor. Since her condo was on the second floor, the ride in the elevator was over before they knew it.

"So, tomorrow I'll pick you up at noon," Nedwyn said when they reached her door. There were only four condos on the second floor, and all four were occupied. Evidently everyone else had retired for the night long ago. The hall was empty. Almost too quiet. And Diana had to inwardly admit it had been a long time since she'd been out this late.

As usual, Nedwyn, being the gentleman that he was, took the key she offered and opened the door for her. She looked up at him. "Good night, Ned. I'll see you tomorrow."

"Good night, Diana."

She was about to turn when he touched her arm. When she glanced back at him, he leaned forward and placed a light kiss across her lips. "Pleasant dreams," he whispered in her ear.

She stood there stunned for a second before taking a step back and entering her home, closing the door behind her. The thought that flowed through her mind was that Nedwyn had never kissed her before.

Until tonight.

When Nedwyn let himself into his own home less than twenty minutes later, he suddenly realized he was whistling and had been whistling since walking out of Diana's condominium building. But then, he thought smiling, he had a lot to whistle about. Diana hadn't had a problem with his dominating her time this weekend, which he considered a blessing.

Walking directly into his bedroom, he went straight to his closet to hang up his jacket, tie, and shirt. He had made it over what he'd perceived as the first hurdle, and planned to continue forward.

He glanced over at the clock on his bedroom nightstand. It was late, way past the time he was usually in bed, but tonight he was so full of energy and his body was pumping so much adrenaline through his system, he couldn't go to bed now if he wanted to.

He might as well pull out his favorite book, *Profiles in Courage* by John F. Kennedy, and reread it for the umpteenth time. He smiled as he finished undressing. As usual, Diana had looked beautiful tonight, and at fifty-seven she still had a feminine figure any man would appreciate, which attested to the fact that she kept herself in good physical shape. And it was plenty evident in that designer pantsuit she was wearing tonight.

He remembered during a part of the play when she had laughed at the actors onstage. He had glanced over at her at the exact moment part of the stage's lighting seemed to shine on her. Her chocolate brown skin still had that smooth, rich glow, and her makeup was flawless. Her eyebrows were arched to perfection, and just the right amount of lipstick had been applied to her lips. The diamond earrings she'd worn had brought out the brilliance in her short salt-and-pepper Afro.

The first word he always thought of when he saw Diana was "classy." She was classy in the way she dressed, talked, and carried herself. He always felt like the proudest of men when she was by his side.

His heart tripped a beat when he remembered the exact moment he realized he no longer wanted her for a friend and that he had fallen in love with her. She had flown into D.C. to attend a Presidential dinner at the White House with him. And when he had arrived to pick her up at the Mayflower Hotel and had walked into the lobby to discover she was there waiting for him, the moment he had looked into her smiling face, it was like he'd been hit with a ton of bricks. He had stared at her for a long time, so long she had eventually asked him if he was okay.

Since that day he had tried to fight it, but it had gotten useless. Now his mind was made up. He had never pursued a woman in his life, but he was intent on pursuing this one. In the end she would be *his* lady.

His very own Lady Diana.

CHAPTER 16

"I'm so nervous I can't stand it," Skye said as Slade took her hand to help her out of the car. They had arrived at the home of Justin's brother Dex and his wife, Caitlin. The couple had been kind enough to host a small dinner party in Skye's honor to introduce her to some of the members of the Madaris family, specifically Justin's parents and his sisters and brothers. Slade had explained that over the course of the summer she would meet the rest of his kin.

"No reason to get nervous. Consider yourself among family and friends. Everyone is anxious to meet you."

Skye was anxious to meet them as well. Vincent had called her earlier that day to say he had arrived with his parents in Houston. The two of them had a long phone conversation in which he told her about his father's two brothers and three sisters.

"They're super," Vincent had said. "And I know I can count on them at any time. I'm blessed to belong to such a wonderful family."

She knew he was right and was proud that he had recognized just how blessed he was. She glanced down at the pantsuit she had chosen to wear as she and Slade strolled down the walkway toward the front door. "How do I look, Slade?"

He smiled. "Beautiful, but I much prefer seeing you without any clothes on."

"Slade!"

"Okay, I'll take that statement back if you want me to, but it's the truth."

She shook her head, smiling. "What am I going to do with you?"

He stopped walking, turned to face her, and took her hand in his and said, "You've done a lot with me over the past twenty-eight hours, but if you're still fishing for more ideas, then—"

"Slade!"

"Just kidding."

She knew that he really wasn't kidding. He had told her about his healthy sexual appetite last night, and all that day he had shown her just how healthy it was. Just thinking about all they'd done had her blushing.

They'd almost gotten caught when Vincent had called. Slade had been trying to coax her into taking a shower with him and wouldn't behave. Luckily, since Vincent had called on her cell phone, he hadn't known she had spent the night in Slade's condo and not her own.

"Remember you promised not to give anything away," she thought to remind him.

"And remember I said that I wouldn't have to. My family knows me."

She frowned. "Well, pretend you don't like me."

He chuckled. "That will be hard to do when I do like you. Then there's Vincent I have to consider. How will he feel if he thinks I don't like his sister?"

Slade did have a point, she thought. "Well, just don't make things too obvious, all right? I want everyone to like me."

He lifted a brow. "And you think they won't if they think you are involved with me?"

"They might think you're the reason I'm here and not Vincent."

"Trust me, they won't think that."

At that moment they had reached the door, and before they could ring the doorbell, the door was snatched open by a smiling Vincent. "It's about time you guys got here," he said, taking Skye's hand and pulling her inside the house.

Slade chuckled as he glanced down at his watch when they entered the foyer. "Dex said seven o'clock, and according to my watch it's exactly seven, so what's your problem, kid?"

"I couldn't wait to see Skye again."

Skye knew Vincent had no idea how much his words had meant. "Well, I'm here now," she said, reaching out and giving him a hug. "But I really didn't expect or need all this fanfare. Your uncle and aunt really shouldn't have."

Vincent smiled. "I told Uncle Dex that, but he insisted."

"And what Vincent is too kind to say," Slade butted in to add, "is that everyone in this family knows how far to go in rattling Dex, so we let him have his way . . . most of the time."

Skye lifted a brow, wondering what Slade meant by that. Before she could ask, a woman she thought was utterly beautiful came around the corner to join them in the foyer. Skye blinked, thinking this definitely couldn't be the lady of the house since she looked so young. This had to be one of Justin's sisters. During their conversation earlier, Vincent had told her that his uncle Dex was forty-four, and this woman didn't look a day past thirty.

"I see our guest of honor has arrived," the woman said, smiling up at Skye. She held out her hand. "Hello, I'm Vincent's aunt Caitlin, and welcome to our home."

Skye knew she had to close her mouth. But then she reopened it when she asked for clarification, "You're married to his uncle Dex?"

The woman laughed as if she understood Skye's confusion. "Yes, I'm married to Dex."

It was Vincent who solved the mystery when he said, "Uncle Dex is eleven years older than Aunt Caitlin. That's why she looks so young."

"Hey, I don't appreciate having my age blasted about, Vincent Madaris."

Skye glanced up toward the boisterous voice and her eyes connected to a man with the most gorgeous set of gray eyes she'd ever seen. They were actually charcoal gray. Other than the eye coloring, she could immediately tell he was a Madaris. He was tall and handsome, and if he was forty-four, as Vincent claimed, he had to be one of the most handsome middle-aged men she'd seen in a long time. But then, she considered Justin handsome, too. Good grief! So far she hadn't met a Madaris man who wasn't handsome.

"Sorry about that, Uncle Dex," Vincent said, grinning.

"And see that it doesn't happen again," Dex Madaris said before playfully grabbing his nephew around the neck. Dex glanced over at Skye and smiled. "Hello. I'm this big-mouth's uncle, and I guess you're the sister I've been hearing so much about."

Skye returned the man's smile. "Yes, I'm the one. Thanks for inviting me to your home. It's simply beautiful."

"Thanks, and you're welcome." He then smiled over at Caitlin. "And yes, this young-looking woman over here belongs to me. I met her when she was twenty-one and I was thirty-three. I tried to fight it, but it was love at first sight."

Skye thought it was sweet that Dex would admit such a thing, but all it took was an observation of how Dex was looking at his wife to know he was still deeply in love.

She shook her head. When she'd first seen Slade and Justin, she'd thought they looked a lot alike. But now after meeting Dex, she thought Slade favored Dex even more. They shared the same height, the same skin coloring, the same bluntly strong and sensuous features. The only difference was the eye color.

"Come on, Skye. I want to introduce you to everyone," Vincent said, grabbing her hand.

Skye found herself pulled into a huge, beautifully decorated room full of people—people she didn't know, other than Justin and Lorren, who smiled over at her.

"Can I have everyone's attention for a minute?" Vincent's

voice rang out over the conversations in the room. "Here she is. I want everyone to meet my sister Skye."

Skye knew there was no way she would remember everyone's name, but she was determined to try. She had immediately determined where Dex had gotten his eye coloring from when she met his mother. She thought Marilyn Madaris was a beautiful woman, who reminded her of Nancy Wilson, and it didn't take long to see that Marilyn was the apple of her husband Jonathan Madaris' eyes.

Neither did it take long for Skye to see that the older couple was everything her parents were not. Jonathan and Marilyn enjoyed being together, and it showed. Even after over forty years of marriage Skye could still see the spark in Jonathan Madaris' eyes whenever he looked at his wife. Then there were the other two people in the room with charcoal gray eyes, who were Dex and Caitlin's ten-year-old daughter, Jordan, and their four-year-old son, Gregory. Their seven-year-old sister, Ashley, favored Caitlin.

Then Skye had met Vincent's other uncle, the one who was an attorney. His uncle Clayton. His wife, Syneda, was also beautiful and actually looked like a model, with her sea green eyes and mane of thick golden bronze hair that fell past her shoulders. According to Vincent she was also an attorney, and she and Clayton had a law practice in the Madaris Building. Their four-year-old daughter named Remington was a little replica of Syneda.

Then Skye met Vincent's aunts Traci and Kattie and their husbands, Daniel and Raymond. When Traci asked if Skye would like to go shopping next week, before she could respond she had gotten pulled away by Justin, who gave her a friendly warning. "Never go shopping with Traci, I don't care how many times she asks you."

He hadn't had to explain. Vincent had already told her that his aunt Traci was a bona fide shopaholic. She smiled. "Thanks, Justin. I'll remember that."

Dinner had been wonderful and everyone had their own "Vincent" story to share. She couldn't help but note that true to his word, Slade had remained in the background, giving her time in the limelight with Vincent so there could not be any attention placed on them.

But still, time and time again she found her gaze seeking him out and, as if he'd known she would, he had been within her scope, and whenever their eyes would meet, he would give her a charming smile and a supportive wink.

It was during those times that her love for him intensified, because even from a distance he was letting her know that he was a man she could count on. And it was sad to think that during her entire twenty-six years she never had a man in her life who'd actually fulfilled that role.

Justin's youngest sister, Christy, had arrived late, and she and Skye struck up a friendship immediately. Christy explained she had just come from dropping her husband off at the airport, where he was off to California on a business trip.

"I would like to invite you over for dinner tomorrow," Marilyn Madaris said later that evening when she and Skye stood alone out on a beautiful terrace that overlooked a swimming pool. "Whenever Jonathan and I aren't the traveling retirees, we like getting the kids and grands together for Sunday dinner. And you're more than welcome to come."

Marilyn then leaned closer and smiled and whispered, "And that invitation also extends to Slade, of course."

It was then that Skye decided that it seemed that she and Slade had not fooled Marilyn Madaris. The woman was sharp and saw it all, just like Vincent had said.

"I can't believe Caitlin is also an accountant," Skye said when she and Slade arrived back at her condo. "Isn't that wild?"

"Yes, it is. I think tonight went okay, don't you?" Slade asked, placing his arms around her waist.

She turned around and smiled up at him. "It went better than okay. I really like your family, and it's hard to believe that's just part of them and there's more."

He chuckled. "Oh, trust me, there's plenty more." He glanced at his watch. It wasn't eleven o'clock yet. "So whose bed will it be tonight?"

Skye frowned. "What do you mean?"

He smiled down at her. "Are we sleeping here or over at my place again?"

Skye shook her head. "You are sleeping in your bed and I'm sleeping in mine. Remember, we agreed that once I started spending time with Vincent, he was to become the focus of my attention."

"Yes, but I thought that was for when Vincent was around. He isn't here with us."

"Yes, but I can't flip back and forth like that. You're a person who needs all of a woman's attention, Slade, and I can't give that to you. If I tried, sooner or later someone in your family would detect something and—"

"This is not about my family, Skye."

"It is to me. I believe that I made a good impression on them tonight, as Vincent's sister. Not as your lover."

"But you can be both."

"I won't! It is not the proper thing to do."

Slade paused. He saw the stubborn glint in her eyes and heard it in her voice as well. The best thing for him to do was back off, play things her way. At least let her assume he was playing things her way. Eventually she would see that when it came to a woman he wanted, there was no stopping a Madaris.

"Okay, look, I don't want to get you upset. I just can't cut my emotions on and off like that," he decided to say, giving it one more try.

"And you think that I can? Even tonight I wanted to cross the room and be with you, to stand beside you each and every minute. But I couldn't. I had to stay focused."

He inhaled deeply. "I think you might be putting too much into this, Skye."

"Well, I don't. I think your aunt Marilyn suspects something already. She invited me to dinner tomorrow and said you were invited, too. But then, Vincent did tell me she was one sharp lady."

"She had to be, raising Justin, Dex, and Clayton, especially Clayton," Slade inclined his head to say. "He was the provincial bad boy of Houston."

"But you do understand, Slade, don't you? Besides, starting Monday I'll be working for you. What would people think if they knew I was sleeping with the boss?"

"I still think you're putting too much into this, but I'll do things your way." *For now.*

"Thanks, Slade."

He lifted her chin so their eyes could meet. "Can I at least kiss you good night?"

Skye smiled brightly, glad he was seeing things her way. "Yes, you can do that."

At first she thought it would be one of his gentle kisses, but then his tongue latched on to hers and it became a kiss that was, in her opinion, downright mentally drugging. In no time at all, he had desire thrumming through all parts of her body. No one could ignite passion within her so quickly and completely like he could.

How long the kiss lasted she wasn't sure. All she knew was she felt a sense of loss the moment it ended. "Think of me tonight," he whispered huskily against her lips.

"And I'm leaving my car for you to use to go to dinner at Aunt Marilyn's place. I can use my truck."

She lifted a surprised brow. "Aren't you going?"

"No. My mom is big on Sunday dinners, too." There. He was letting her see she couldn't have it both ways. "Do you need directions?"

She shook her head. "No, I'll use my laptop and look up the directions on MapQuest."

"Okay then. I'll check on you tomorrow before I leave for church. Unless you want to go to church with me. My parents would love meeting you."

Skye wished that she could flatly refuse to consider the idea, but then another part of her, the part that wanted to be with Slade, be around him, was pushing for her to say yes. She conceded. She would love to meet the parents who had raised such an outstanding man.

"Yes, I'd love going to church with you and meeting your parents."

He smiled. "Good. Be ready at ten. Service starts at eleven. It annoys Mom if I'm late."

"Okay."

He then pulled her into his arms for another kiss, and the thought that ran through Skye's mind was that she would definitely miss sleeping with him tonight.

CHAPTER 17

"Mom. Dad. I'd like you to meet Skye Barclay, Vincent's sister."

Church service had ended for only a few moments and already Skye had met a number of other Madarises. Deliberate or otherwise, Slade had failed to mention that this particular church was considered the Madaris family church, and in addition to seeing a few of the same people she had seen last night at the dinner party, she'd also been introduced to more of Slade's numerous family members.

So much for her and Slade keeping low-key.

The moment Skye looked into Slade's father's face, she could tell where he and Blade got most of their prominent features. Milton Madaris III was a handsome man just like his sons, and the woman standing by his side, Fran Madaris, was short compared to her husband and sons but had beautiful features and a smile that radiated sincere warmth. And Slade's other brothers, Quantum and Jantzen, were also quite handsome.

"Skye," Fran said, reaching out and gripping her hand in a firm hold. "I've heard so many nice things about you from Vincent, Slade, and Blade. I know you must be happy to find Vincent after a year of looking."

She returned the woman's smile. "Yes, I am."

"And I understand you're spending the summer here in Houston and will help out at the office with Blade and Slade. Don't let either of them work you too hard."

Skye chuckled as she glanced up at Slade. "I'll make sure of that."

"And if you ever get tired of that condo and want some real space, come out to our ranch and visit us. It's not as big as some, but it's where we've lived now for over thirty years," Milton was saying. "And we love people to come visit."

Skye truly believed that.

"And if you don't have any plans for today, you're invited to dinner," Slade's mother said.

"Skye already has made dinner plans, Mom. Maybe another time," Slade interjected.

Skye saw the disappointment in the other woman's face. "Okay, then maybe another time. The invitation is always open. Like Milton said. You don't need a reason to come visit."

A few minutes later Skye got to meet Slade's grandfather Milton Madaris Jr., the oldest of the original seven Madaris brothers. Vincent had already told her that his granduncle Milton, being the oldest male of the clan, considered himself the head of the family and sometimes liked to rule with an iron fist, but that deep down he was nothing but a marshmallow. In other words, he was all bark and no bite.

On the drive back to the condo, Skye glanced over at Slade. "Why didn't you tell me that most of your family would be at church today?"

He shrugged. "You didn't ask. Did it bother you that they saw us together at the service?"

"No, I guess not. It did at first, but then I guess considering your family, it makes sense for them to worship together. I assume most families do."

Slade nodded. He had to constantly remind himself that she didn't come from a large family and sometimes his could be overwhelming. "This is the church most of us attend who live in Houston, but the real family church isn't far away from Whispering Pines, Uncle Jake's ranch. It's called Proverbs Baptist Church. My great-grandparents Milton and

Felicia Laverne Madaris helped to build that church, and my great-gramma is one of the oldest living members. At least twice a year, usually on a fifth Sunday in a month, we all travel back there for service and make a big day of it by having a picnic on the church grounds. Great-Gramma Laverne is the mother of the church."

Skye nodded. She and her parents were Catholics; however, they were far from being considered devout. In fact, before today she couldn't remember the last time she had gone to mass. She had truly enjoyed the church service. It had been different from anything she was used to.

She glanced over at Slade. "Thanks for letting your mom know I couldn't make dinner with her today."

"No problem. She likes you and wanted you to eat with us. Maybe you'll be able to do so at another time."

Skye didn't want to commit to anything. She saw her Sunday evenings spent with Vincent and doing the things that he wanted to do. "I know I've said this more than once, Slade, but you have a wonderful family and you should be proud of them."

He smiled over at her. "I am and I never forget how blessed I am, especially when I read about kids being abandoned or single mothers raising kids without any strong, positive male influence. That's not the case in my family. When Uncle Robert was killed in 'Nam, all my uncles stepped in and helped Aunt Diana with the raising of Felicia. That's what families are for. They come together when there is a need. They are there for each other."

His words were food for thought. Skye had always considered Aunt Karen family and wondered how much better things would have been if everyone in the Barclay family had gotten along. But she could vividly recall when she was younger her father having to play referee for her mother's and aunt's disagreements.

Skye made up her mind then and there that if she ever got

married, she would raise her kids differently. She would in-
still into them the value and importance of family.

Diana's breath caught when Nedwyn came up behind her
and looked over her shoulder at the sauce she had simmering
on the stove. "Umm, that smells delicious," he said, looking
into the pot. "I hope Felicia's not upset about me taking you
away today. I'm sure she looks forward to having you over
for dinner on Sundays."

"Yes, but Jolene's in town," she said of Trask's mother.
"And she wanted to take the kids to the country fair, so in a
way it will give Felicia and Trask a quiet evening at home
alone."

Nedwyn smiled at her. "I'm sure they'll appreciate that."
He then watched as she placed a lid on the pot. "Well, that
about covers it. I've grilled the steaks and potatoes. You got
your own brand of steak sauce simmering, and the salad is in
the fridge. What did we forget?"

Diana returned his smile and said, "The bread."

Nedwyn nodded, grinning. "And not just any bread. Texas
toast. And if you're through in here, I want to show you something that I came across earlier today while cleaning out one
of the closets in the garage."

"Okay."

Taking her hand, he led her through the dining room and
into the living room. Diana glanced around. Nedwyn had
purchased this house many years ago, while Felicia was in
high school, and since he'd spent so much time in the nation's capital he'd rarely been in Houston to enjoy it. However, once he'd made the decision to retire from the Senate,
he had begun thinking about purchasing another home, one
more in tune to his current style and taste. He was taking a
leisurely time packing up stuff so when the time came for
the transition, he would be ready.

The house sat on two acres of land, with a lake in the

back. Since the both of them enjoyed fishing, he'd kept the lake well stocked, and many Saturdays would find the two of them out here pulling the fish in. She had accepted many, many years ago that he was her best friend. Some women needed another woman as a best friend, but she'd felt she was blessed to have Nedwyn.

He was a good person to talk to and he always offered good, sound advice. He'd been there to listen to her woes when it seemed Felicia wouldn't put aside her wild and reckless ways, and he'd been there to calm her fears when she'd heard that Trask and Felicia had started seeing each other. The two had never gotten along since childhood, so Diana couldn't imagine anything really serious between them. Nedwyn had assured her things would work out, and they had. Trask and Felicia were happily married, with a son and a daughter.

"Okay, what do you have to show me?" Diana asked, sitting down on the sofa.

"This," he said, pulling a huge photo album from under one of the tables. "Take a look and tell me how many of those you can remember."

Diana flipped open the album and the first photo she came to was of the two of them at Felicia's first play when she was in the third grade. A smile touched Diana's lips. "Oh, I remember that night. The Madaris family came out in droves. You would have thought a star had been born, and the only part she had was as the daffodil flower that only said two words."

Nedwyn chuckled. "Yes, I remember."

Diana flipped to other photos. All held special memories in her and Felicia's life, and Diana suddenly realized just how much a part of their lives Nedwyn had been. Felicia had had enough uncles, so she'd always considered Nedwyn her godfather, and it was a role he'd taken seriously.

When Diana came to the last photo, she noted it was one that had been taken a few years ago, one she hadn't seen before. Someone had captured her and Nedwyn on the dance floor at a huge gala given for breast cancer awareness. She remembered that night well since it was the night she'd realized he meant more to her than a friend, that she had fallen in love with him.

"I don't recall this photo being taken," she said softly, as she continued to study it, noting how good they looked together, how good they fit, and how he was holding her in his arms.

"A private photographer took it to appear in the *Cancer Society Memoirs* booklet and wanted to know if I wanted a copy. I told him I did." He paused a minute and then said, "We looked good together that night, didn't we?"

She smiled because she'd thought the same thing. "Yes, we did." She closed the book, once again thinking of just how much a part of her life he'd been and how much she'd been a part of his. When he'd asked how Felicia had felt about canceling her regular dinner date with her, Trask, and the kids, Diana hadn't told him everything. She had taken her daughter into her confidences a couple of years ago and had told her how she truly felt about Nedwyn. Felicia, being Felicia, had made a number of suggestions on what Diana should do, saying the modern woman didn't wait around for the man to make the first move.

Diana had decided if that was the case, she would continue being a traditional woman instead of a modern one. It wasn't in her persona to pursue a man, even if he was one she wanted. She felt if it was meant for them to be together then eventually he would wake up and realize how deeply she cared for him, and if he didn't, well, she would still have him as a friend. A very special friend.

It was then she noted the two of them were sitting close together on the sofa and neither had said anything for a few moments, as if both were deep in their own individual thoughts. Thinking she needed to say something, she said, "I had fun going grocery shopping with you yesterday." She chuckled. "It was quite an experience."

He leaned back against the sofa and crossed one leg over the other and grinned. "Why? Because you discovered my lifelong secret that I love Klondike bars?"

"Yes." They had driven to three different stores looking for them.

"Usually I don't have a problem finding them," he said, smiling. "I guess with the beginning of summer and this heat wave we're having, they're in demand."

"Evidently," she said, trying to keep the smile out of her voice. He'd been like a kid, desperate for another toy. He was intense about getting those bars. A shiver went down her spine at the thought of him ever being that intense about her.

She inhaled deeply, trying to recall the last time she had made love with a man, and decided it had been so long ago she couldn't remember. Then she did.

Harrell Fletcher.

Most men hadn't bothered asking her out for fear they would encounter too much of her brothers-in-law's scrutiny. But once, years ago when Felicia was away at college, Diana had met someone, someone she'd liked. They'd dated for almost a year, and he had asked her to marry him. For some reason Harrell had been jealous of her friendship with Nedwyn, and when he'd asked her to end the friendship, she had refused. They had stopped seeing each other right after that. It was hard to believe that that had been almost twenty years ago.

Once again thinking that things had gotten too quiet between her and Nedwyn, she decided to ask, "So, how are things coming for your retirement party? The one Jake and Diamond are giving you."

A smile touched his lips. "I passed the guest list on to Jake a couple of weeks ago, and knowing him and Diamond, it will be larger than I'm expecting. They like doing things in a grand style."

Diana nodded, chuckling, knowing that was true. "Anyone on the guest list that I know?"

"Umm, Hillary has been invited. I know how much you

admire her. And before you ask, yes, she's bringing Bill. Then there are several other senators and congressmen coming. Oprah has accepted, and so has Bill Cosby. Denzel is out of the country filming, but Sterling Hamilton and his lovely wife, Colby, are coming as well as Kyle and Kimara Garwood. As you know, they're regulars at any party Jake hosts."

"Yes, I know." Diana then decided to ask something she had wondered about since he'd confided in her that he was going to retire over a year ago. "Ned, you were a senator for over twenty-five years. If you could do anything different now, what would it be?"

She turned slightly and studied his features and saw the sadness that crept into his eyes. It was a long moment before he finally spoke. "I regret my inability to detect that in addition to being vindictive, Senator John Harris was also a very sick man. Only a truly demented person could have done what he did to those teenagers."

She knew what he was talking about. The once-popular senator from Pennsylvania had gotten arrested a few years ago, along with a few noted others, as part of a cartel that kidnapped teens all over the country to be shipped to other countries to be sexually exploited. Her niece Christy Madaris had broken the story and had placed her life on the line in doing so, as she herself had gotten kidnapped.

"But you didn't know," Diana said quietly.

"No, I think when he was exposed, it came as a surprise to everyone. But still, when I think of all those kids, some he even had killed . . . I hope he rots in jail. Being given life with no chance of parole was being too kind to him."

He didn't say anything for another long moment; then he said, "And then I wish I would have been more forceful in my stance about us going into Iraq. I voted against it, but I should have gotten more of my colleagues to support my position. Instead, they believed there were weapons of mass destruction buried somewhere."

She nodded. "Now what do you think is your greatest

accomplishment? What bill did you help get passed that was important to you?"

He smiled. "Now that one is easy. The King Memorial. I thought it was long overdue, and I was proud to give it my full support."

Taking a deep breath, he then glanced at the clock on the wall. "It's getting late. I think we should enjoy dinner now, don't you?" he asked, coming to his feet.

He offered her his hand and she took it. "Yes, I think that we should."

Skye let herself into her condo around seven that evening. She knew that Slade was home since she'd parked the car he'd loaned her next to his truck. A part of her wanted to see him and to tell him what a great afternoon she'd had with Vincent and the other Madarises, but she decided not to bother him. Besides, she was trying to wean herself from having so many Slade moments. She loved him, but knew nothing could ever come of it. At the end of the summer she would be returning to Maine, and he would continue his life here. Since Vincent would be living in Dallas, she could fly there to see him and not to Houston, which meant it would be rare for her and Slade's paths to cross unless, like before, he was visiting Justin and Lorren when she visited.

Tossing her purse on the sofa, she decided to call her parents, hoping they had regretted what they'd told her the last time she'd seen them. Being around Marilyn and Jonathan Madaris had again made her notice things about their interaction with each other that she had never noted with her parents.

And then there was the way all the other married couples interacted as well. Everyone was loving toward each other. She chuckled. She found that Clayton and Syneda rarely agreed on anything, and they had gotten into a rather heated debate as to who would become the next president. The one thing they had agreed on was who would be the best person for the office of vice president. They both thought that at forty-three, Senator Ryan Baines, from her own home state of Maine, was the top contender.

Syneda had pulled her into their discussion by asking if Skye knew the very handsome and single Senator Baines, who was fast gaining popularity across the country. She responded by telling them that she didn't know him as well as she knew his father, retired Congressman Baines, a man she considered like a godfather to her since her father had been his personal accountant for years.

After her response, Syneda and Clayton moved to another topic—one they didn't agree on. A laughing Lorren told her not to mind them because the couple was known to never agree. But Skye figured they evidently agreed on some things when she and Vincent's aunts, Kattie and Traci, accidentally walked in on them an hour or so later, sharing a very passionate kiss in Marilyn Madaris' kitchen.

Sighing deeply and with a yearning to speak with her own parents, Skye pulled her cell phone out of her purse and begin dialing her parents' number. It was picked up by Helen.

"Yes, Helen, are my parents home? I'd like to speak with them."

There was a slight pause and then the older woman said, "Sorry, Ms. Skye, but your parents said not to disturb them if you were to call."

Skye held her breath for a moment, fighting the hurt that settled around her heart. How could her parents treat her this way just because she was doing something that she wanted to do? Something that made her happy.

She let out her breath and then inhaled deeply. "Very well, then. Please let them know that I called."

Skye flipped shut her phone and returned it to her purse. She wrapped her arms around herself, feeling a shiver touch her body. How could herself parents put a hurtful ending on what had otherwise been such a beautiful day? It just wasn't fair, and why couldn't they see that? Why couldn't they see that if she did what they wanted her to do, which was cutting off all contact with Vincent as well as marrying Wayne, both would ultimately destroy her? Didn't that matter to them?

She closed her eyes, fighting the need to walk across the hall to Slade and be held in his arms. He had a way of taking her hurt away, and she needed that now.

She reopened her eyes, knowing this time she would not turn to Slade. Doing so would only start something she couldn't afford to finish. In the past when she felt lonely and needed a shoulder to cry on, she'd had no one, and now she would have to go back to being her own comforter.

Her parents had made their decision and she would have to find a way to live with it.

Slade quit pacing the floor when he heard Skye return. He'd waited awhile to see if she would come over to his place, and when she hadn't he pulled out one of his favorite old movies and slipped it into the DVD player.

He kept telling himself the same thing he'd tried convincing himself all day. He didn't need any hassles in his life now. And if Skye didn't want to pursue anything with him, then that was fine.

He inhaled deeply when he slipped his body between the sheets. "Hell, no, it's not fine," he angrily muttered to himself. He didn't like what she was doing to him. To them. Why couldn't she see that she could have it all? Him and Vincent? Slade understood her need to spend time with Vincent, but he wanted to spend time with her as well. Why was she being so stubborn and difficult?

He flipped on his back and stared at the ceiling. Was she upset because he hadn't warned her that a lot of his relatives were going to be at church today? Pretty soon she would see he had relatives practically everywhere. Tomorrow she was to start work for him. Sexual chemistry was something they hadn't been able to deal with very well.

It was going to be a challenge for them to work together in the same office, and he wondered how they would handle it.

CHAPTER 18

Slade glanced down at his watch. It was just a minute or so past ten. He had only been in his office a couple of hours, and he wasn't handling Skye's presence very well.

He had not called to ask if she wanted a ride to the office that morning. Instead he'd called to let her know his car was available for her to use. In a very professional tone she had thanked him and then told him that that wouldn't be necessary since a rental car was being delivered to her. She didn't think it would look good if she drove the "boss's car" on a continuous basis.

She had arrived to work on time and he had taken her around to introduce her to everyone. Blade had an early outside appointment, so he wasn't in yet, but she was introduced to his secretary and his staff. Then Slade had taken her to see Sherri, the person Skye would be replacing for the summer. The two hit it off immediately, and he'd left her in Sherri's competent care. But that hadn't stopped him from thinking of her, from remembering all the things they'd done together that past weekend. How could she cut her emotions on and off like that? Or could she?

A part of him was dying to find out by boldly walking across the hall to where she was in the accountant's office and kissing her senseless. But what would he accomplish by doing that, other than cause unnecessary office gossip about the boss and the temporary employee? Most of his staff considered her a family member, since Vincent, who had arrived an hour ago, had quickly spread the word that she was his sister.

He turned at the knock on his closed office door. "Come in."

He lifted a brow when Blade walked in smiling. "What are you smiling about this early?" he couldn't help but ask.

"I just saw Skye. It's nice seeing another beautiful face around here, isn't it?"

If Blade was trying to get him riled up, Slade decided it wouldn't work. "Yes, it is. Now what do you want? I'm sure you have a lot to keep you busy today like I do."

Blade chuckled. "Umm, I heard while you were at Mom's yesterday, Skye was at Aunt Marilyn's. What's up with that?"

Slade narrowed his eyes. "I don't know. You tell me what you think is up."

"That sounds like the two of you are cooling things between you for a while. Or that there's trouble in paradise. That you've gotten into short-term affairs like me. Hell, Slade, I don't know and I don't like guessing. So tell me what's up with you and Skye."

Slade pushed away from the drafting table. He knew his brother well enough to know that he wouldn't leave his office until he got answers, and since they'd always been honest with each other, Slade said, "Skye's worried about what the family might think if they knew we were involved. She's afraid they'll think it's not her interest in Vincent that brought her here for the summer but her interest in me."

Blade looked confused. "Maybe I missed a piece somewhere along the way, but does it really matter?"

"Yes, to her it does. I get the feeling that while growing up she had to adhere to a very strict code of principles and standards. A few of them she can't easily let go of. She only wants to focus her time and attention on Vincent this summer."

"So where does that leave you?" Blade asked.

Slade shrugged. "Frankly, I don't know. But I do know

I'm not going to make things easy for her. She'll eventually realize that one doesn't have anything to do with the other."

"Well, good luck. Now you see why I prefer playing the field. Women are too much trouble to settle with just one. They'll send you to an early grave trying to figure out how their minds work." A slow grin spread across his face when he added, "I'd much rather concentrate on working another part of their body."

"Bye, Blade. I'm sure you have something to do," Slade said, turning back toward the table.

He shook his head when he heard the door close shut behind his brother. If he could think like Blade, it would definitely be easier for him to deal with Skye. But he couldn't think like Blade. They were twins, but when it came to women they definitely thought differently.

Diana walked into her daughter's lingerie shop when it opened on Monday morning. She looked around and made a few purchases that she didn't think were too outlandish for her to wear to bed. Not that anyone would see her in them, but still, when it came to nightclothes she thought sensibly. She liked silk and lace but thought she was too old for all that overly-sexy stuff. Wearing a thong was something she would never be comfortable doing, physically or mentally.

"Hi, Mom, how did your date with Uncle Ned go?" Felicia asked her mother when Diana went to the counter with her purchases.

Diana glanced around. She was glad no one else had heard her daughter's question. "It wasn't a date, Felicia. We merely had dinner together at his place."

Felicia shrugged. "Sounds like a date to me. In fact, I always considered the two of you dating when you didn't."

"Only because Ned is nothing more than—"

"Your best friend. But you love him. You told me so. So why won't you let him know how you feel?"

"Because things don't work that way."

"Maybe in your generation but not in mine. And I'm going to teach Madaris to go after what she wants in life, whether it's a man, career, an education, whatever."

Diana believed her. Thanks to the spoiling by her uncles, Felicia always had done pretty much whatever pleased her. Diana thought Felicia and her husband, Trask, made a beautiful couple and Trask was just what she needed. They had known each other forever, so Trask was used to her airs and didn't tolerate them much. He knew how to keep Felicia in line most of the time.

"So what's next?"

Diana looked up into her daughter's smiling face. "What do you mean, what's next?"

"When is the next date—I mean best-friend get-together?"

Diana rolled her eyes. "I'm his escort at the retirement party Jake is giving him in a few weeks."

"Umm, that's sweet. Honestly, I can't imagine any other woman walking in on his arm but you."

Diana smiled. Neither could she. She and Ned had gotten into a routine, and people were used to seeing them together. "Well, I got to run," she said.

She decided not to mention to her daughter that Ned was taking her to lunch. Knowing Felicia, she would read more into it than there was.

"I think you made some nice purchases, Mom. But I wish you'd consider that outfit over there. I think it would look good on you. Just the thing for you to lounge around wearing. And it would be appropriate for you to wear to entertain a certain man."

Felicia scanned her mother's toned limbs and ripe curves. The dress she was wearing was very flattering. In fact, all of the clothes she wore always looked gorgeous on her, but if only she could interest her in buying those hot sexy items that were guaranteed to raise a man's temperature up a notch. "You have a nice figure, Mom. You've kept it up over the years, and I think you should wear outfits—both inside and out—that flaunt it."

Diana glanced over at the outfit her daughter was talking about. It was on display in the middle of the store on a mannequin. The outfit didn't just flaunt; it bared all. Gracious! It was a beautiful lounger, but it left nothing to the imagination. It was something way too bold for her taste. She couldn't imagine what Ned would think if he were ever to see her in something like it.

"That's not me, Felicia."

"Then make it you, Mom. Go ahead. Be bold and daring just once. Here," she said, reaching under the counter and pulling out the same outfit. "This one is your size and I know it's the senator's favorite color. Consider it a gift."

"Felicia, I can't possibly wear some—"

Felicia put the item in a bag, then placed the package into her mother's hands. "Yes, you can. Humor me, will you? And take it a step further and take advice from your daughter for a change instead of giving me advice. You are *woman*. That entitles you to go after what you want. Men are slow about certain things, and it takes a woman, a strong, confident woman, to be bold enough to make the first move. I think one of the reasons my godfather has never taken things further is because he's not sure it will be reciprocated. He probably assumes friendship is all you want. Once he knows that's not the case, then your worries are over and you'll live happily for the rest of your life."

Felicia leaned closer over the counter and whispered, "And don't you want that, Mom? Wouldn't you rather curl up at night with a good man than a good book? Umm, just think of the possibilities."

Diana felt the blush that came into her face. The possibilities were too numerous to think about or share with her daughter. She quickly gathered up all her bags. "I'll see, Felicia."

"Remember what I've told you, Mom," Felicia called after her.

Diana didn't look back as she headed for the exit door, thinking there was no way she could forget.

Slade walked out of the office to leave for the day the exact moment Skye was leaving with Vincent. He smiled when he saw them. "Hello, Skye. Vincent, how did things go your first day?"

"Great! I got to spend time with Glenn, and he showed me how he takes the plans you draw and checks to make sure they will work for the environment. I thought it was cool. Tomorrow I get to ride out on a job site with Blade," Vincent answered excitedly.

"That's good. I see the two of you are calling it a day."

"Yes. Skye and I are going to that pizza place for dinner. You want to come?"

He glanced over at Skye. Although she was looking at him, there was nothing in her features that gave him the impression that she wanted him to tag along. "Thanks, but I have some work I need to finish up at home. The two of you go and enjoy yourselves."

It was then Skye spoke. "Are you sure, Slade? You are welcome to join us."

Although she had issued the invitation, he knew she preferred time alone with Vincent, and he was fine with that. What he wasn't fine with was that she didn't want time alone with him. "I'm sure. Besides, Mom sent me home with a to-go box filled to capacity. I have enough food to last for a week."

He took the elevator down with them, and he and Skye listened while Vincent recapped his day some more. When they got to the fifth floor the elevator picked up Syneda and Clayton. They were caught up in another heated debate as to whether or not the Texans, who were Clayton's favorite team, would beat the Cowboys, who were Syneda's favorite team, in football this coming season. They broke off the torrid discussion long enough to find out how Skye and Vincent's first day at work had gone.

Slade walked Skye and Vincent to her rental car before getting into his truck. He watched them pull off and sat there awhile in his truck. Skye seemed to be handling things pretty well. Evidently his presence in the office didn't bother her like hers had bothered him today.

He'd caught a glimpse of her several times that day while she'd followed Sherri, learning her way around the office. And each time he thought she looked stunning. Although his office had a pretty lax dress code for the summer months, she had worn a very sharp business pantsuit. Several times he'd been tempted to corner her somewhere and take the suit off her.

He rubbed a hand down his face before pulling out of the parking lot. He'd made it through day one; now there were only eighty-something more to go.

"I wish Slade could have joined us."

Skye glanced over at Vincent, hearing the disappointment in his voice. A part of her wished Slade could have joined them, too. "You really like him, don't you?"

"Who? Slade?" At her nod Vincent said, "Yes, he's cool. But then Blade and Luke are cool, too. All my older cousins are cool, but Slade is one of the coolest. He used to spend a lot of time with me when I was little, and would make me feel special and made me think I was so smart that I could do anything."

Skye nodded. Every child needed someone in their life who was a mentor, a role model. Just plain someone who cared.

"Was there anyone who made you feel special and smart when you were growing up, Skye?"

Skye thought long and hard over that question. Besides her aunt Karen there had been one other person. "Yes, the man who I consider my godfather, although he's really not. My father worked as Congressman Baines's accountant for many years, and I remember going to the office with my father on Saturdays and the congressman would be there." Skye smiled. "Come to think of it, he was always there visiting the office and would ask how I was doing and would tell me that I would grow up to be a special young lady one day. He used to tell me that so much that I believed him. And he would always buy me a special present for my birthday."

"That was nice of him."

Skye's smile widened. "Yes, I always thought he was a nice man. I still do, although I don't get to spend as much time with him now as I did when I was younger. Maybe that will change now that he's retiring from politics."

"Like my uncle Nedwyn Lansing. He was a senator, but he retired a few months ago. He's not really a family member, but we all think of him as one. We had another senator in the family, Mama Nora's brother. His name was Roman Malone. He was a good friend of Grampa Jonathan. They had gone to college together, but he died two years ago. He was a nice man. He's the one who introduced my dad to my mom."

"Well, thanks for sharing some more family history," Skye said, smiling, as she pulled into the parking lot of the pizza shop. "I'm learning more and more about the Madaris family every day. But while we're eating pizza I want to learn all there is to know about *you*. What you like. What you don't like. What's your favorite color?" Her eyes twinkled when she said, "How many girlfriends do you have?"

Vincent couldn't help laughing. Before unhooking his seat belt he said, "Skye, there are some things a guy don't even tell his sister."

CHAPTER 19

Slade stood at the window in his office looking down at the pond. Below he could make out his cousin Dex. Caitlin had brought him lunch, and the two were sitting on the park bench eating.

For the first time ever, a shiver of envy went through Slade's body at what he didn't have. A woman who loved him and who enjoyed his company. A woman who wanted him around.

He glanced over at the calendar. It had been two weeks since Skye had come to work for him and Blade. Two weeks of fighting the attraction for her both in and out of the office. During the day they exchanged professional pleasantries, and then most evenings she spent her time doing one thing or another with Vincent. But Slade was aware of each and every time she came home. He didn't go to bed each night until he knew she was safely inside her condo.

He closed his eyes for a moment as memories washed over him. They were memories of his and Skye's weekend spent together, of them making love, of him making her his. He reopened his eyes, thinking the sad thing was that he couldn't be mad at her. She had explained how things would be several times. But he'd assumed she would still want to be with him, at least some of the time. However, she was more concerned with appearances than emotions.

He turned when he heard the buzzer go off on his desk.

Crossing the room, he reached on his desk to hit the "speak" button. "Yes, Claire?"

"Guess who I have on the phone for you, sir?" his secretary said, almost breathless.

"Who?"

"Diamond Swain-Madaris, sir. Can you believe she's on the line?" Claire asked excitedly. "I've seen all her movies, some more than once, and—"

"Thanks, Claire," Slade said, smiling as he shook his head. "Please put my aunt through."

He made it a point to always refer to Diamond as his aunt when speaking to others, as if that could erase the time he'd been in high school and college and had a huge pinup poster of her on his bedroom wall. Hell, how was he to know he'd been lusting over someone who'd one day become his aunt?

"Slade?"

He smiled. It always amazed him that her voice was as beautiful as the rest of her. "Diamond, how are you?"

"I'm fine. In fact, everyone is fine. Granite is getting over a nasty cold, but he'll survive. He's pouting because I wouldn't let him go out riding the range with his daddy this morning. Unfortunately, he had to be stuck in the house with me."

Slade decided not to tell her that there were a lot of men who had fantasies of being stuck just about anywhere with her. "And to what do I owe the pleasure of this call?"

"The guest list for this weekend's affair. Jake mentioned that you might be bringing someone, but he didn't have a name."

Slade remembered that conversation he'd had with Jake weeks ago. At the time Slade had been certain he would be bringing Skye, but now . . .

Damn. He simply refused to give up on her. He would ask and if she turned him down, oh well. "Her name is Skye

Barclay," he heard himself say. "I haven't asked her yet, so I'll have to get back to you on that."

"Skye Barclay? That's Vincent's sister, right?"

"Yes."

"I'm looking forward to meeting her. I'm hearing such wonderful things about her. Will you ask her tonight and have an answer for me tomorrow?"

"I can do even better. I can ask her now and call you back in about an hour or so."

"That would be wonderful! Thanks, Slade. I'll look forward to your return call."

Skye made her way toward Slade's office wondering why she'd been summoned. His secretary had buzzed and said that he wanted to see her. Surely he didn't have any complaints about her work, since she was definitely on top of things and had been since Sherri had left last week.

"Mr. Madaris said for you to go right in," Slade's secretary, said, smiling at her.

"Thanks."

Skye opened the door to find Slade standing at the window, staring out. She silently closed the door and studied his profile. She had noted the difference in the way he and Blade dressed for the office immediately that first day. Blade liked wearing designer jeans with a sports coat, where Slade was strictly a suit-and-tie man. He was someone who took the rule "dress for success" to another level. In the two weeks since she'd been here, she was yet to see him wear the same suit twice, and he had to own more ties than a department store. He was definitely a sharp dresser.

"Slade, Claire said you wanted to see me."

He slowly turned around and the dark eyes that lit on her almost made it impossible for her to breathe. It had been a while since she'd seen him look at her that way, slowly moving his gaze over her from head to toe. Whenever they passed

in the halls or attended business meetings together, the look
he gave her was indifferent. But not this time. Not now.

"Yes. I want to know if you have anything scheduled with
Vincent this Saturday night."

She shook her head. "No, in fact, Vincent is spending the
weekend, starting Friday evening after work, with his
cousins. Kattie and Raymond's sons."

Slade nodded. "In that case, is it possible for you to be
my date to the retirement party my uncle Jake is hosting for
his friend Senator Nedwyn Lansing?"

She had heard of Senator Lansing and all the good things
he'd accomplished while he'd been in office. She thought
about Slade's invitation. It had been hard to convince Vincent that it was all right to go visit his cousins. She hadn't realized just how much of his time she'd been monopolizing.
She had been doing the very thing she had promised herself
that she wouldn't do, and that was crash in on the time he
could be spending with the Madarises.

She could now admit she'd made a mistake by putting her
time with Slade on hold. Whenever she met any members of
his family, they would be more than kind to her and they always referred to her as Vincent's sister and made no refer-
ence to anything going on between her and Slade other than
friendship. And what if they did think otherwise? Would that
be so awfully bad?

It had taken Vincent to make her see the light when he
had come out and asked her last night if she and Slade had
had a fight about something. She told him no and asked why
he would think that. And he said he noticed they didn't
spend time together anymore. He'd then gone on further to
say that it wouldn't bother him in the least if Slade was her
boyfriend. In fact he would think it was cool.

She'd then asked Vincent why he thought Slade would
want to be her boyfriend. Vincent had merely shrugged,
smiled, and said, "Because I think he likes you."

She didn't tell him that at one time that might have been

the case but that was before she had put distance between them.

"Skye?"

It was then that she realized Slade was waiting for an answer. She smiled over at him. "Yes, I'd love to go to the party with you Saturday night."

She could tell her answer both surprised and pleased him. "Good. I'll call Diamond back and let her know."

They stared at each other for a long moment; then he said, "I'm leaving in a few minutes for the airport. Blade and I have a business meeting in Atlanta and won't be back until Saturday morning. If there's anything you need while I'm gone, advise Vincent of it. He'll know which one of his uncles to call."

"I really don't think that will be necessary."

"Maybe not. But promise you'll do it anyway."

She nodded, smiling. "Okay, I promise."

Slade then crossed the room to do the one thing he said he would not do. Mix business with pleasure. "I'm going to miss seeing you around, Skye," he said softly when he came to stand in front of her.

"And I'm going to miss seeing you around as well, Slade."

Again she could tell her response had surprised him. He said nothing for a while. And neither did she for being caught up in the scope of his dark eyes. Then his head began lowering toward her lips. She tilted her mouth toward his.

"Slade."

He thought his name was a sweet, delicious sound from her mouth. And the moment his lips touched hers and he fully invaded her mouth with his tongue, two weeks of longing sent shivers all the way down his spine. This was the taste he'd gone without. The taste he'd missed. The taste he wanted so badly.

It was the same for Skye. For one crazy moment she was tempted to tell him how she felt, had felt for a long time, toward him. But considering how she'd put distance between them for the past two weeks, she knew he wouldn't fully believe her. When he returned she would have to show him. And show him she would.

He slowly pulled back. "I'm going to be gone for three days."

She smiled. "They'll fly by fast and you'll be back before you know it."

He doubted it. "Got any big plans for Friday night?"

"Christy invited me over. Her husband had to go out of town again, and like you, he won't be back until Saturday. She thought we could grab dinner Friday night and do a movie."

A smile touched the corners of his lips. "Sounds nice, but not as nice as this." And then he leaned down and kissed her again.

"What do you think of this outfit?"

Marilyn turned from browsing a rack of clothes and smiled at her sister-in-law. "Oh, Diana, it looks simply beautiful on you."

Diana glanced down at herself. Over the years, although she'd tried to stay in shape, there were some things a woman her age just couldn't hide. She didn't care how many stomach crunches she did every day, she could never get a flat tummy out of it. Thank goodness for body shapers. "Are you sure? It's not the style I normally wear. It's a bit daring, don't you think?"

Marilyn waved off her words. "I told you what I think. You have the body for it, so why are you hesitant about getting it?"

She shrugged. "Because Ned is the honoree and as his date, the spotlight will be on me as well. I don't want to wear anything that will draw a lot of attention."

Marilyn shook her head. Diana had to be one of the most modest women she knew. She really didn't know just how attractive she was. "Well, personally, I think you deserve a lot of attention, especially from Ned. And this outfit will definitely do the trick."

Diana looked down at herself again. She did like the dress. Made of soft material, it was tea-length, with a crystal scoop neckline and a beaded hem. It had an elegant look, and she knew the right accessories would definitely set it off.

She smiled up at Marilyn. "I'm going to buy it."

Marilyn chuckled. "I was hoping that you would. That dress was made for you, and when Ned sees you in it he'll think so, too."

Marilyn and Diana took a break from shopping to dine for lunch at one of the restaurants in the Galleria. For years they had enjoyed getting together at least once a week for lunch or a day of beauty at a spa where some of their other sisters-in-law often joined them. It was an enjoyable time when the older Madaris women got together.

After the waiter had taken their order, Diana asked, "So you have met Vincent's sister?"

"Yes, and she is absolutely stunning. I think she has already caught a Madaris man's eye."

Diana lifted a brow. "Whose?"

"Slade. He happened to be visiting Justin and Lorren the day she showed up. It's very obvious he's quite taken with her, although he tried to downplay his interest the other night over at Dex's." She chuckled. "I recall when Alex used to try the same thing with Christy. Jonathan and I caught on real fast. The boys never did."

Marilyn took a sip of her wine, then said, "Then Clayton thought he had me fooled with Syneda. But I have an observant eye."

Diana smiled as she studied the wine in her glass. "Are you hinting at something?"

Marilyn laughed. "Yes, I guess I am. I've started noticing you and Nedwyn."

Diana chuckled as she looked up. "And?"

"And I've noticed interest. And on both sides. That night Jonathan and I joined the two of you for dinner was really an eye-opener. Until then I had no idea." She reached across the table and took Diana's hand in hers. "I'm truly happy for the both of you."

Diana shook her head. "Trust me, Marilyn, it's not what you think. What you saw was love shining in my eyes for him. Ned has no idea how I feel and I'm afraid he won't reciprocate my feelings, so I'd rather not tell him."

Marilyn's hand tightened on Diana. "Oh, but I think you're wrong. I think Ned is just as taken with you as you are with him."

Diana lifted an arched brow. "What makes you think that?"

"Because of what I saw that night. The way he was looking at you when he knew you weren't looking back. I saw something shining in his eyes as well."

Diana swallowed. She didn't want to get her hopes up, but Marilyn was good at noticing things. But still . . .

Diana pulled her hand back and picked up her wineglass to take a sip. "You might be wrong."

"But what if I'm right?"

The thought of Marilyn being right sent shivers all through Diana's body. She hadn't made love to a man in over twenty years, and the thought of curling up with Ned instead of a good book, like Felicia had hinted, was formulating thoughts in her mind that shouldn't be there. And age didn't have a thing to do with it. She knew that Marilyn and Jonathan still had an active sex life. The last time she and Marilyn had gone to the spa for a day of beauty, all the passion marks she'd seen on Marilyn's body had proven that.

Just the thought of her and Ned sleeping together, making love, waking up in the same bed together the next morning, was almost too much to think about. She could just imagine how hot his naked skin would feel against hers and how—

"Diana?"

She glanced guiltily up at Marilyn, hoping her sister-in-law, who was good at reading people, wasn't a good mind reader as well. "Yes?"

"What if Nedwyn feels the same way about you that you feel about him? What then?"

Diana was silent for a moment. Then she looked across the table and a smile touched the corners of her lips. "There's this outlandishly sexy outfit Felicia gave me a few weeks ago when I dropped by her shop. I took it home and stuck it in a drawer. If I even thought Ned's feelings were anywhere near mine, I would pull it out and wear it for him."

Marilyn chuckled. "Then you might as well pull it out."

CHAPTER 20

Slade glanced at his watch the moment he stepped off the plane. He should have arrived back in Houston around noon, but because of a delayed flight it was four o'clock already. He had just enough time to make it home, shower, and get to the senator's retirement party.

Skye had left a message on his cell phone that she would meet him at the party. Since Alex was out of town and she and Christy hadn't come in from the movies until late, Skye had ended up spending the night. It seemed that Alex's plane had also gotten delayed coming in from Illinois and he wouldn't be arriving in town until later. So he would also be joining Christy at the party.

God, he'd missed Skye. More than once he had picked up the phone to call her but then had changed his mind, not wanting to interrupt any time she was spending with Vincent. And then at night when he figured she would be at home, he'd gotten stuck with wining and dining potential clients. Blade, not surprisingly, had met some woman he'd become enamored with and had made himself scarce for several nights.

But Slade figured all that was good, since he was home and couldn't really be mad at his brother. Blade was no more ready to settle down with the right woman than the man in the moon. But Slade felt different. In fact, he'd come to realize something very vital while in Atlanta. He'd fallen in love with Skye.

Exactly when it had happened he wasn't sure. It might have been the moment he'd opened Justin's door to find her standing there. Or it could have been the moment he had shared their first kiss.

He smiled. But then again it might have been the day he had picked her up from the airport. He had definitely felt something other than lust when he'd seen her that day. Or, he thought, smiling further, it could very well have been the first time they'd made love.

Just thinking about that night had memories racking his mind as well as his heart. That night had been one filled with passion and desire. He remembered every shiver of pleasure she'd felt, because he'd felt them as well. And when he had entered her body for the first time, it had been one of the most precious moments of his life.

He was glad that things hadn't worked out for her and her ex-fiancé. The man hadn't appreciated just what he had. Slade knew he would not make that same mistake. He would appreciate her every day of his life.

He couldn't help wondering how she felt about him. He knew she didn't love him, but he did believe she could grow to love him. He would not force his love on her, but he would ply her with all the love and affection any one woman could handle, and then he hoped that one day she would return the feelings.

Now that he knew just how much he loved Skye, there was no way he would ever let her go.

Skye glanced around the elegantly decorated room. Never in her life had she been under the same roof with so many important people. First she had to recover when movie actress Diamond Swain-Madaris had opened the door to greet them and invite them in.

Skye knew she had to have stood there a full five minutes staring with her mouth open. The woman was simply beautiful, and according to what Christy had shared with Skye on the ride over to the ranch, Diamond was as beautiful on the inside as she was on the outside. Everyone in the family loved her, and their uncle Jake simply adored her, and with good reason. She had brought so much love and joy into what had been Jake's lonely life on Whispering Pines.

Skye had seen the Clintons shortly after that, along with Oprah. When she spotted George Clooney standing by the terrace talking to fellow movie actor Sterling Hamilton, she thought she'd died and gone to heaven. Later, Christy had introduced her to Sterling, who was considered a close family friend because of his friendship with Christy's uncle Jake. Skye had also been introduced to Sterling's beautiful wife, Colby, as well as another couple who were close friends of Jake's—Kyle and Kimara Garwood. When they'd walked away from the couple, Skye had almost flipped when Christy had whispered to her just how many kids they had. She shook her head. Unbelievable.

Skye smiled. She was really enjoying her friendship with Christy. Not only were they the same age, but their birthdays were just days apart. And she could tell from talking to Christy that she had a very close relationship to Slade, Blade, and Luke and simply adored her three older cousins.

Christy checked her watch. "I wonder what's taking Alex so long to get here."

Skye had wondered the same thing about Slade. "I'm sure it was pretty hectic getting from the airport. He'll be here soon."

Christy smiled. "God, I hope so. I miss him so much. I wanted to go with him on this trip, but he felt it best that I stay home this time."

Skye nodded. Last night after she and Christy had come in from the movie—a new Denzel release the two of them had practically drooled through most of the scenes of— Christy had told Skye all about her love for her husband, a love that had lasted from the time she'd been thirteen. She'd also told Skye about her adventure two years ago when she'd gotten kidnapped.

"I can't wait for you to meet Alex," Christy was saying. "He is simply wonderful."

Skye took a sip of her wine before she was tempted to say that she thought Slade was simply wonderful, too, when she turned and noticed what had to be one of the most gorgeous men she'd ever seen. He was standing across the room talking to Jake Madaris. It was apparent he wasn't from this country but was from the Middle East.

"Who is that?" she asked in a strained voice. The man was smiling at whatever Jake was saying, and his smile . . . oh my gosh! It was simply beautiful. He was tall and had dark piercing eyes. The color of his skin was a medium brown, and straight black hair flowed loosely around his shoulders. He was dressed in a business suit, and it was apparent the outfit cost a lot.

Christy followed the direction of Skye's gaze and grinned. "He's simply gorgeous, isn't he? Alex is handsome, but the sheikh is in a class by himself."

Skye's brow rose. "The sheikh?"

"Yes, Sheikh Rasheed Valdemon. He's the one I was telling you about, who bought me for a million dollars from those bad guys to get me out of harm's way." Christy chuckled. "Of course he never had to pay the million dollars."

As far as Skye was concerned, it didn't matter. She couldn't imagine being close enough to the man to breathe the same air. Christy was right. Skye thought that Slade was an extremely good-looking man, but the sheikh took "good-looking" and gave it an all new definition.

"Skye Barclay?"

Skye quickly turned, wondering who on earth at this party would know her. She smiled when she saw it was Congressman Baines and his son, Senator Ryan Baines. It had been the senator who'd spoken. It then occurred to her that most of the time when the two men were together, it was the congressman and not the senator who did most of the talking. Although the senator was always friendly to her, she'd always gotten the impression—and to be honest she really didn't know why—that he avoided her whenever he could, which really didn't make sense. But the congressman did just the opposite. She couldn't recall a time during any part of her childhood that he hadn't been a part of it.

She smiled and quickly gave the congressman a huge hug. She hadn't seen him in quite a while.

"Congressman Baines, how are you?" She then turned to the senator and offered him her hand. "And how are you doing, Senator Baines?"

"I'm fine, Ms. Barclay, and you?"

"I'm fine also." She then introduced the two men to Christy.

"I'm curious as to why you're so far from home," the senator said, looking at her curiously. "Do you know Senator Lansing?"

Skye shook her head. "No, I just met him tonight. However, since I'm here visiting with the Madaris family over the summer, I—"

"You're visiting the Madaris family?" the senator asked, seemingly surprised.

Skye smiled. "Yes, in a way." She met the congressman's gaze, knowing her father confided in him about a lot of things. "I'm sure my parents told you that once I discovered I was adopted, I wanted to find my biological brother."

The congressman nodded. "Yes, but I thought they said you had made a trip to a town near Dallas."

"I had. But since my brother, Vincent, was spending the summer here with his family, the invitation was also extended to me to come for the summer as well."

The congressman smiled. "That was very kind of his family."

"Hello, beautiful."

At that moment a very handsome man walked up and placed a kiss on Christy's lips. Skye immediately assumed it was Christy's husband. Introductions were made and when Christy introduced him she said, her eyes glowing with love, "I want everyone to meet the best private investigator in the entire world: Alexander Maxwell."

Skye couldn't help but grin. All last night Christy had sung her husband's praises. Skye shook the man's hand. "It's nice to meet you, Alex."

He smiled. "Likewise." He was then introduced to the congressman and senator.

"I hear you're almost a man wonder at finding people, Alex," Skye said jokingly. "It took the private detective I hired almost a year to find Vincent. When I'm ready to locate my biological father, I'll make sure and give you a call."

Alex chuckled as he brought Christy closer to his side. "Yes, you do that. I'd be happy to take you on as a client."

"Hello everyone."

Skye swallowed. She would recognize that deep masculine voice anywhere. She turned and met Slade's smiling eyes. "Slade. Welcome back," she said, smiling at him and at the moment not caring who saw how glad she was to see him.

He came to stand next to her. "Thanks. And I'm glad to be back." He said hello to Christy and Alex, and then he glanced over at the two men he didn't know. Skye quickly introduced him to the congressman and senator.

Slade then glanced over at Skye. "Would you like to dance?"

Skye stared up into what she thought was Slade's gorgeous dark eyes. She had missed him. The time she had spent with Vincent had helped, but late at night when she'd been alone in her bed she had thought of Slade. She had hoped that he would call her, but he hadn't. But maybe that had been a good thing, since it had given her time to think. There was a reason she and Slade had met the way they had, a purpose to why they had connected so easily, establishing first friendship and then a level of intimacy that took her breath away just thinking about it.

"Yes, I'd like that," she said, smiling up at him. She turned to everyone else. "Excuse us." She then walked away with Slade toward the area where other couples were dancing.

The moment Slade pulled Skye into his arms he leaned down and whispered, "If only you knew how much I missed you."

A sensuous shiver raced down Skye's spine with his words, and she seemingly melted into him. He held her close, and at that moment she didn't care who might be watching and assuming there was more between them than mere friendship. This was Slade, the man she loved, and a part of her wished she could tell him just how she felt.

Slade was also having a hard time holding on to his emotions. Holding Skye this way—in their first dance together—reminded him of how wonderful it felt to hold her in his arms, whether standing or lying down. At the moment he ached to lie down somewhere with her, make love to her, claim her as the woman he wanted in his life for always.

When he had walked into the party and seen her, everything and everyone else in the room had faded into a state of non-existence. His eyes had been trained solely on her. She looked radiant in the gown she was wearing, a vision of beauty that nearly had him breathless. It was slinky and sexy all rolled into one, and he couldn't imagine any other woman wearing it. It seemed to have been made for her and her alone.

Thinking he needed to talk to take his mind off of leaning down and kissing her right then and there, he said, "I see you aren't the only person from Maine here tonight."

She smiled up at him. "No, it's nice seeing the congressman and senator here. But then there are so many other important people here as well." Her eyes widened. "I even saw a sheikh."

Slade released a soft chuckle. "That was Rasheed. He's a close friend of the family."

"It seems the Madarises have a lot of friends."

"Yes, they do."

At that moment the music ended, but Slade didn't release her, so Skye assumed they would remain on the dance floor for the next song. But then he leaned down and said, "Please come outside with me for a minute."

It was hard for Skye to swallow. She nodded and Slade took her hand in his and led her outside on the terrace. When they kept walking, she asked, "Where are we going?"

He smiled down at her. "For a walk."

She lifted a brow. "At night?"

Slade chuckled. "There's a well-lit walking path on the other side of this patio."

"Oh."

She noted how beautiful the night was and that the lit trail they were following was lined with numerous bluebonnets. They kept walking, neither saying anything but both enjoying the beauty of their surroundings. She and Christy had arrived before it had gotten dark, and Skye had seen the beauty of the Whispering Pines ranch. This was definitely a working ranch, and its beauty was absolutely spellbinding.

When they were a good distance away from the terrace, Slade stopped walking and turned to her. As though their minds were on the same page and their desires in sync, she tilted her head back the moment he leaned his down. His arms slid around her waist the same moment hers slid around his neck.

"Skye."

He whispered her name in a voice that sounded achingly low, unbearably sexy, and then their mouths connected on a blissful sigh. His hand moved from her waist to settle in the small of her back and bring her body closer to the fit of him at the same time he deepened the kiss.

Slade thought this was heaven. The sweet, succulent taste

of her always amazed him, always made him greedier for more. Desire ripped through every part of him, making his already hot body even hotter. A helpless groan murmured from deep in his throat, and he continued to taste her while she was doing likewise and tasting him as she mated with his tongue, enveloping it in the wet warmth of hers.

He finally pulled back but gathered her closer to him, breathing in deeply while holding her in his arms. God, he'd needed that, but it only made the desire in him that much keener, sharper. He looked down at her, felt the love that was overflowing in his heart almost hit a bursting point. He inhaled deeply, needing to get things in control, but that kiss had his entire body spinning.

"You're going back to your place tonight, right?" he asked, not sure if she'd made plans to spend another night over at Christy's.

She looked up at him, smiled, and leaned closer when she whispered, "No. I was hoping that I was going back to yours." She could tell by the look that flickered in his eyes that he was surprised by her response.

His voice was packed with desire when he reached out and touched her chin with the tip of his finger. "Baby, if that's what you want, then that's what you'll get."

"And what if I told you that's not all I want?" she asked with a little laugh.

"Then I would say that your wish tonight will be my every command."

"And what if I were to tell you that your wish tonight will be my every command as well, Slade?"

He chuckled softly. "Then I would say I can't wait to leave here."

She shook her head, grinning. "You just got here. It's too soon to say good night and leave."

He knew she was right. What she didn't know was that the wait to get her back to his place would probably kill him. But he would wait because he knew she was worth it.

He leaned down and kissed her lips again, thinking so what if they were missing a good party? They were doing their own brand of celebrating right here.

"Did I tell you just how beautiful you look tonight in that dress, Diana?" Nedwyn asked as he and Diana moved around the dance floor.

She smiled up at him, glad Marilyn had convinced her to buy it. From the moment he'd arrived to pick her up, he had let her know that he really liked her in this particular dress. "Yes, you did, several times, but you can tell me again and it won't hurt my feelings."

He chuckled softly. "Okay then. Diana, I really think you're absolutely stunning in this dress. But then I think you're beautiful in anything that you wear."

A sweet shudder went through her with his words. "Ned, that's so kind of you to say something like that."

"I'm not being kind; I'm being honest."

Diana didn't know what to say after that other than, "Thank you."

Nedwyn pulled her closer to the fit of him, but decently so, since he knew that with him being the honoree, a lot of eyes were on them. Saying she looked beautiful in that dress had been an understatement. The moment he had walked into her house and seen her in it, something inside of him, something he'd held under control for a number of years, had fought to escape.

His intense desire for her.

He doubted she even realized what she did to him, even without trying. Whenever he was around her he was like a schoolkid around the girl he had a crush on, only what he was enduring was the wants and desires of a full-grown man. A man who didn't need Viagra to stimulate his sexual urges. Diana being Diana was the only stimulant he needed.

They were both given guest cottages for the weekend and would remain at Whispering Pines until Sunday afternoon.

He had to fly to Savannah on Wednesday regarding some rental properties he had there, and he wanted to ask her to go with him. Would she? She'd flown to D.C. to be his escort for several functions, but they'd never actually flown anywhere together, just the two of them, mainly to avoid people speculating about their relationship. He was no longer a public servant, and he wanted to begin spending more time with the woman he loved.

"There's something I want to ask you about later, after the party. If you're not too tired, would it be okay if I drop by your cottage later?"

She gazed at him questioningly and then said, "Yes. I think Jake and Diamond put us in adjoining cottages."

He nodded. Jake had at his request, but he wouldn't tell her that yet. "I'll call you on your cell phone, and if you're too tired for company, I'll understand."

She shook her head. "I doubt I'll be tired, so you dropping by later will be fine."

"Thank you."

They continued to dance. Diana couldn't help wondering what Ned wanted to ask her. She would look forward to later tonight when she found out.

CHAPTER 21

Slade could barely hold himself in check when he and Skye stepped onto the elevator to go up to his condo. At the end of the party when most of the invited guests had left, Christy and Alex had gathered the family together to announce they were having a baby.

Slade smiled, remembering the moment and not sure who the news affected the most, his aunt and uncle, who were thrilled at the thought of becoming grandparents again, or his three cousins—Justin, Dex, and Clayton. They'd always been overprotective toward their baby sister and the thought that Christy was having a baby had deeply touched them. At least it wasn't a mystery anymore as to why Great-Gramma Laverne had been dreaming about fish.

Slade glanced over at Skye. The hour-long drive from Whispering Pines had tested his endurance, and he had appreciated her attempt at making things easier on him by discussing a number of topics, from the recent political scandal to the movie she and Christy had seen the other night. He had heard what Skye was saying, but he hadn't really been listening. His mind had been centered on one thing, and that was making love to her again.

In the tight confines of his car, her scent had gotten to him and he had wanted her even more with each lung-filled breath he'd taken. And now he was as helpless as a newborn puppy. He had put up a valiant battle while at the party, but now he was quickly losing the fight. Especially when memories encroached his mind of how things had been with them the last time they'd shared a bed. And now that love had been added to the equation, it was taking all he had to retain his sanity until he got her up to his place. But as soon as the elevator door swooshed shut, sealing them inside, the question that suddenly flared through his mind was . . . why wait?

It was late, almost two in the morning, the building was quiet, and other than the security doorman downstairs, there wasn't another living soul stirring. Besides, this particular elevator was a private one that only went to certain floors. It was like having an elevator all to themselves.

Slade turned to Skye. She saw the look and the intent in the darkness of his eyes and backed up a little and chuckled. "You're not thinking what I think you're thinking, are you?"

A slow smile spread across his lips as he began removing his jacket. "Yes, I probably am," he said, dropping the jacket to the floor. He then snatched off the tie from around his neck.

She backed up some more. "Don't you think we ought to wait until we get up to your place?"

He chuckled as he tossed his tie to join his jacket on the marble floor. "You can initiate foreplay anywhere." She probably wouldn't be interested to know that his cousin Clayton had shared that piece of advice with him a few years ago. Nor would she be interested to hear that Clayton believed as long as you had a private spot, you could make love to your woman just about anywhere and anytime you pleased. Clayton's philosophy was that mundane constituted boredom, but variety was the spice of life.

"That's what you're doing? Initiating foreplay?" she asked, barely able to get the question out.

Slade pushed the elevator button on "stop" and then smiled at her and said, "I'll let you decide."

He advanced on her and she backed up even more. "But what if others want to use this elevator?" she asked.

"What others? This is a private elevator that only goes to the tenth, fifteenth, and twenty-fifth floors. Most of the people living on those floors are older, more settled couples who wouldn't be caught out this time of night."

She glanced up and looked around. "What about security cameras? A lot of buildings install them in their elevators."

"We didn't. Remember, Blade and I built this building."

"But . . ."

He heard whatever she was saying, but had once again gone into the not-listening mode. Desire, a degree he'd never encountered before, was pulsing everywhere, but especially heavily in his groin. He had taken off his jacket, but what he should have done first was release the zipper of his pants to take off some of the pressure; however, politeness demanded that he not be that bold. Any other time he might he considered a slow burn, but tonight with Skye he was a fast burn. It wouldn't take much for him to go up in smoke.

"Come here, Skye."

His eyes never left hers and he knew the exact moment she decided to go along with his *I-can't-wait-any-longer* approach. Instead of retreating any farther, she took a couple of steps forward. As soon as she was within arm's reach, he sneaked out his hand, curled his fingers around her waist, and pulled her body close to his. He heard her breath hitch when she realized just how aroused he was. He wanted her to know just what she was capable of doing to him.

"Open your mouth and take me in," he leaned forward and whispered against her mouth. Her lips parted immediately and he swooped his mouth over hers. While his tongue was mating deliciously with hers, he decided to use his hands to get reacquainted with the feel of her body by caressing all her curves and the firmness of her backside.

He broke off the kiss to murmur against his moist lips, "You're perfect."

The stark desire in the eyes looking at Skye had heat blazing through all parts of her body. She had a feeling that he wasn't through with her yet. This kiss was just the beginning. The dark, heated look in his eyes promised as much.

The corners of his lips turned up as he took a couple of steps forward, backing her up against the elevator wall. She felt cornered. She felt hot. She felt ready to take him on and do whatever crossed his mind. Tonight she wasn't Skye Barclay, the woman who only did what she was told to do. She was Skye Barclay, the woman who wanted to be as daring tonight as she could be.

Daring with Slade.

His arms went around her waist and gently lifted her feet off the floor. "Wrap your legs around me, Skye."

She did and he bunched the dress up to her waist while bracing her back against the paneled wall. He stuck his hand underneath it to poke a little hole in the seat of her silken panty hose. Then he inserted his fingers and smiled when he didn't encounter any panties.

"You don't have to wear them if you wear hosiery with the panties made in them," she quickly explained, not wanting him to think she made a habit of not wearing underthings.

He smiled. "I don't have a problem with that," he said softly. "In fact, it makes what I need to do a lot easier."

She heard him ease down his zipper, and when he tunneled his fingers back through her ripped panty hose, he had something else with them. Evidently he intended to do more than initiate foreplay. It seems that he was going to go straight for the gusto.

She felt the firm head of his hot shaft brush against her thigh, and she literally moaned out an anxious breath. And when he found the spot he wanted, took aim, and pushed in, sinking deep into the warm wetness of her, she groaned deep within her throat.

"You mentioned that other time we made love that you

were on the pill. Nothing has changed, has it?" he asked, barely able to get the words out.

She shook her head. "Nothing has changed," she said, not sure she was speaking coherently. Although they had used condoms the first couple of times before, once she'd told him she was on the pill they had stopped, preferring the intimate feel of being skin to skin, heat to heat.

"Good."

And then he began his thrusting motion, driving back and forth, in and out, deep inside of her. Pleasure, as keen as it could get, rammed through her whenever he withdrew, then plunged back in. And his rhythm was relentless, achingly accurate. Never had she been made love to this way, and it produced sensations that had her entire body trembling.

She purred out his name, and then he leaned forward and captured her lips. She felt the moment an orgasm struck him, and he increased the pace and tightened his hold on her lips, plunging in deeper. He then broke off the kiss to throw his head back while sucking in a deep breath.

"Skye!"

She then felt ecstasy hit her the moment he cried out her name, shattering her body into tiny sensuous pieces. She felt hot, tingly, filled to capacity all the way to her womb. Sensations hammered through her and he covered her mouth in time to stop her from screaming. He gave her one ravenous kiss and the arms she had twined around his neck tightened as he continued to grind his shaft inside of her, making sure she got it all. Her internal muscles clenched him to make doubly sure as well.

Moments later, when he eased her back on her feet, she could barely keep her balance. He kissed her again before starting the elevator back up. He reached down and picked up his coat and tie before reaching out and sweeping her off her feet and into his arms.

"Slade! I can walk."

He smiled down at her. "I bet you won't say that in the morning."

Diana moved toward the door the moment she heard the knock. It was almost three in the morning, but like she'd told Ned, she was still awake. She had undressed, taken a shower, and slipped into a long, flowing robe that she felt was appropriate enough to greet a male caller, even at this hour. Besides, she was curious as to what he wanted to ask her.

She opened the door and smiled. He had changed out of his tux and was wearing a pair of jeans and a chambray shirt. He looked just as good in casual clothes as he did in the expensive business suits that he wore. "Come in," she said, stepping aside.

"Thanks, and again I want to apologize for coming so late, but it's something I need to discuss with you."

She nodded as she led him into the sitting room. She sat on the sofa while he sat in a chair. "So what's this burning question?" she asked, glancing over at him and leaning forward in her seat, giving him her full attention.

He hesitated for a moment and then he said, "I'm leaving early Wednesday for Savannah. I bought some investment property there a few years ago and I'm thinking about expanding my interest, and need to go there for a few days to check on a few things."

He paused for a moment and then said, "I'll be gone through the weekend, probably returning sometime on Sunday, and I would like to take you with me."

Diana blinked. Was he inviting her on an out-of-town trip with him? She needed further clarification. "Will you be attending some important function where you'll need an escort?"

He chuckled. "No. It's strictly a personal trip. The reason I'm asking you to go is because I want to spend some time with you."

She wasn't going to let him get off that easily. "Why?"

He inhaled deeply and then said, "Do you really have to ask me that, Diana?"

She lifted a brow at the incredulity in his voice. Was she missing something? Was there something she was supposed to know? "Yes, I think that I really do have to ask that, because evidently I'm missing something here."

Their eyes held for a second, and then as if he'd made up his mind about something, he stood and crossed the room and when she scooted over he sat down beside her on the sofa. He took her hand in his and studied it for a moment before saying, "For the longest time I've considered you one of my very best friends."

"You no longer do?"

He chuckled. "Oh yes, I still do. In that regard I think we share a very unique and special relationship."

She had to agree with him on that. "And how do you define it?" she asked.

He thought about her question for a minute before saying, "I define it as a relationship where there's mutual trust, respect, and admiration. There's nothing I wouldn't do for you, and I believe there's nothing you wouldn't do for me."

"Yes, that's true. But it still doesn't explain what you meant earlier, Ned."

He sighed deeply. "I recently discovered something . . . and in truth it wasn't all that recent. . . . I just decided to finally acknowledge it and act on it."

"Acknowledge and act on what?"

He gazed into her eyes for several long moments before saying, "That I've fallen in love with you, Diana."

She blinked. She moved her lips but found herself unable to speak. Her voice actually felt trapped within her throat. She swallowed, tried again. Her hands tightened around the hand that still held hers. "Oh, Ned. That is the most beautiful thing you could ever say to me, because I love you, too."

He shook his head, thinking she really didn't understand what he meant. "No, Diana, I'm talking about real love, here. Not best-friend love. What I'm saying is that I love you the way a man loves a woman."

She nodded, clearly understanding. Her heart was almost bursting with happiness. "I know what you meant because I love you, too, the way a woman loves a man."

He stared at her for a moment, as if at a loss for words. Then he asked, "For how long?"

She chuckled softly. "For quite some time."

He was surprised. "Why didn't you tell me?"

She raised a dark brow as a smile touched the corners of her lips. "I'm going to ask that same question. Why didn't you tell me?"

He managed a tight smile. "Because I didn't think you'd want to become involved with someone as deeply into politics as I was."

"Oh, Ned, every time you called and asked me to accompany you to some political function or whatever, I became involved."

"But the media could be cruel."

"I know. I see what they try doing to Sterling and Colby and Diamond and Jake at every turn. Their job is to create sensationalism to sell papers. I think it was in last week's tabloids that Jake supposedly asked Diamond for a divorce to marry Tyra Banks."

Ned laughed. "So I heard."

"You need to have a strong relationship or marriage to endure such garbage."

"And I agree," he said.

"You didn't think we had that?"

He inhaled deeply. "I didn't know what we had because I was too afraid to find out. I didn't want to ruin what we shared if you didn't feel the same way I did."

"And I had taken that same position," she softly admitted.

Nedwyn's heart felt like it was ready to burst in his chest; he was filled with elation. "So this trip to Savannah will be sort of like a beginning for us. The start of a different type of relationship."

Diana nodded in agreement. "Yes, it will be." If this was a dream, then she wasn't ready to wake up yet. It seemed that Marilyn had been right. She had detected more than friendship in Ned's eyes.

"You know what I want to do more than anything, Diana?" he asked, his voice going husky and deep.

She saw his face inching closer to hers and automatically she moved her face toward his mouth. When his lips latched onto hers, she released a sigh of pleasure from deep within her throat. This was the kiss she'd dreamed of sharing with Ned so many times, the kiss she thought would never take place between them. And now it was happening.

Her muscles began to quake, her entire body began to ache, and the air surrounding them seem to crackle. She couldn't recall the last time she had shared a kiss with a man, but it hadn't been anything like this. She had forgotten how it felt to be French-kissed by a man, to have your mouth devoured like you were the best thing he'd tasted since gingerbread.

Moments later he slowly pulled back, releasing her lips, but that didn't stop him from trailing a few kisses down her throat. "Are you sure you want to spend five days with me, Diana, knowing I'm in love with you and that I want you?"

"I could ask you the same thing about me, you know," was her soft response.

He pulled back, looked at her, and smiled. "This should be an interesting trip."

"And I think it will be."

He then leaned in and kissed her again, just as thorough and deep. Then he pulled back and stood. "I'd better go before I get us both in trouble. But be forewarned, Diana Madaris, in Savannah I'll only stop when and if you tell me to."

Her voice was filled with both anticipation and desire

when she said, "I'll remember that. And I'll also hold you to it."

And before she could say anything else, he turned and quickly walked out the door.

Wayne came awake when the phone rang. He glanced at the illuminated digital clock on his nightstand. For crying out loud, it was three in the morning. Who would be calling him at this hour? He reached out and grabbed it and barked into it. "Hello!"

"Get your ass in gear and do something! You told me you could control her and I paid you a lot of money to do just that; now start earning it!"

Wayne recognized the voice and sat up in bed, rubbing a hand down his face. "I told you I had matters under control. When she returns from Texas, I—"

"She plans to hire some private investigator to find her father, and you know how I feel about that."

Yes, Wayne did know.

The person continued talking. "I will not lose all I've gained if she decides to go snooping. I'm willing to double what I was offering you before if you marry her. But not only marry her, you have to keep her under control and rid such foolishness out of her head about ever finding her biological father."

There was a pause and then the caller said, "And there's something else you might need to know."

Wayne sighed as he moved to sit on the side of the bed, feeling annoyed. Skye was beginning to be more trouble than she was worth. "What?"

"Getting her to marry you might not be as easy as you think, because there's a possibility that she's falling for someone she met in Houston. A man by the name of Slade Madaris. He's a cousin to her brother. So it will be to your advantage to do something now."

The caller then hung up.

CHAPTER 22

"Had enough yet, sweetheart?"

Before Skye could respond to Slade's question, he lowered his head and captured a swollen tip of her breast in his mouth, sucking on it, licking it, torturing it as she released groans of pleasure.

He then glided his tongue to the other one, perked and firm as it could be, as if waiting for his mouth to give it the same treatment it had given its twin. Then there were his hands that refused to stay still. They were busy, stirring and brewing the wet heat pooling between her thighs, sharpening her awareness of him, increasing her need. Making the desire building once again inside of her almost unbearable.

She closed her eyes and moaned, inhaled the scent of sex that filled the room. They had made love almost non-stop once they'd made it to his condo. First in the living room several times before finally making it to the bedroom. Each time she and Slade made love, he not only touched her body, he touched her heart as well. He had the ability to awaken every sensation she possessed, and with the way his tongue was gliding across her breasts, making her gasp, squirm, and moan, she knew he had her just where he wanted her and just where she wanted to be.

"You like that, don't you?" he asked huskily.

She didn't know why he was asking when he knew she did. She liked everything he did to her, and with an intensity that overwhelmed her. "Yes, I like—"

Before she could get out the final word, he had lifted his mouth from her breasts and captured her lips, swallowing up whatever word she was going to say. His tongue tangled with hers in a way that had her heart pounding while mirroring her innermost emotions, fantasies, and dreams. But then this was also a taste of reality, and the realism was that she was just where she wanted to be, in Slade's arms. In his bed.

Now if she could only wiggle into a part of his heart.

She loved him, but other than knowing he enjoyed what they were sharing, she didn't know how he actually felt about her. She refused to entertain the unwanted notion that this summer was all he wanted for them. She had to believe that deep down he wanted more like she did.

He released her mouth. "Open your eyes and look at me, Skye."

She did what he asked, and the intensity of the dark eyes looking down at her almost took her breath away.

"Now tell me what you see," he requested softly as he shifted his body in position over hers.

She gazed into his eyes for a long moment and then said, "I see a deeply aroused man. A man who wants me as much as I want him. A man who's shown me the meaning of being desired to the utmost and not holding anything back, and a man who has introduced me to so many incredible experiences."

He reached down and gently brushed a twisted curl from her cheek and she shivered, an automatic reaction from his touch. "What about love, Skye? Do you see a man who loves you?"

She stared at him and she did see it now. It was there, shining in the dark depths of his eyes, and it was so profound it made tears form in her eyes. "I didn't know," she said in a broken whisper. "All I knew was that I had fallen in love with you, Slade. I had no idea you loved me, too."

"Well, I do. I love you very much. I didn't realize how much until we were separated these past three days. My wanting desperately to get back here to you was more than just wanting to sleep with you. It was about loving you. I think I've loved you since the moment I first opened Justin's door to find you standing there."

"And I believe that's when I fell in love with you, too. There were so many things about you that were so unlike Wayne. I didn't know a caliber of man like you existed. You have completely and irrevocably captured my heart, Slade Madaris."

He leaned down and captured her lips with his as the wet heat of their mouths fused together, igniting every kind of nerve in their bodies. Their tongues tangled; they mated in the most intense form possible, sending erotic sensations all through the both of them.

Slade pulled his mouth back slightly and whispered against her moist lips, "I love you and will always love you until the last breath leaves my body," in a deep voice filled with love and passion.

The look in his eyes and the words he'd spoken made Skye's insides quiver. During a time in her life when her parents had practically written her off, and the only person she thought she had was a newfound brother, Slade had provided her a beacon of hope for a better and brighter future, one filled with his love. She couldn't stop the tears that came into her eyes, and he leaned down, cupped her face in his hands, and kissed the tears away.

And then he was kissing her again, letting her feel the power and depth of his love. Then he pulled back and stared down at her as he lowered the bottom part of his body, gently pressing forward, entering her, going deeper, and filling her completely as he joined their bodies as one. And when he had gone to the hilt, a storm of emotions ripped into him. This was the woman his heart had chosen, the woman he would love for all eternity.

And then he began making love to her, his thrusts powerful, driving her deeper and deeper into the firm mattress. She screamed out his name as she began climaxing. Her body shuddered and quivered beneath his, triggering his own powerful, explosive release.

"Skye!"

And then moments later he was kissing her again. This time his kiss was gentle, tender, and filled with love, and Skye felt it all the way to her toes, but especially the tingling sensation that settled in her stomach. He was still embedded inside of her, and she tightened her arms around him, savoring the feel of their bodies still joined.

She closed her eyes as sensations continued to rack her body and she wondered if Slade's prediction would be correct and she wouldn't be able to walk in the morning.

Skye glanced over at Slade across the breakfast table. "Will your mom be upset that you skipped church and won't be coming to dinner today?"

Slade smiled at her. Although it was past lunchtime, they were just eating breakfast. After they took a bath together in his oversized Jacuzzi tub, he had shared one of his bathrobes with her, and they'd been satisfied with cereal and milk.

"Mom and Dad spent the night at Whispering Pines," he said. "Uncle Jake has several guest cottages, and instead of making the long drive back to Houston, most of the family spent the night there."

Skye nodded, then smiled brightly. "So what would you like to do today?"

At the look he gave her, she shook her head and quickly said, "Besides that. I can barely walk this morning."

He chuckled. "You asked for it. Over and over again."

She blushed because she had. In fact, she had been the one to awaken first this morning with a burning desire to mate with him. All she had to do was wake him up, let him know her interest, and then the heat was on. "You shouldn't make it so good," she said teasingly.

"Baby, for you that's the only way I intend to make it." He glanced at his watch. "What time do you expect Vincent back?"

"This afternoon. He'll be spending the night over at Dex's

place, since I understand his grandparents are hitting the road again."

Slade grinned. "I want to be like Uncle Jonathan and Aunt Marilyn when I grow up. They use their time as retirees to full advantage and enjoy putting their motor home on the road."

Skye thought of her own parents. She had called them several more times over the past few weeks, and each time Helen had delivered the same message to her. They would not talk to her until she agreed to their terms. They were treating her like a naughty child being punished instead of the twenty-six-year-old woman that she was.

And when she had checked her cell phone after her bath with Slade, she saw that Wayne had called. She had no idea what he wanted but had no intentions of calling him back to find out. She had called her parents to make sure they were okay and that he hadn't been calling about them. Again Helen had answered the phone and said Skye's parents would not talk to her.

"What are you thinking about?"

She glanced over at Slade. "My parents. They still won't accept my calls."

The sadness in her voice caused a pain to rip through his heart. He couldn't imagine any parents deliberately treating their child the way Skye's parents were treating her. He thought of his own parents. He and his brothers had done a lot of things in their lifetime that their parents hadn't approved of, and of course they had let their sons know it. But at no time had his parents ever turned their backs on them. It was the strangest thing he ever heard of. Parents, at least the ones he knew, weren't usually that hard on their kids, especially when they were Skye's age. Her parents were treating her like a child instead of the adult she was.

He stood and slowly walked over to her and pinned her with his gaze. "Tell me, sweetheart. What can I do to make you happy?"

Skye blinked back tears. In all her twenty-six years, no

one had ever asked her that before, and only a man like Slade would be asking her that now. "You made me happy last night when you told me that you loved me, Slade," she said softly, looking up into his eyes. "Because now I know that if my parents never come around and talk to me again, at least I have you and your love. And that means so much to me. I love you so much."

"And I love you, too. For always." And then he bent his head down to kiss her, pulling her out of the chair and sweeping her off her feet and into his arms in the process.

When he broke out of the kiss she said, "Slade, I can walk."

He grinned down at her. "Yes, but barely. That's why I made sure you took a hot-tub bath instead of the shower. I'm taking care of you from now on."

"Oh, Slade." She laid her head on his chest when he cuddled her in his arms to carry her into the bedroom. Sunlight was streaming in through the window when he placed her on the bed. Fighting the intense desire raging through him, he gently took off his robe that she was wearing, leaving her completely bare. He then pulled back the covers. "Come on, get under this. I'm going to hold you for a while."

She slipped her naked body beneath the covers; then he removed his own robe and got underneath the covers with her. He gathered her into his arms and held her. Entwining their limbs, his arms bracketed her, holding her close. They were skin to skin, heart to heart, his naked chest to her bare shoulder blades. He fought to ignore his aroused shaft that was resting against her backside, and every time he breathed, he picked up her scent and it had his nostrils flaring. He loved her. He wanted her. But now more than anything he just needed to hold her.

Within minutes he heard her even breathing and knew she had drifted off to sleep, and he continued to hold her even while she slept.

CHAPTER 23

"With all due respect, sir, you might be who you claim, but unless I hear from Ms. Barclay, I cannot grant you entrance to her home without her permission."

His lips curling angrily, Wayne glared at the doorman. "In that case I'll try reaching her again on her cell phone."

"Thank you, sir, and if she is your fiancée as you claim, then I'm sure you understand that I take my job of keeping her, as well as everyone else in this building, safe very seriously."

Wayne angrily walked away to sit on the sofa in the lobby while he tried to reach Skye again on her cell phone. He had left three messages since Sunday, and she had not called him back. When he saw her again he intended to make certain things absolutely clear with her. First, whether she wanted it or not, the wedding was back on, so she could bank on the Christmas wedding like he had announced to his family before leaving Maine for this god-awful place. The air here was humid. The weather unbearably hot. Renting a car at the airport and getting on that interstate had been almost suicidal. Why would someone want to live here? Skye would pay dearly for what she was putting him through. He'd had enough of her nonsense.

His insides quivered at the phone call he'd received Sunday morning. The caller was angry and had threatened to cut off his money supply if he didn't get Skye back in line, and he had too many gambling debts not to follow orders. He needed money. Plenty of it. It would take Skye's trust as well as his own, along with any extra income he could make on the side, to continue to live the lifestyle he was accustomed to. Yes, Skye had pissed him off and he was determined to let her know it.

He glanced up when two people walked into the building. He recognized Skye immediately and could only assume the lanky teenager walking by her side was the brother she had traveled to this horrific state to visit. Neither of them glanced his way as they headed toward the elevator.

He stood immediately. "Skye?"

She turned toward the sound of his voice and stared at him. Surprise was etched all over her face as he walked over to her. "Wayne? What are you doing in Houston?"

He pasted a smile on his face, although her question made him even more pissed. "You act like you're not happy to see your fiancé, sweetheart."

He noted the lifting of the boy's brows. He turned to Skye and said, "I thought you weren't getting married."

She smiled up at Vincent and said, "I'm not."

Wayne chuckled, leveling a cool stare. "Of course you are. We're getting married on Christmas Day. How could you forget?"

She glared at him. "Easily. What are you doing here, Wayne?" she asked him again.

"We need to talk." Then glancing at the kid, then back at her, Wayne said, "Privately."

"We have nothing to say."

"I think we do."

"Ms. Barclay," the security doorman said, coming to stand beside her and Vincent. "If this man is bothering you, I can escort him out of the building."

Skye smiled up at the doorman. "That won't be necessary, Ron. He's leaving."

She then turned her attention back to Wayne. "Good-bye, Wayne, and have a safe trip back to Maine."

Skye touched Vincent's arm, and the two of them then

walked off toward the bank of elevators, leaving Wayne standing there, staring at them.

Wayne sat in an area of the parking lot waiting for Skye to return. He had watched her leave with her brother over an hour ago, and, thinking she was taking the kid home, decided to sit and wait for her to come back.

There was no way he could go back to Maine until she understood just where he stood and that there would be a Christmas wedding. He had made the necessary phone calls and warnings had been put in place. He was to use whatever means necessary to get Skye to cooperate . . . and he would.

He watched as her car pulled into the same parking space it had been in earlier. She got out and had begun walking toward the entrance to her condo when he got out of his car and called after her, "Skye?"

She stopped and turned around at the sound of his voice, saw him, and then turned back around and quickly began walking toward the entrance door.

Rage ripped through him and he called out to her and said, "If you care about your brother's welfare, I suggest you don't walk away from me, Skye."

She stopped, turned around, and met him with anger flaring in her eyes. "What did you say?"

He slowly began walking toward her. "You heard what I said, and I meant every word. All I have to do is make a call and that brother of yours is history."

Skye stared at him, not believing what she was hearing. She had determined a while ago that Wayne was ruthless, but she refused to believe he could be capable of doing bodily harm to anyone.

He evidently read her thoughts. "I wouldn't chance it if I were you. I have too much to lose by not marrying you. I wouldn't harm your brother personally, but I know of others who will upon my orders. They will fix it so he'll never be heard of again, and you wouldn't be able to prove a single thing. If you want to think I'm bluffing, then take a chance, go ahead and try me. It's your brother's life we're talking about."

Skye took a step back and stared at Wayne. She saw the cold look in his eyes, his entire stony face. "You're crazy," she said softly. "You're really crazy."

He shook his head and chuckled. The sound was just as cold as the look in his eyes. Both sent shivers down her spine. "Not crazy, Skye. Desperate. And just so we understand each other, someone is paying me a lot of money to keep you under control, and I intend to do it. I stand to lose too much if I don't, so don't think for one minute that I'm not telling you the truth. Unless you do what I say, then I can't be held responsible for the kid's untimely accident. And trust me, there will be an accident."

He then crossed his arms over his chest. "And if that doesn't get your attention, then that new so-called boyfriend of yours might be next."

At the surprised look on her face he said, "Oh yeah, I know about him, too. Get rid of him, Skye. You have forty-eight hours to return to Maine and start planning our wedding or you'll be sorry. And just so you'll know I'm serious, maybe your friend will tell you about what almost happened to him tonight. Trust me, that was a warning. We're going after the kid next and then your friend again."

Again? Skye shook her head as she continued to back up. "No, Wayne, I refuse to believe this. You might be capable of some things, but not that."

"That just goes to show that you really don't know me, doesn't it? You will marry me and we will have a long and wonderful life together. Forty-eight hours, Skye. That's all the time you have. Call me to let me know what plane you're taking and I'll pick you up from the airport."

Skye then watched as he turned and walked back toward the car he had gotten out of.

"Ms. Barclay? Are you all right?"

She turned around and saw Ron. No, she wasn't okay.

"Do you know if Mr. Madaris has come home yet?" Slade had left the office early for a business meeting downtown.

The older man shook his head. "No, ma'am. He hasn't arrived."

"Thank you."

She quickly headed inside and pulled her phone out of her purse as she headed for the elevator. She had turned it off earlier when she kept getting calls from Wayne, not knowing that he was here in Houston. She sucked in a deep breath when she saw she'd missed a call ten minutes ago from Slade. She quickly punched the button to redial the number.

"Hello?"

Remembering what Wayne had said, she quickly asked, "Slade, are you okay?"

"Yes, I'm okay, but my truck's not. I'm having it towed."

Panic thickened her throat and she had a hard time swallowing. "What happened?" she asked, stepping off the elevator.

"Someone ran me off the road. Probably some teenager out driving recklessly when he should be home doing homework. I hit the curb and blew a tire. Nothing major."

She almost dropped the phone out of her hand as Wayne's threats rang loud and clear in her ears: "*Trust me, that was a warning. We're going after the kid next and then your friend again.*"

Her head started spinning. How did Wayne know about Slade? Was he having her watched? Then she suddenly recalled something he'd said: "*Someone is paying me a lot of money to keep you under control and I intend to do it.*"

Chills ran down her spine. Who was this someone he was talking about? Would her parents go that far to control her that they would harm Vincent or Slade? And if so, why?

"Skye, are you all right? I tried calling you because Vincent called me, upset, saying some man was at the condo claiming he was your fiancé. What's going on, Skye?"

A lone tear fell from her eye as she opened the door to

her condo. She knew what she had to do. She didn't understand any of it, but she knew more than anything she could not and would not let anything happen to Vincent and Slade.

She inhaled deeply and tried to keep her voice from breaking up when she said, "I'm leaving Houston, Slade, and returning to Maine. I have to go start packing."

"Why? Has something happened to your parents?"

"No."

"Then why are you leaving?"

She closed her eyes and leaned back against the door. "I've decided to marry Wayne after all." Then without giving Slade a chance to ask her anything, she clicked off the phone.

Skye had hoped to be packed and gone before Slade got home, but she had no such luck. She knew it was him by the insistent knocking at the door. He had called twice, but she hadn't answered the phone.

"Open up, Skye. I know you're in there, so let me in and tell me what the hell is going on."

Inhaling deeply, she moved toward the door. She took another deep breath before opening it. Then there he stood, his features a mixture of irritation and anger. "What do you mean you're marrying that guy after all?"

Skye swallowed. "I have to marry him, Slade."

He stepped around her and came into the condo. "Why do you *have* to marry him? You told me that you and that guy were history. You also told me just yesterday that you were in love with me. What the hell is going on here, Skye?"

She tried to hold herself together when she said, "I was wrong about us. My place is back in Augusta."

"As that bastard's wife? The same man you told me treated you like crap? So what were you doing here with me, Skye? Using me to make him jealous? And what about Vincent? You're just going to up and leave tonight without telling him anything, after dropping into his life the way you did? Just what kind of sick game are you playing?"

Skye knew if she had to endure Slade's anger a minute longer she would fall apart and she couldn't do that. Under no circumstances could she let him know about Wayne's threats. That way he and Vincent would be safe. "Please leave, Slade. I'll be out of here as soon as I finish packing. I'm spending the night at a hotel and will be flying out in the morning. I'm sorry if I caused you and Vincent pain. I'm truly sorry."

Slade stood there and stared at her for a long moment. He then turned and walked out the door, slamming it shut behind him. It was then that Skye dropped down on the sofa and gave way to the tears she'd been holding back.

Slade went across the hall to his own condo and slammed the door shut. Full of an anger so intense, he knew he'd never felt it before, he went into his bedroom and pulled off his jacket and slung it across the bed. The same bed he and Skye had shared Saturday night and practically all day Sunday. The same bed where he'd told her he loved her and she had told him that she loved him as well.

Lies. She had told him nothing but lies. How could he have been taken in by her? How could he let her convince him she was something that she wasn't? How could he—

Something snapped inside of him. No! He refused to believe she had told him lies. He refused to believe she wasn't what she'd claimed to be all along. All he had to do was close his eyes to relive the memories of all the times they shared together, everything they did and the conversations they had. Skye was not a phony person. She was a very caring one. There was a reason she was going back to Maine to marry that bastard, and Slade refused to believe it was because it was something she wanted to do. What was she afraid of? Why couldn't she confide in him and tell him what the hell was going on? Why was she letting the bastard call the shots and meekly following orders? Why?

There was only one way to find out.

Slade turned, retraced his steps, and walked out of the

condo. Crossing the hall, he lifted his hand to knock when he picked up the sound of her crying beyond the door. His heart clenched as he silently turned the knob and went in without knocking. She was there, lying across the sofa, weeping like a newborn baby.

He quickly crossed the room to her. "Skye, please tell me what's going on."

She jumped up at the sound of his voice and quickly began wiping her eyes. "Why did you come back, Slade? And nothing is going on. I merely changed my mind about things and have decided to return to Maine to marry Wayne."

"Are your parents forcing you to do this? Are they threatening you in any way?"

She turned away from him, refusing to look at him. "I don't know what you're talking about. Please leave, Slade. We don't have anything else to say to each other. I'm sorry, but I want you to leave."

Her words hurt, but he refused to walk away. "Turn around and look into my face and tell me that you don't love me, Skye. Tell me your words of love to me were nothing but lies. Do it and then I'll leave."

She turned to him, lifted her chin, and met his gaze. "I don't love . . ." She couldn't get that last word out of her mouth. Tears came into her eyes. "Please, Slade. Don't do this. You have to let me go to keep you and Vincent safe. I couldn't bear it if anything happened to you."

He stared at her. "What are you talking about?"

She shook her head. "You have to leave."

He reached out and pulled her to him. She resisted at first, but when he tugged her into his arms and held her there for a moment, she then clung to him and began sobbing into his shirt. "You have to let me go. You have to."

He continued to hold her. "I can't do that, Skye. Letting you go is like losing a piece of my heart. It's okay. Whatever is wrong, we'll deal with it. Don't let that bastard make you a victim. Tell me what he said to you."

She lifted her tear-stained eyes. "I can't. Telling you will put you and Vincent in danger."

Slade frowned. "Is that what he told you? That if you didn't return to Maine and marry him, something would happen to me and Vincent?"

She dropped her face back in his shirt and nodded. Slade reached up and lifted her chin and saw the fear in her eyes. "Tell me what he said, sweetheart. We're in this together; always remember that. Tell me."

Skye sighed deeply before saying, "Wayne gave me a warning tonight. Someone deliberately tried to run you off the road. It was no accident. He told me something would happen."

Slade thought about what she had said; then anger began consuming him. "And he told you that something would happen to Vincent if you didn't leave as well?"

She nodded. "Yes, and I can't let anything happen to either of you. I can't. You're going to have to let me go."

He pulled her tighter into his arms. "That's not even a possibility, Skye. We're going to sit down and you're going to start from the beginning and tell me everything that bastard said, every single word. Then I'll handle things. No one makes threats against a Madaris and gets away with it."

"No, I can't let you get involved, Slade."

"I'm already involved. Are your parents that desperate for you and Wayne to marry that they would go this far, and place other people's lives in danger?"

Skye shrugged. "I don't know if my parents are, but someone is. Wayne said as much. He said someone is paying him a lot of money to keep me under control. It could very well be my parents, but why would they do that?"

Slade sat down on the sofa, then pulled Skye into his lap. "I don't know, sweetheart. But I want you to start at the beginning and tell me exactly what he said. Then I'll handle things from here."

CHAPTER 24

Slade persuaded an emotionally drained Skye to go into the bedroom and lie down while he made a few phone calls. After she had told him every word Wayne had said to her, Slade had held her while she cried in his arms. She just couldn't understand why Wayne would make the threats he made, and if her parents were involved, then why?

Slade put on a pot of coffee, knowing it wouldn't take long for the men he had called to arrive. The one thing he had quickly learned while growing up as a Madaris was that in his family you never fought your battles alone, especially those that might have a major impact on the entire family.

He had known just who to call, and he knew they would help him achieve the goal he wanted. He wasn't worried about the threat made against him, although he got pissed every time he thought about his slight accident tonight being deliberate. What really concerned him was the threat made against Vincent. Bigelow didn't know the grave mistake he'd made by making a threat against Justin Madaris' son. Justin was known for his warmth and sensitivity; however, mess with someone he loved and there would be hell to pay.

The coffee had just finished brewing when Slade heard the doorbell. He quickly crossed the room before the sound could awaken Skye. He would have to wake her up soon enough, because he was sure the men would want to talk to her.

He opened the door and the first thing he noticed was that

Justin was still in town from attending the senator's retirement party. Although Justin was holding it in check, Slade could tell his cousin was pretty angry.

Slade stepped aside to let them in. Not surprisingly, it was Clayton who spoke first. "How's Skye doing?"

Slade inhaled deeply. "She's okay. I got her to lie down for a while and she dozed off to sleep."

"That's good," Justin said, walking into the center of the living room. "She probably needs her rest."

"Trask and Alex are on their way, although I didn't have time to go into any details of what was going on," Dex Madaris said, taking a seat on the sofa.

Slade shook his head. He didn't know of any other man who looked more ready to kick butt at any place or at any time than Dex.

"Where's Vincent?" Slade asked.

"He's at Whispering Pines," Dex answered with a cocky grin on his face. "I'd like to see anyone try to touch him there. Jake and his men would gladly take them apart."

Slade knew what he meant. Whispering Pines had the look and feel of a fortress. No one got on its lands unless invited by Jake. "What did you tell Vincent?" he asked Justin.

Justin met his gaze. "The truth. And of course he's worried about Skye. I promised him I'll make sure she's okay and I intend to keep my promise."

At that moment the doorbell sounded again. "That must be Trask and Alex," Slade said, heading for the door.

It was more than Trask and Alex. Somewhere along the way they had picked up Trevor Grant, a good friend of the Madaris family.

"Jake called," was the only explanation Trevor gave when he walked in. He glanced around the room. "Okay, what's going on? All Jake said was to get over here."

It was Clayton who spoke. "A threat has been made against Vincent's and Slade's lives."

There was a hint of a smile in Trevor's voice when he

asked, "And just what stupid ass would be foolish enough to do such a thing?"

Slade chuckled. Trevor had expressed his sentiments exactly. "A man by the name of Wayne Bigelow," he spoke up and said. "He's Skye's ex-fiancé. It seems it's more than a mere case of a man wanting to reclaim what he lost. I think he's getting paid by someone to make sure he marries her and keeps her under control."

Trask frowned. "Who?"

Slade shrugged. "My guess is her parents."

"Sheesh," Trevor said, rubbing his hand down his face. "I've heard of people who're anxious to become the parents of the bride, but aren't they taking it a little too far?"

"I'd think so," Alex said, speaking for the first time. "Besides, that doesn't fit their makeup from that report I did."

All eyes went to Alex. "What report?" Justin asked.

"Oops," Alex said, smiling, lowering his head, studying the floor.

All eyes then went to Clayton, who merely smiled and said, "Hey, I told you I wanted to make sure Skye was who she claimed to be, Justin."

"You had Skye investigated?" Slade asked his cousin incredulously.

Clayton met Slade's astonished gaze defensively. "Yes. You ought to know I'm nothing like Justin. I don't take anything or anyone at face value. We had no proof she was who she said she was. However, after I got the report, then I was satisfied she was legit, and no harm was done." He smiled. "In fact, I think she's a real classy lady. I doubt you'll do better, so if I were you, I'd be the one planning a Christmas wedding instead of this Bigelow guy."

Slade had a very serious look on his face when he said, "Trust me. I'm thinking of doing just that."

Justin sat down on the chair opposite the sofa. "Okay, Alex, what else were you able to tell from the report about her parents?"

"Not a whole lot, but there's nothing to indicate they're the type that will go so far as to pay someone to commit bodily harm just to keep their adult daughter under control. They are pillars of their community, devout Catholics, old money. In fact, I don't see where they stand to gain anything if Bigelow marries Skye; it's the other way around. Give me a couple of hours to do more research."

Alex then turned to Slade. "And how did this guy know about you? Had Skye mentioned you to him?"

Slade shook his head. "She hasn't spoken with him since she left Maine almost three weeks ago. She thinks he had someone watching her here."

Trevor nodded. "That's a good possibility if he was that desperate to make sure she returned to Maine to marry him."

"He shouldn't have expected that," Slade said angrily. "Their engagement ended months ago; but according to Skye, Bigelow refused to accept it, although he was the one to break it. He told her if she went to Dallas to meet Vincent, they would not get married. She went anyway."

"Called his bluff, did she?" Dex said, smiling. "Gutsy woman. I knew I liked her right away for a reason."

Trevor sighed. "Okay, it's time for us to hear Skye's side of things."

Slade nodded. "I'll go wake her."

Skye glanced around the room at the six men. She had met all of them at different times over the past three weeks; however, all together in one room and at the same time, they looked imposing, larger than life. Slade said they were there to help and had teasingly referred to them as the Madaris Coalition, and in a way she thought that term fit.

They had taken turns asking her questions about Wayne and her parents. Clayton, being the attorney, had asked the majority of the questions, and most of them were pointed, intended to make her think. She had answered each truthfully to the best of her ability and knowledge. Alex, who would smile over at her occasionally, didn't do much talking but spent a lot of his time jotting stuff down on a notepad.

"I just have a few more questions for you," Clayton was saying. "About this trust fund you're to inherit when you turn thirty, can you tell us about it, since it seems greed is the driving factor behind what Wayne Bigelow's doing?"

Skye nodded. "I didn't know anything about it until a year and a half ago, about the same time I discovered I was adopted. I think as a way to convince me to give up my interest in finding my biological mother, my parents told me about it and said that I could stand to lose it if I continued on the path I was going."

Alex glanced up, frowning. "I wonder why they said that. From what I gather, the trust that was set up for you didn't come with any stipulations like the one that was set up for Bigelow. You're to receive it upon your thirtieth birthday, no matter what, married or single."

Skye nodded. "The reason they said it was to keep me in line. They thought they were dangling a carrot in front of me, a carrot I'd want more than finding out about my mother."

"Were your parents always controlling?" Justin asked quietly. He couldn't imagine having parents who thought controlling someone the way they had done to Skye was normal. Anything she did had to be acceptable to them.

"To be honest, Justin, I never thought they were controlling. To me it was a way of life. I did what I was told and everything was fine. However, as I got older and became more defiant and wanted to think for myself, that's when the trouble started between us. My mother thought I was being difficult."

"And what about your father?"

A smile touched her lips. "I think in a way my father understood; however, he wasn't strong enough to stand against Mom."

"How did you meet Bigelow?" Trevor asked.

"My parents introduced us the month after I graduated

from college. I was given what I now see as a coming-of-age party. At the end my parents told me that he was the man who'd been chosen for me to marry and that everything had been decided."

Dex lifted a brow. "Just like that?"

"Yes, and that a wedding would take place sometime before my twenty-eighth birthday."

No one said anything for a moment; then Alex asked, "What sort of man do you perceive Bigelow to be?"

Skye thought on that question. She'd perceived him to be a lot of things but never one who'd go as far as he'd gone now. "He's always been arrogant, conceited, and wanted things done his way. He's an attorney, so I knew he could be cunning when he wanted to be, and he always handled me as the child who was to do what she was told. Like my parents, he would get upset whenever I thought for myself."

"Was there no one you had in your corner while growing up? No one you could go to and talk to when your parents became overbearing?" asked Justin.

She smiled. "Yes. There was my aunt Karen, who's my father's sister. She and I are close. Then on occasion there was Congressman Baines."

Alex raised a brow. "Congressman Baines?"

"Yes. My father has been his personal accountant for years. While growing up I remember the congressman a lot, since he would always be there at the office whenever I would go in on Saturdays with my father, and we would talk. He would ask me how things were going, was I happy, and that sort of thing."

"Did you ever go to him to complain about your parents being overbearing?"

She shook her head. "No, I never did. He was a family friend, but I wouldn't discuss my parents with him that way."

Trevor then asked the next question. "Because of what happened to Slade tonight, we're concerned that maybe you've been watched since coming to Houston. Have you noticed anyone familiar? Anyone you recognized as someone you knew back in Maine?"

Skye bunched her brows in thought; then after a few moments she said, "No. Other than seeing Congressman Baines and his son, Senator Baines, Saturday night at that party, I don't recall seeing anyone."

Alex lifted a brow. "If I recall, I was introduced to the two of them right before Slade arrived, right?"

Skye smiled. "Yes."

"And then you introduced Slade to them," Alex said, as if thinking out loud.

"Yes, and soon after that Slade asked me to dance and I don't recall seeing the congressman or the senator any more that night."

"Other than those two, can you think of anyone else you might have recognized or who would have recognized you? How about when you and Vincent spent time together? Did you perhaps notice someone always there? The same person?" Trevor asked.

Skye shook her head. "No. I never really paid much attention, but I think if it had been the same person, that would have caught my attention."

Alex closed the notepad he'd been writing on. "Give me a few hours to check out some things and talk to a few contacts. If we find out the name of Bigelow's financer, then we can determine why there's a rush to marry Skye and get her under control."

"I'd like to know why anyone thinks she needs controlling," Dex said to no one in particular. He turned to Skye. "I know your parents were totally against you wanting to find your biological mother and then establish a relationship with Vincent. Is there anything else they are absolutely totally against that you might have suggested doing?"

Skye inhaled deeply as she thought about Dex's question. She didn't say anything for a long moment and then she remembered. "Yes, there is this one thing."

It was Slade who asked. "What is it, sweetheart?"

She looked at him. "They literally freak out anytime I mention any interest in finding out the identity of my biological father."

The six men stepped onto the elevator. Once the door closed shut behind them, it was Trevor Grant who spoke. "Okay, Alex, I was watching your face during Clayton's line of questioning of Skye. You're on to something."

Alex smiled. The one thing he wished he were on to was his wife. He had left her in bed after getting the call from Dex, and she had promised she would stay awake and wait for his return.

"Alex?"

He turned to look at Trevor. "I might. A number of things don't make sense, and then some things she said sent out red flags."

Justin looked over at him. "What?"

"I'd rather not say until I check a few things out. When can we get together again?"

"I have a court date in the morning," Clayton was saying. He looked over at Justin. "You had plans to return home tomorrow, didn't you?"

Justin nodded. "Yes, but I'm not going anywhere until this matter is resolved. No one better touch a hair on my son's head."

"And they won't," Dex assured him. "Right now he's at the safest place he can be. But all of us might want to keep a close watch on the family if this asshole finds he can't get to Vincent and Slade and turns his attention elsewhere, to another family member he thinks means a lot to Skye."

"We have forty-eight hours to figure things out."

Trask shook his head. "Bigelow really expects her to show back up in Maine and meekly agree to a forced marriage?"

"Evidently," Clayton said when the elevator came to a stop on the ground floor.

Dex chuckled. "This may come as a surprise to the bastard, but I doubt Slade is going to let Skye out of his sight until this is over. Has anyone contacted Blade and Luke?"

"Yes," Clayton answered. "And they'll watch Slade's back. But just to be on the safe side, Jake contacted the sheriff. He promised to keep a low profile while we checked out everything," Clayton said of the man who was a fishing friend of Jake's and a huge fan of Diamond. "He also told Jake that he knows the police chief of Augusta, if he needs to intervene."

"That's good," Dex said.

"He's also having one of his men keep an eye on this place as well as the Madaris Building," Clayton added. "It's my guess that Bigelow is on his way back to Maine, fairly certain that warning stunt he pulled tonight will send Skye flying back to him in forty-eight hours."

As they stepped off the elevator, Alex said, "I plan to have everything wrapped up before then, and Bigelow and whoever is involved will regret the day they started this."

Slade crossed the room to sit beside Skye on the sofa. "You've gotten quiet on me," he said, reaching out and taking her hand in his.

A sob welled up in Skye's throat, but she forced it back down as she met Slade's gaze. "I can just imagine what your family think of me, especially Justin. None of this would have happened had I not decided to get to know Vincent. I should have seen long ago that Wayne wasn't wrapped too tight, and ended things between us. I should not have been so weak as to let my parents dictate how my future was going to be and with whom."

Love, more than any man had a right to have for any one woman, flowed through Slade. He gently tightened his hold on her hand. "First of all, my family, specifically Justin, think the same thing that I do, that you are a beautiful and wonderful person. And don't ever think any of our lives would have been better had you not shown up that day at Lorren Oaks. Surely not Vincent's and definitely not mine. Vincent had a right to know about you, just like you had a right to know about him. I think your biological mother would have wanted that. And as for me, just think of how my life would be now without you in it."

Leaning forward and holding her within the scope of his stare, he whispered huskily, "You are the best thing to ever happen to me. We're in this together and pretty soon everything will be over. And if it's your parents who are the ones pushing Bigelow to do what he's doing, then we'll deal with it. But no matter what, we won't let them or anyone come between us. I love you and I will always love you."

"Oh, Slade."

A sigh shook her petite frame as his words rang in her head and settled deep in her heart. He gathered her into his arms, then shifted his body for the two of them to stretch out together on the sofa. Luckily it was large enough to accommodate the both of them.

He kissed her, his mouth hot, hungry, and urgent. He wanted to remove her fears and to let her know that everything would be all right. She could unleash passion so quickly within him, and as he began removing her clothes and then his own, he knew that what Clayton had said tonight was true. She was one classy lady, and if anyone married her, it would be him.

Wayne Bigelow checked his watch as he moved around the Atlanta airport to catch his connecting flight to Maine. He smiled, pretty sure that he and Skye understood each other.

He had a couple hours' layover, so he found a good spot to make a call. The party picked up on the second ring. "What do you have to report?"

Wayne smiled, knowing the caller would be happy with his news. "Everything has been arranged. Skye is returning to Maine in two days."

There was a pause. "And she agreed to do it?"

"Not willingly at first, but then I showed her I meant business. She knows what she stands to lose if she doesn't cooperate."

"I hope you're right."

Wayne chuckled, feeling pretty confident. "I'm right. You'll see."

Alex slipped out of bed beside his sleeping wife and went into a room in his home that he used whenever he preferred working away from the office. It contained some of the same equipment and was set up like a command center with so much state-of-the-art equipment.

He went to a special detailed telephone and punched in one number. It connected to a computer that sounded a lot like a fax machine kicking on. He then went to the keyboard on his computer and began typing several names. The machine blinked a few times before information started appearing on the screen. He pushed the printer button.

He turned and switched on the coffeepot he kept in the room as he sat down and watched the printer spit out pages and pages of information. He rubbed his hand down his face, thinking of the hot spot he'd given up beside his wife in bed and that it was destined to be a long night.

CHAPTER 25

"Okay, what do you have?" Justin asked when everyone had arrived at Alex's office in the Madaris Building around ten the next morning. Alex had called everyone to say he'd found out some rather interesting information he wanted to share. However, he preferred that Skye not hear it now.

It had taken a lot for Slade to leave her alone at the condo to attend the meeting. It was only after another Madaris family friend by the name of Drake Warren had shown up and assured Slade that he would remain downstairs in the lobby as a watchdog until Slade returned did he relent.

Sir Drake, as he was known to everyone, was a former Marine and CIA agent. After one look at him no one in their right mind would want to tangle with him. But just to make sure, Marine colonel Ashton Sinclair, also another family friend, decided to keep Drake company.

Trevor, who was a former Marine himself and a close friend to Drake and Ashton, was the one to pick Slade up from the condo. No one wanted to risk his being alone in case Wayne decided to pull another warning stunt.

Clayton was glad his appointment that morning at the courthouse had gotten canceled. The last thing he wanted was to miss anything Alex had to say. All of them had known Alex long enough to know that he took his job as a private investigator seriously, and that when it came to handling a case, he was very thorough. He had contacts in high places and had a method of digging up information some people would rather keep hidden. No one questioned his sources. They didn't have to. He always delivered.

"These are theories and not absolutes. I'm still obtaining information, but I found out a couple of things you all might find interesting."

"Such as?" his brother, Trask, asked.

"After listening to what Skye said last night, there were two things that bothered me," Alex said. "This whole issue of a trust fund and what's driving Bigelow. I do have concrete proof that Wayne Bigelow is a compulsive gambler. In fact, he's so buried in debt that it isn't funny. He definitely sees Skye as a meal ticket, as well as seeing his own trust fund that he'll be able to inherit as a blessing. However, he has to marry Skye to get it."

"Who made that decision?" Justin asked. He knew in certain countries such a thing was the norm and that here in some parts of our own country arranged marriages were a growing trend instituted by family members or religious leaders. He and Lorren had been asked to join one sort of private organization that prided itself on making sure their offspring were surrounded by other children of the same social and economic class, which would make things easier years later when they got ready to choose their mates. Justin and Lorren had turned down membership after deciding to let their children be the ones to determine the people they wanted to spend the rest of their lives with.

"Bigelow's grandfather. He died eight years ago," Alex said.

"Why did he choose Skye?" Slade asked. "Was he close to the Barclays?"

"No," Alex said. "And I have nothing to indicate the two families even knew each other. But there is a family name that kept popping up a lot during my investigation."

Clayton lifted a brow. "And what name is that?"

"Baines."

Trask also lifted a brow. "As in Congressman Baines and Senator Baines?"

"Yes. It appears that Bigelow's grandfather and the congressman were good friends who became business partners around thirty years ago, before the congressman got into politics. For some reason, the two agreed on a marriage between Skye and Bigelow before the two of them were ten years old."

Dex, who'd been pacing, finally stopped and asked, "Why would the congressman care enough about a kid who wasn't related to him to do such a thing?"

"That's what I'm going to find out," Alex said. "Someone didn't want any of this information revealed and did a good job of covering it up by several means. It was one heck of a maze trying to trace back everything and fit together pieces of the puzzle, including who set up this very generous trust fund for Skye in the first place."

"And who was this very bighearted individual?" Clayton asked.

Alex glanced at all five men before he finally said, "Congressman Baines and his deceased wife."

He waited for the men to digest what he said before delivering the final piece. "Another thing I discovered. Although it was hard to do, because Maine has some tough privacy laws thanks to my database and numerous contacts I was able to."

"What?" Trask asked.

"When Tom and Edith Barclay adopted Skye some twenty-six years ago, it was a very, very private adoption."

"It couldn't have been too private, since Skye managed to find out the identity of her biological mother," Slade said.

"Well, someone made a mistake there," Alex said. "A possible error on a nun's part in recording the information when she shouldn't have. But anyway, it seems Skye's biological mother's parents convinced her to give the child up

for adoption since she was only sixteen. They sent her out of
the country, away to London, to do it. Kathy Lester lived at
the convent there for six months before she delivered. The
only stipulation was that the baby was to be adopted by an
American family."

Trevor nodded. "And that was the Barclays?"

"Yes, but what Skye probably doesn't know is that the
very private adoption was arranged secretly, even without her
biological mother's or grandparents' knowledge, by none
other than Congressman Baines."

Skye tried to keep busy while Slade was gone and had
cleaned the bathrooms and kitchen twice. She wished there
was some way she could go into work and stay busy, but
Slade had said that was out of the question. They would take
the day off and enjoy it. Of course that was before he had
gotten called away.

The sound of her cell phone interrupted her thoughts. She
hoped it was Slade and not Wayne calling. Everyone had
agreed that if Wayne called, she should continue to convince
him she was going to do as he'd ordered and return to Maine,
and that she was still packing to leave.

When she got to the phone she was surprised to see the
caller was neither Slade nor Wayne but her father and he was
calling from his office. She wasn't sure she should answer it
but decided to do so. She hadn't spoken to either of her parents since leaving Maine; however, as she flipped up the
phone she had to remember it had been their choice.

"Dad?"

"Skye? It's good to hear your voice."

She lifted a brow. "Is it, Dad? I called to talk to you and
Mom several times over the past three weeks and both of
you refused to talk to me."

"Well, that was before you came to your senses. Wayne
joined us for breakfast this morning and told us the good
news."

Skye's father's words pierced whatever hope she was holding that he'd called because he was concerned about her. Her heart felt crushed. The only reason he was calling was because he'd heard that his difficult daughter had decided to become manageable again.

"I guess I don't have to tell you how happy your mother and I are that the wedding is back on. We think you've made the right decision."

Conscious of the dull, painful ache in her heart, she asked, "But what if things don't work out between me and Wayne? What if after marrying him I find he's not acceptable to me as a husband?"

"He's the right man for you, sweetheart. You'll see. With all that money the two of you will be getting, you'll be plenty happy."

She frowned. Her father thought all it took for happiness was money.

"Your mom has been in contact with Marjorie Bigelow. The two of them are getting together for lunch."

And plan my wedding the way they want it to go, not caring what I would want, Skye thought. They'd never asked her for any suggestions of what she preferred in the way of colors, flowers, cake . . . nothing. They'd even gone so far as to tell her who would be her bridesmaids. Daughters of women who were within their inner circle, regardless of whether they were her actual friends or not.

"Well, I'd better let you go," her father was saying. "When can we expect you?"

"Sometime tomorrow afternoon," she said, making sure her arrival time was within the forty-eight hours.

"Wayne mentioned that he would be the one picking you up from the airport. He has your engagement ring and intends for you to start wearing it again."

The thought of that actually made Skye feel sick.

"Good-bye, Skye."

"Good-bye, Dad. Oh, and please tell Wayne he doesn't

need to pick me up from the airport tomorrow. I can take a cab."

She hung up the phone the exact moment she heard a key in her door. She looked up as Slade walked in. Evidently he read the expression on her face and saw the phone she still held in her hand, and he asked in a concerned voice, "Who was that?"

She inhaled as she crossed the room to him. "My dad. He was just calling to let me know that Wayne had breakfast with him and Mom and they are happy the wedding is back on again."

Slade took her into his arms. He knew that was the last thing she wanted of her parents. She had wanted them for once to be in her corner.

She pulled back out of his arms. "How did the meeting go? Did you find out anything?"

He knew he had to tell her what Alex had uncovered so far and, as a result, in what directions their thoughts were headed and what their plans were. Slade was a person who never liked putting puzzles together. But with this particular one, things seemed to be falling into place. The key had been the uncovering of vital information about his adoption. More than likely, the congressman figured he had pretty much covered his tracks. Thanks to Alex the man would soon find out just how wrong he was. Once again Slade's great-grandmother's famous saying "Anything you do in the dark will eventually come to the light" hailed true.

He looked down into Skye's anxious face. In a way she was a lot stronger than she had been when he'd first met her. She had made decisions that had gone against what her parents wanted for her, and she was still doing that. Deciding not only to find Vincent but also to establish a relationship with him had been her first defiant act in declaring her independence. But he doubted even doing that had prepared her for all the problems confronting her now.

As well as the truths she still had to face.

However, he, as well as every other member of the Madaris family—along with family friends—would be there with her. She wouldn't have to face any of it alone. And in the end, he intended to make her his in the most legal way possible. He planned to ask her to be his wife. But for now, he had to tell her what she needed to know.

"Come on," he said, taking her hand. "Let's go sit on the sofa."

She nodded as he led her to the sofa and sat down beside her. Before he told her anything, he needed to ask her something to help start her thinking. "I want to ask about your relationship with the Baineses."

He saw confusion light her gaze. "The Baineses? The congressman and the senator?"

"Yes."

"I've told you that I consider the congressman a longtime family friend, so over the years I sort of considered him my godfather, although there was never an official christening or anything like that. Come to think of it, I always thought of Mrs. Baines the same way—as a godmother."

Slade lifted a brow. "You knew her?"

Skye smiled. "Yes. I think she died when I was twelve, but before then I remember a lot about her. I especially remember how good she smelled and how nice she dressed. And I remember how kind she was to me. She spent a lot of time with me when I was small."

"Was she a friend of your mother's?"

Skye shook her head. "No," she said bluntly, as if she could never imagine such a thing. "Dad was their private accountant and for some reason he did all his business with them on the weekends, at either his office or their home. He would always take me with him and the Baineses would be there. While Dad worked on the books, the Baineses entertained me."

"And why do you think they spent so much time with you?"

She shrugged. She'd never thought of a reason before. "Mainly because they were nice people. And I also felt they were lonely people. I knew they had an older son who was always busy, so I figured they were lonely. I remember asking Dad why the Baineses liked to play with me and I think that's what he said. They were lonely people. And even after Mrs. Baines got sick and died, Mr. Baines continued to come those weekends. Then I remember him getting elected as a congressman and not being around much anymore. But those times with the Baineses were special times with me because they did something my own parents basically never did."

"And what was that?"

"They spent time with me. And it was time that wasn't all serious and full of censure. It was doing fun stuff, like coloring in a huge coloring book, watching cartoons, and just talking."

A part of Slade was glad the Baineses had given her that. "Now what about their son, the senator?"

Skye waved a dismissive hand. "Pleeze. The senator never gave me the time of day. Like I said, he was busy most of the time, so I rarely saw him. In fact, the first time we actually met was at my college graduation. He was there with his dad and he gave me the impression he was somewhere he didn't want to be. And afterward, if our paths would cross he would give me a curt nod and nothing else." Skye shook her head. "He's one standoffish man."

With a lot to hide, Slade inwardly thought.

"Slade? Why are you asking me about the Baineses?" she asked, tucking a twisted curl behind her ear.

He took her hand in his. "In the midst of Alex's investigation he discovered a number of things regarding the Baineses. First, were you aware that it was the Baineses who set up that trust fund for you? The one you're to receive when you turn thirty?"

Skye's eyes widened in surprise. "No, I didn't know that. Are you sure?"

"Yes, I'm positive. And you probably didn't know that it was Congressman Baines who arranged the private adoption between your biological mother and the Barclays twenty-six years ago, although we can find no record that your mother was aware of the Baineses' involvement. She was never to know who adopted you."

Skye's head began spinning. "I don't understand. Why would they do that? How did he go about handling such a private arrangement?"

Slade paused. "It's my guess that he wanted to make sure he and his wife knew who adopted you and that you would be in arm's reach of them."

Skye leaned forward toward him. "But why?"

Slade paused again. "This is just a theory and not an absolute, but we have reason to believe Congressman Baines is your grandfather, Skye, and that your biological father is his son, the senator."

CHAPTER 26

Skye pulled away from Slade and jumped to her feet. "No, that's not possible," she said adamantly. "I refuse to even consider that being a possibility."

"Think about it, Skye," Slade said softly. "Considering everything I've told you, I think it *is* possible. Alex was also able to uncover the fact that your parents, the Barclays, received and have been receiving an annual allotment from the Baineses for your care."

She turned to him with tears misting her eyes. "If what you're saying is true, then instead of being parents, they were paid caretakers and that's all. They never were real parents."

"Skye, I'm not saying they didn't care for you; all I'm saying is—"

"You don't have to say it, Slade. My history speaks for itself. I always felt a little softening over the years with my father, but with Mom I never felt that, and now I know why."

Slade caught her arm and pulled her down into his lap. He cradled her in his arms. "Listen, Skye, remember it's only a theory. Alex is trying to fit more pieces of the puzzle together to determine if indeed what I've just told you is an absolute."

She inhaled deeply. "And if it is?"

"Then we're traveling to Maine to confront all the parties involved. I doubt the congressman knows what's going on with Wayne."

Slade then told her how it was also uncovered that the

congressman was the one who had arranged her future marriage with the grandson of his former business partner over sixteen years ago. "In the congressman's defense," Slade said, "I think he thought the two of you would make a good match, and since Wayne was only thirteen at the time the agreement was made, no one knew he would eventually grow up to be a jackass. He's also a compulsive gambler, by the way. That's one of the reasons he needs to get his hands on your trust fund."

"But he has one of his own," Skye implored.

"Yes," Slade agreed. "But he intends to keep doing what he's doing, and he'll need all the money he can get to do so."

Skye didn't say anything for a long moment. Then she asked, "What about my parents? What do they stand to gain if I marry Wayne?"

Slade paused, almost too ashamed to say. "Once your marriage to Wayne becomes legal, they'll receive a cash bonus of a million dollars."

"And Congressman Baines arranged for that?"

"No. Actually, it was Wayne's grandfather's decision, so I can only assume he knew your true identity and it was his way of making sure your adoptive parents did what had to be done to assure the marriage took place."

Skye stared at him in stunned amazement, not wanting to believe what she was hearing. She again got quiet, and when she did speak, her voice was low, could barely be heard, when she said, "When will Alex know for sure if any of this is for real?"

"In a few hours."

"And if they're absolutes?"

"Then we're traveling to Augusta to have a talk with the congressman. I don't think he knows what's going on with Wayne or Senator Baines's possible involvement. The way I figure it, the senator has a lot to lose right now if anyone were to get wind that he has an illegitimate daughter that he never acknowledged, especially one where a private adoption was established. With him staring a possible candidacy for Vice President in the face, the last thing he would want is any of his past deeds to surface, especially if those deeds call his character into question."

Skye stared at Slade. "So you think the senator is the one pushing Wayne into marrying me?"

Slade shook his head. "I'm still not sure. Your parents are still suspects. All three of them have a lot to lose, but given political power, I think the senator has more to lose than anyone."

Skye nodded. "So, we won't know anything else until Alex calls?"

"Yes. But for now I've given you a lot to think about, haven't I?"

Skye sighed deeply. He most certainly had.

Alex picked up the phone after shutting down his computer. He would make only one call, but he knew that word would reach the others. Time was of the essence. They needed to be in Maine within the forty-eight hours to put an end to what Wayne Bigelow had started.

"Yes, Alex?"

"Notify the others. There are no longer theories, only absolutes. The senator is definitely Skye's father. And if he's the one involved with Bigelow, I have a feeling Congressman Baines has no idea what's going on."

Clayton nodded. "Okay. I'll inform the others."

Slade hung up the phone and swore softly before turning to Skye. The two of them had just finished watching a movie on television. "That was Clayton. Alex has determined there are no longer theories."

"So it's true? The senator is my biological father?" she asked weakly.

"Yes." He held out his arms to her, and when she made a move, her steps faltered, so he quickly crossed the room and swooped her into his arms.

"Remember what I told you? What we talked about earlier? That I will be with you and that no matter what type of life you might have had in the past, I promise you a future filled with all the love any one person can handle."

She held his gaze. "Yes, I remember," she said softly.

"And that we're going to get through this and one day we're going to look back and determine this is what made our love stronger than ever."

Skye inhaled, thinking that this beautiful man was nothing short of magnificent. And yes, she would get through this because she had him by her side. She had his love, and his love was making her stronger in ways she didn't think were possible.

"So what's next?" she asked.

There was a moment's pause, then he said, "We have a plane to catch later this evening. Clayton is flying out earlier and will join us there. Justin is getting the Cessna ready, and because Bigelow expects you to arrive on a commercial airline, Clayton is booking you on Delta, just in case Bigelow decides to confirm you're on your way to Maine."

She furrowed her brow at all the details. Slade and his family had practically thought of everything. "What happens when we get to Augusta?"

He laid a hand over hers. "The first person we'll touch bases with is Congressman Baines."

"Is anything wrong, Ned?"

Nedwyn turned to glance over at the beautiful woman who was sitting on the sofa in his hotel room. They had arrived in Savannah a few hours ago, and not wanting to assume anything about their sleeping arrangements or to rush her into anything, he had gotten connecting hotel rooms. However, she had opened the connecting door and had left it open.

"That was Jake. He wanted my personal opinion about former colleagues in the House and Senate." There was more to it, but he wasn't planning to go into any details at the moment. Both Slade and Vincent were her nephews, and Nedwyn and Jake had agreed to hold off mentioning anything to her until everything had been resolved. There was no need to upset her needlessly.

Placing his cell phone on the desk, he walked over to where she sat and did something he'd always wanted to do. He reached out for her hand, and when she gave it to him he pulled her up into his arms and kissed her. With firm lips he moved them leisurely over hers, and when he felt her tremble in his arms he brought her closer to the fit of him. She parted her lips on a ragged sigh, and he swept his tongue into her mouth for the taste he knew awaited him there.

He felt her arms when they wrapped around his shoulders at the same moment he deepened the kiss. Her tongue met his every stroke. Desire, hot and heavy, filled his entire being, poured through every vein, sparked every cell, and when she uttered a small moan deep in her throat, he felt a luscious heated sensation in the pit of his gut. This was nothing like the kiss they'd shared a few days ago when he'd visited her guest cottage at Whispering Pines. It was totally different, unique and so doggone delicious it was making his insides quiver.

He pulled back slightly and whispered against her moist lips, "We can go out somewhere to eat or we can order in. Which do you prefer?"

She didn't say anything at first and then she whispered honestly, "At the moment, I want to do neither," looking at him in a way that made all kinds of sensations shoot up his spine.

He released a deep chuckle. "Okay, I take that to mean you aren't hungry."

"Oh, I'm plenty hungry, Ned, but the food I'm craving is sexual in nature."

His heart skipped a beat with her words. It was then that he noticed what she was wearing. It wasn't what she'd had on earlier and it definitely wasn't anything you could wear out in public. It had to be the sexiest outfit he'd ever seen on a woman. He took a deep breath after forcing air into his lungs.

"Y-you look gorgeous in this," he said, taking a step back to allow his gaze to take in all of it, looking her up and down. Certain parts of it were sheer, leaving nothing to his imagination; then other parts teased him mercilessly. It was flesh tone with spaghetti straps that tied at the shoulders and a long flowing skirt that stopped at her toes. The outfit was made of thin, sheer material with a long split on both sides with satin bows.

It was obvious from the cut of the outfit that she wasn't wearing a bra or underpants, but he thought that in itself was a testimony to what a well-toned body she had and what fantastic shape she was in. He knew the gentlemanly thing to do would be to stop staring, but he couldn't stop. Instead he reached out and touched the side slit at her waist and felt her body quiver. His body became that much more aroused in knowing his touch had done that to her.

He then reached out and slid his hand beneath the V-neck of her bodice to rub his finger across the rigid tips of her breasts. "Tell me to stop, Diana," he whispered hoarsely. "Tell me now because I won't be responsible for my actions later. I might be a man looking sixty real close in the face, but I'd better warn you that at the moment I feel like I have the stamina of a twenty-year-old," he said, smiling, as he slowly began releasing the buttons on his shirt. "And none of it is from a pill. It's one hundred percent pure authentic male-produced testosterone."

Diana suddenly felt the nipples on her breasts harden even more when she whispered, "Oh my."

"No, Diana, it's oh, yours," he said, reaching out and pulling her closer to him when he had completely unbuttoned his shirt. He kissed her again and their tongues played a game as they mingled and lingered, seemingly not getting enough. He pulled his mouth back and began walking her backward toward the bed.

"You're sure about this, right?" he asked her.

She smiled at him as he continued to walk her backward. "Just as sure as I am about loving you."

He met her sexy, confident smile. "And I love you, Diana Madaris. And tonight I'm going to show you how much. And I want to do this right. I want us to get an understanding now that this isn't something just to pass the time away. I want us to be together forever. I want to marry you, Diana."

He reached inside the pocket of his pants and pulled out a small white box and flipped it open. Inside was a beautiful ring. "Will you marry me?"

Diana had stopped walking. Her breath caught. She forced herself to believe this wasn't a dream. She stared at the beautiful ring; then she lifted her head and searched his gaze. Emotions surged through her. Tears misted her eyes as she stared at him for several long seconds before asking softly, the same question he'd asked her moments ago. "Are you sure, Ned?"

He smiled, didn't hesitate as he reached out and took her hand and slid the ring onto her finger. "Just as sure as I am about loving you."

And then he lowered his head and kissed her again, with as much tenderness as he could, considering what state he was in. Every nerve in his body had sparked to life, every cell ignited.

She broke off the kiss and reached out and began pulling the tail of his shirt from the waistband of his slacks before pushing it from his broad shoulders. She drew in a ragged breath when her hands went to the snap fastener of his slacks and eased it open before going to his zipper and slowly sliding it down.

"I might as well warn you that although you might have the stamina of a twenty-year-old, I feel like a virgin on her wedding night. I haven't done this in quite a while, Ned."

"I heard it's like riding a horse," he teased huskily. "Once you're back in the saddle it'll come natural as to how you go about managing things."

She released a soft chuckle. "I hope you're right."

She gazed up at him when she had the zipper down. The heat of his stare through hazel eyes sent sensations rumbling all through her as she watched him step back to take off his pants. She inhaled deeply. The man had an awesome body.

"Now can I take off your outfit?" he asked.

"Yes."

His large hands reached out, and in one click of the wrist he undid the ties at her shoulders, and the outfit shimmied down her body, leaving her totally bare. The deep look in his eyes caused her heart to pound furiously in her chest. "I want you. I've always wanted you. And I love you so very much," he whispered. Tell me that you will marry me, Di. You're already wearing my ring and I have no intention of taking it back. Make me a happy man and tell me."

She leaned close and kissed his lips. "I will become a happy woman as well, and yes, Ned, I will marry you, and I will live the rest of my life trying to make you happy."

He smiled. "And I will do likewise. And I don't want a long engagement," he said, advancing on her again, causing her to resume her walk backward.

"How soon?"

How about before we return home? If Felicia wants us to do it all over again, that's fine. But I don't want to leave here without making you Mrs. Nedwyn Lansing. If I can arrange things, will you marry me? Here in Savannah? Tomorrow?"

Love and happiness flowed all through her. "Yes," she agreed. "Tomorrow."

When they finally reached the bed, he gently lowered her onto it and then gathered her to him and kissed her. Diana tasted his hunger. She also tasted his passion, and as a sensual tension made its way through her entire body, she knew what she was about to share with Nedwyn was special. Their friendship had lasted a lifetime, and she believed their marriage would do the same.

His gaze held hers captive when he eased his body in place over hers, and the moment he began entering her, she felt her body stretch to accommodate him.

"It feels good being inside of you," he whispered moments before he began moving his body in smooth, easy strokes.

She couldn't stop the murmurs that flowed from between her lips when he set a rhythm for them. Her pulse was pounding right in tune with their bodies. Then she felt something swell inside of her, a sensation that started at the top of her head and swept all the way down to the bottom of her feet.

She fought to prolong the feeling but couldn't, and when he whispered into her ear, "Let it go," she did.

"Ned!"

"That's right, Di, let it go. Let go in my arms," he muttered against her hair.

And then she heard him growl out her name. Then he made a sound that was a half moan, a half groan, before he slipped his hands under her hips to lift her up for a closer and deeper connection. And like her, she knew he was whipping through the waves of ecstasy, soaring past the stars.

And when they finally came back down to earth he kissed her again, and she knew that this night with him would be seared into her heart forever, and tomorrow, when they married, it would be the beginning of the rest of their lives together.

Justin Madaris was an expert pilot, Skye thought when he landed the small plane on a private airstrip in Augusta. It had been smooth flying, and other than making a pit stop to refuel in Memphis, they had stayed in the air the entire time.

She had taken little catnaps most of the way, and whenever she would come awake she would find Slade talking to

Justin and the other man who'd come along, Drake Warren. The man, whom everyone called Sir Drake, wasn't someone with a lot of words and seemed bigger than life. He had a muscular build and strong, bold, handsome features. She got the distinct impression that he was someone you wouldn't want to cross. And from what she'd been told, he was a former CIA agent who would be able to relieve Justin at the controls if he got tired. And according to Slade, there wasn't too much of anything Drake couldn't do.

Whether it was fact or fiction, Slade claimed Drake and his wife, Tori, also a former CIA agent, had rescued the President's niece when she'd gotten kidnapped a few years ago. Since Skye didn't recall reading of any such rescue in the newspapers, she could only assume Slade was pulling her leg.

"We're visiting the congressman first thing in the morning," Slade said, gathering their belongings off the plane. "Tonight we're staying at a hotel."

"Anyone know we're here?" she asked, no longer bothered by who knew she and Slade were going to spend the night together.

"No one that we don't want to know, and we're going to keep it that way," Justin answered, smiling at her. "Don't worry; we'll get through this," he assured her.

She returned his smile. She was no longer worried. Everyone was confident that Vincent was safe. And then Slade was with her and she had his love and to her that was what was important.

Hours later, after checking into a hotel and taking a shower, she walked out of the bathroom to find Slade stretched out on the bed, shirtless, with just his jeans on, and watching television. He glanced over at her and smiled. They had planned on taking a shower together, but he'd gotten a call from Blade concerning a job they were doing.

She went and stretched across the bed beside him. "How do you think things are going to go tomorrow when we see Congressman Baines?"

He folded his hands behind his head and said, "Fine. Like I said earlier today, if his son is involved, I really don't think he knows about it. He and his wife went through too much to assure you had a future and that they were a part of it. Wayne Bigelow is not the man the congressman thinks that he is."

Skye nodded. She then thought about the man who Slade was convinced was her biological father. He was considered by many to be a top contender for the Vice Presidency. Would news about her ruin his chances of getting the political position he'd aspired to all these years?

"What are you thinking about, sweetheart?"

She glanced over at Slade. "I was just thinking about the senator. How different he is from his father."

"It happens that way sometimes. But just so you'll know," he teased, grinning over at her, "I want our son to be just like me."

Skye lifted a brow. This was the first time they'd ever talked about having children together. "A son, uhh?"

"Yes."

"And what if I have a daughter?"

"Then she can be like you."

Skye smiled. "Thanks."

And then before she could say anything else, Slade was pulling her into his arms and kissing her with a passion that she felt all the way to her toes. And she quickly decided that no matter what tomorrow brought, she would have tonight.

Wayne smiled as he opened the hotel room door and saw the lone figure standing across the room. "I checked the airlines and she's booked. Her flight arrives tomorrow evening around five," he said.

"You did a fine job. You both surprised me as well as pleased me," the individual said, walking toward him.

An arrogant smile touched Wayne's lips. "Don't I always? You worry too much," he said, placing the hotel key aside as he began removing his shirt and then unzipping his pants. "You're going to get everything you've worked so hard for. That will teach Edith a lesson for talking so damn much and telling you all her secrets. I told you from the beginning that I had no intention of letting you down, Helen."

Not giving the older woman a chance to respond, he pulled her naked body to his, feeling victorious at the way things were going and deciding when a feeling of intense need seeped into his bones, that they would have plenty of time to talk, as well as to celebrate, later.

CHAPTER 27

"Are you all right, Skye?"

Skye blinked, realizing Justin Madaris was talking to her. She had been in another world, thinking about what was yet to come.

They were standing in the lobby of the hotel, and Slade had excused himself to go to the men's room, which left her alone with Justin, Alex, Clayton, and Sir Drake. When Slade returned they would be leaving for the congressman's office, showing up unannounced. Alex had used his contacts earlier to check to make sure the congressman would be there. He'd also checked to make sure the senator would be available to meet with them.

Alex, Clayton, and Sir Drake were engrossed in their own conversation, and Justin, she noted, was waiting for her to answer his question. "I'm sorry, Justin, my mind was elsewhere," she said, smiling. "And yes, I'm all right. I'm just thinking about what's yet to come. How will Congressman Baines feel about what we're going to tell him?"

Justin smiled softly. "It really doesn't matter how he feels at this point. Serious threats were made, and either he gets to the root of the problem or we will."

Skye knew he was as serious as he sounded. She also knew he had not only come as Vincent's parent but as Slade's cousin as well. And that was what she found so amazing about the Madaris family. She truly believed that even if no threats had been made against Vincent, these same men would still be here because of her.

"Why, Justin?" she asked, needing him to explain it to her.

He lifted a dark brow. "Why, what?"

"Other than the threats made to Vincent and Slade, why does anyone even care about the outcome, especially with Wayne wanting to force marriage on me? Why not tell me to marry the man? It would certainly make all of your lives easier."

Justin's face was without a smile when he said, "But it certainly wouldn't make yours easier, now would it? The Madarises don't operate that way. We would never build our happiness upon someone else's unhappiness. Besides, you belong to Slade and that means that you also belong to us."

Justin's words touched her. Hearing him say them didn't bother her, mainly because she had now accepted her place in Slade's life. She did belong to him. And he belonged to her.

"Ready to go?" Slade asked, returning to the group.

Alex glanced at his watch. "Yes, the congressman should be at his office now."

"Okay then, let's go," Clayton said.

Skye felt Slade take her hand in his and she inhaled deeply. It was a beautiful day, and she wished everyone were in town visiting her city for another reason. She would be glad to take them around, show them the sights. She had missed Augusta, but not as much as she thought she would. She had discovered since falling in love that home was where the heart was, and although Slade hadn't mentioned anything about the two of them getting married, a part of her felt that eventually he would.

But at the moment there were other more important issues to resolve, and facing the truth of her birth was one of them.

"There's a group of people here to see you, sir."

Congressman Baines lifted a brow at his secretary's announcement. He didn't recall having any appointments this early in the morning. Now that he'd retired, a number of members of special interest groups liked to drop by every now and then and bend his ear in hopes he would pass their views and opinions on to his son, the senator. "Who are they?"

"Skye Barclay, along with a group of men, Slade Madaris, Justin Madaris, Alex—"

Curious, the congressman stood. "Please send them in."

His forehead furrowed. What was going on? Why would Skye be coming to see him and why had she brought others along? It was his understanding that she would be in Houston spending time with her brother for the entire summer.

The congressman walked around his desk the moment his door opened and his secretary escorted everyone in; however, his gaze went immediately to the lone young woman walking in with the men. "Skye, this is a pleasant surprise," he said, automatically reaching out and giving her a hug. He then gazed at the four men. He remembered seeing all of them at some point or another at the party given in Houston for Senator Nedwyn Lansing. And one of the men he distinctively remembered Jake introducing as his nephew Dr. Justin Madaris.

"Thanks, Congressman Baines, and I hate arriving unannounced, but things couldn't be done any other way. I'd like to introduce everyone." She then made introductions.

He offered everyone a seat. "I'm confused, Skye. Why couldn't you let me know you were coming? You're always a person I enjoy seeing, but I talked to your father last week and he said you weren't returning home until the end of the summer."

"Yes, that was my plan, but something has made me change that plan. A threat was made against two people I care deeply about unless I return home and marry Wayne."

The congressman frowned. "But I thought you and Bigelow had called off your engagement."

"We have. But he is forcing me to marry him and has

threatened the lives of my biological brother, Vincent, and Slade unless I do what he says. That's why Justin and Slade are here. Clayton is Justin's brother, Alex is a brother-in-law, and Drake is a close family friend. They are as concerned about the threats as I am, especially since Wayne gave a warning and actually had someone run Slade off the road."

Congressman Baines' expression reflected his anger. "That's simply preposterous. Has the man gone mad? He can't force you into a marriage against your wishes."

Slade spoke up. "That's true, sir, especially since I'm the one who intends to marry Skye."

Skye turned to Slade, who was sitting beside her on the sofa. Their eyes met. This was the first he'd mentioned their marrying, and a part of her felt good that he was declaring his intentions not only to her but to everyone in the room.

The congressman smiled and a part of Skye felt it was sincere. "Then let me congratulate the both of you."

"Getting back to the threats that were made against my nephew and cousin," Clayton said, deciding it was time to deal with the real issue as to why they were there, "we're hoping that you can intervene, since we have reason to believe your son is involved as well."

Surprise shone in the congressman's eyes. "Ryan? Why would he be involved in any way with Wayne Bigelow?"

"That's what we're trying to determine, sir," Slade said, taking Skye's hand in his. "We might as well tell you that once the threats were made, we contacted Alex here to find out why Bigelow would be so determined to marry Skye, and everything came back to control. Someone wants her controlled so she won't ever entertain any thoughts of finding out the identity of her father the way she did her mother."

The congressman was quiet for a long moment; then he said, "Oh, I see."

Skye could tell from the look in his eyes that he did see. She decided to speak up. "I know the truth now and I'm fine with it," she said softly, leaning forward, meeting the congressman's gaze and holding it. "And if the senator doesn't want to claim me as his daughter, then that's fine, but I refuse to—"

"It's not that he doesn't want to claim you, Skye," the congressman said, his voice sounding tired and exhausted. "It's just that he doesn't know about you."

Shock appeared on Skye's face. "I don't understand. How can he not know about me?"

The congressman hesitated in responding at first. Then he leaned back in his chair and said in a defeated voice, "Because his mother and I decided not to tell him everything."

"With all due respect, sir," Justin said, "maybe you ought to start at the beginning and tell us *everything*."

"Yes, Dad, I agree that that would definitely be a good idea."

Everyone turned at the sound of the masculine voice and saw the man standing in the doorway. Senator Ryan Baines.

CHAPTER 28

"Ryan, I wasn't expecting you until later today," Congressman Baines said, standing as his son came into the room.

The senator glanced around at everyone. "I thought so, too, but I received a message that you needed to see me and that I should come right away."

"I sent that message," Alex said with a dry smile, not the least apologetic for having done so.

The senator nodded as he took the only available chair in his father's office. "Okay, I'm here and I'm just as anxious as everyone to hear what you have to say, Dad."

The senator's gaze then went to Skye. "From the little bit I overheard, It appears that I don't know everything there is to know about you, Ms. Barclay. Presently, the only thing I do know is that you're the daughter of Tom Barclay, the man who's been my father's accountant for years."

He then turned to his father. "I take it there's more?"

The congressman closed his eyes briefly. "Yes." When he reopened his eyes he started talking. "Twenty-six years ago we received a call from Charles and Maureen Claremont. They had sent their daughter, Kathy, to this exclusive all-girl camp for the summer and she returned pregnant after engaging in a summer affair with another teen she met at one of the neighboring camps for boys. They said Kathy had given them Ryan's name as the father of their child."

Skye had expected the senator to outright deny it. Instead

he said to his father, "I remember you and Mom questioning me about it and telling me Kathy had gotten pregnant. And I also remember admitting to the two of you that Kathy and I had been intimate and that if she was pregnant, there was a very strong possibility that the baby was mine."

"Yes, you did," the congressman agreed slowly. "You were seventeen and about to leave for college. Your mother and I told you that we would handle it."

"Yes, and when I came home for Thanksgiving I asked you about Kathy. You said it was over, she had miscarried. Are you now saying that was not the case?" the senator asked.

"Yes. That was not the case," Congressman Baines replied after a tense few moments. "The Claremonts were wealthy ranchers from Texas and they weren't ready for their sixteen-year-old to become a parent any more than your mom and I were ready for you to become one. Both you and Kathy had your lives ahead of you. She had plans to go on to college in two years, and you had just entered Harvard. The Clare-monts made a decision to send Kathy to London to live at a covent until the baby was born; then the child would be put up for adoption. Your mom and I thought it best not to tell you of their decision. We agreed it was the most excellent solution for all involved."

It was a long, silent moment before the congressman spoke again. "The only bee in the bonnet was your mother, Ryan. She could not accept the thought of knowing we had a grandchild who we wouldn't claim as ours. The thought of it almost broke her heart, and I loved her too much for that to happen. So I decided to do something. Without telling the Claremonts what we planned to do, your mother and I estab-lished a private adoption for Kathy's baby, so we would al-ways know where she was and how she was doing."

He paused; then said, "Tom and Edith Barclay were our choice as parents. We had known them for some time and they couldn't have children of their own. We made an offer to them that if they adopted our grandchild and provided a loving and caring home for her, we would make sure they were taken care of. We then put everything in place to secure a good future for our grandchild as well. We established a trust fund that she was to receive on her thirtieth birthday. And later when she got older, we even went so far as to select someone for her to one day marry who would continue to provide for her financially."

"An arranged marriage?" Senator Baines asked, lifting a brow.

"Yes, an arranged marriage, but her trust fund was not dependent on her marrying the person we selected, who happened to be the grandson of my business partner at that time."

Skye had been watching the man who was her father the entire time. He appeared calm, cool, collected, but she had a feeling he was taking in everything his father was saying, emotionally and mentally.

"Your intentions may have been good, Congressman Baines," Slade was now saying. "Unfortunately, the Barclays were not the loving and caring parents you assumed they were."

Congressman Baines jerked his head around to stare at Skye. "Is that true?"

It seemed to Skye that all eyes were on her. "They weren't monsters or anything like that, but Mom was very controlling and Dad just wasn't strong enough to stand up against her, although I felt he was on my side most of the time. As a child I could never do anything to please her, although I always tried. But I really can't complain, because I'm sure there are other children who had it worse than I did."

A smile touched her lips when she added, "I think while growing up, the brightest highlight of my week was when I knew Dad would take me into the office on Saturday and you and Mrs. Baines would be there to spend time with me. I didn't understand why the two of you were there, but now I do."

"And I would always ask if you were okay and if you were happy and you always said that you were," the congressman said softly.

"Yes, I know. Both you and Mrs. Baines would always ask. And although you were very kind to me, I couldn't say anything about how I truly felt. What could I say? No, I wasn't okay and wasn't happy? The Barclays were my parents, and I thought they acted like all parents act. I didn't know there was a difference . . . until I met the Madarises," she said, smiling at Slade, Clayton, and Justin. "I saw how Lorren and Justin interacted with Vincent. I could feel the love and I saw how quick they were to show it, and then I realized what I had missed out on while growing up."

The room got quiet and the congressman held his head down for a moment, and when he lifted his head the hurt and pain reflected in his eyes tore at Skye's heart. She had been deeply loved even when she hadn't known it.

"Marie and I did all that we could to assure that you were taken care of," the congressman was saying. "We couldn't imagine strangers taking you into their homes and our not ever knowing where you were or how you were. I guess in my selfishness I made a mess of things."

Skye's voice cracked a little when she said, "No, you didn't make a mess of things, because you did know where I was and you and Mrs. Baines did spend time with me. I just never knew who you really were to me."

"And it was our intention that you never found out," Congressman Baines said. "Because we had lied to Ryan, we knew we'd lost the privilege of you ever knowing you were our grandchild."

"At any time did you ever consider telling me the truth, Dad?" the senator asked his father.

Congressman Baines glanced over at Ryan. "Yes, many times. That day I persuaded you to go to her college graduation with me was one of those times. But I had lost your mother and I couldn't stand the thought of losing you as well once you discovered the truth. I'm sorry that I lied to you, but I thought what I was doing was for the best for everyone. I came close to telling you again after the Barclays had informed me that Skye had discovered she'd been adopted, and she had mentioned to them that she also wanted to find out the identity of her father. But by then I thought it was best to leave well enough alone, and that if you discovered the truth, then it was meant to be."

Ryan nodded as he glanced over at Skye. "And how did you put two and two together, Skye?"

Skye sighed deeply and gazed into the eyes of the man who was her father. "I didn't. When those threats were made I—"

"What threats?" the senator asked, frowning deeply.

"The ones made by Wayne Bigelow. Do you know him?" she asked.

The senator nodded. "Not personally, although I know who he is. His grandfather and my father were business partners many years ago. Over the past couple of years, I can remember seeing him once or twice."

"So the two of you are not engaged in any business dealings together?" Clayton asked carefully.

The senator shook his head again. "No. Did he say that we were?"

"No, but threats were made against the lives of Skye's biological brother and Slade that unless she returned to Augusta by this afternoon and promised to marry him as planned by Christmas, something would happen to them."

Senator Baines leaned forward. "No one can force her into marriage," he said, not believing such a thing.

"We know that, but evidently Bigelow doesn't. He will lose his trust fund unless he and Skye marry by Christmas Day. And from what we can gather," Clayton continued, "he's a compulsive gambler who needs as much money as he can get his hands on to feed his habit. In addition to that, he's heavily in debt."

"But what does any of that have to do with me?" the senator asked, still not understanding.

It was Slade who broke it down for him. "Evidently there's someone who wants Skye controlled so that she'll never go through with locating her biological father. Someone doesn't want that information known, so much to the point they would harm others to keep it hidden."

"So you assumed it was me?" the senator asked, not believing what he was hearing.

"You were the logical choice, Senator," Clayton said, staring straight at the man. "With your eye on such a high political prize, you stand to lose quite a bit if news of an illegitimate daughter surfaces. So in that case, you were our number-one suspect."

"Was I the only one?"

"We had considered her parents," Clayton replied. "However, we discounted them when Slade became involved. Skye never mentioned him to her parents. But you saw them together at Senator Lansing's retirement party. Somehow Bigelow found out about Slade soon after that and knew he was someone who meant enough to Skye to use him to threaten her."

"And you assumed I was the one who told Bigelow about him?"

Before anyone could answer, Congressman Baines said, "I might have been the one to do that—not that I passed anything on to Wayne Bigelow. However, I had been so excited about seeing Skye that night and when I got back to my hotel room, I called Tom and Edith to let them know I'd seen her. I also mentioned the comment she'd made about hiring someone to locate her biological father and that I noticed her ardent interest in Slade."

He turned to look at Skye. "It wasn't that I was reporting

to them, I was merely letting them know I'd seen you and that you seemed happy and content. I even told them that if you did discover the identity of your father it would not bother me."

Clayton nodded. "Then there's a possibility that they are the ones who might have mentioned something to Bigelow." He then glanced back at the senator. "Considering the million-dollar bonus they'd get if they were successful in marrying Skye and Bigelow, I can understand why they are so desperate to see it happen. But is there any reason why the Barclays would want to guard your identity as her biological father?"

The senator glanced over at his father. "Since you know these people better than I do, Dad, I'm going to have to let you answer that question."

The congressman shook his head. "No, I can't think of a reason. It really makes no sense, and a part of me can't believe that Tom would be involved in something like that."

"What about Edith Barclay?"

"I really don't want to think that about her, either, but after hearing what Skye's childhood was like, I really don't know."

"Well, everyone, there's only one way to find out who is behind what Bigelow is doing," Clayton said.

"And what way is that?" the senator asked.

"Set him up. If Skye lets him know she's decided not to marry him after all and that she plans to report his threats to the police, he'll make contact with someone, his accomplice. When he does, we can have him followed."

Slade angled his head and glanced over at Skye. "What do you think?"

Skye's gaze touched everyone in the room. "I think it's time for us to put an end to things."

Sir Drake, who hadn't spoken the entire time, spoke up

and said, "I'm glad everyone is in agreement, because I've had Bigelow under surveillance since early this morning."

"Are you sure you don't have to be at the airport to pick up Skye?" a naked Helen Stone asked as she sipped on her champagne. They had ordered a bottle sent up to their hotel room to celebrate Skye's homecoming.

"No, I offered, but she refused. I expect her to be in a little snit for a while and I'll let her. Then I plan to let her know who's boss."

"Good. Edith will stand her ground, but if Tom tries to interfere, don't let him. He's often soft where Skye's concerned."

At that moment Bigelow's cell phone went off and he reached across the bed to pick it up off the nightstand. He checked the number and silently mouthed the name *Skye* to Helen.

"Yes, Skye, have you made it to Augusta yet?"

"No, and I've decided not to come, Wayne," Skye said, reciting the script she had been coached to say. "I won't let you force me into a marriage that I don't want."

Wayne jumped from the bed. "Now you look here, Skye, evidently that warning to Madaris wasn't good enough for you. Next time I'll have my man go after your kid brother."

"Not if I go to the police first. I refuse to let you bully me. I'm protected by the Madarises, and there's nothing you can do."

"The hell there isn't. You just wait and see just what I'll—"

At that moment the hotel room door was flung wide open. Helen Stone let out a startled scream before doing everything she could to cover her nakedness when four men walked in, along with Skye, who was still holding the cell phone in her hand. Skye looked at a speechless Wayne, whose mouth was gaped open, before moving her gaze to the woman in bed with him.

"Hello, Helen. It's not even amusing finding the two of you together like this," Skye said with disgust in her voice.

Fearful of jail time, Wayne Bigelow spilled his guts. He claimed that a week after the announcement of his engagement to Skye, Helen had approached him, after finding out about his gambling habit, with an offer of a deal, along with the enticement of an illicit affair. Edith had confided in Helen regarding the person who was Skye's biological father. The reason Helen hadn't wanted the identity of the man known was because she had planned to use it in her grand blackmail scheme to get money out of the Barclays, the congressman, and the senator.

Charges were being filed and a press conference had been called by both the congressman and senator to explain what the charges were about and why. Skye chose not to attend the press conference, nor did she want to see it on television. What she wanted was to get as far away from Augusta as she could. Slade had granted her that wish, and plans were under way for them to leave to return to Houston later that day.

She and Slade had just finished enjoying a late lunch in their hotel room when there was a knock on the door. Her parents had called, eager to talk to her to tell their side of the story, not wanting her to think they knew what had been going on with Helen and Wayne. They had even apologized, saying they had never meant to hurt her and that deep down they did love her as a daughter. A part of Skye had wanted to believe them, but then another part, the one that had taken their mental abuse for years, could not.

"Who do you think that is?" she asked as Slade headed for the door.

"Probably Justin to let us know what time the plane will be ready."

It wasn't Justin. It was the senator. "Sorry to show up like this, but I just came from the press conference and was wondering if I could talk to Skye."

"Certainly," Slade said, inviting him in.

And to give them the privacy he felt they needed, he said, "I'm going across the hall to Justin's room to check with him about something. I'll be back later."

As soon as the door closed behind him Skye glanced over at the senator. "Would you like to sit down?"

"Yes," he said, taking the seat she offered him.

He stared at her for a few seconds before saying, "I can see the resemblance. You favor Kathy."

She nodded. "You do remember her, then."

"Yes, I remember her. I thought she was very beautiful. I'm not going to lie and weave some story of a summer love that I never got over, because that wasn't the case. I was seventeen, away from home for the summer, and she and I met. We liked each other right away and eventually became involved. I remember that night being special because it had been the first time for the both of us. At the end of the summer we exchanged addresses and phone numbers and said we would keep in touch, but we never did. I returned home with my focus on attending Harvard."

"So, you never talked with her again?" Skye asked, tilting her head to look at him.

"No, I never did, and after my parents told me she'd lost the baby, I thought of sending her a card and flowers but decided against it. I figured it would be best that we both moved on with our lives."

Skye didn't say anything for a long moment, then said, "May I ask you something?"

"Yes."

"Whenever I saw you, you always seemed to be distant to me. Why was that?"

"Because of my father. He was fascinated with you, always singing your praises or mentioning your name, and I never knew why he'd taken such an interest in you. He never would say, so I could only form my own opinions."

Skye looked shocked. "You thought your father and I were involved in some way?"

"I didn't want to think it, but it's been known to happen. My mother had been dead a number of years and one day I accidentally came across a bank account he had set up for you. I do know that older men get attracted to young girls. It's been the career downfall of several of my colleagues."

Skye understood where he was coming from in light of the most recent scandal in the Senate, where a well-known senator was accused of having an affair with a young woman—twenty-two years younger—who had worked in his office last summer. The pregnant young woman had come forward to tell her story.

"But I want you to know that today I publicly announced that I recently discovered that I have a twenty-six-year-old daughter who just happened to have been born on my eighteenth birthday."

Skye lifted a brow, surprised. "I didn't know that."

He smiled. "Neither did I. Dad told me. He and Mom thought that in itself was a special blessing for the both of them. I'm glad they got to spend time with you while you were growing up."

"I'm grateful for that time as well. Your mother was so nice to me. I used to hate it when the time came to leave. Then all I had to look forward to was the next weekend. I'll never forget how I felt when I got word that she had died."

The senator leaned back in his seat. "I guess the big question is just where do you and I go from here, Skye? You are my daughter and more than anything I want to get to know you."

Skye's heart didn't feel as heavy when she said, "And I want to get to know you as well. I'm returning to Houston and I will make my home there with Slade. He's asked me to marry him and I've accepted. But you and Congressman Baines are welcome to be a part of my life. I really want that."

A smile touched the senator's lips. "I want that as well, and I know Dad does. And you're not the only one contemplating marriage. I'm giving up my bachelor status and I'm asking Addy Peterson, the woman I've been seeing for a couple of years, to marry me."

Skye grinned. "That's wonderful, and congratulations." Automatically she crossed the room and gave her father a hug. He held her tight and she felt it: a tie and bond were established between the two of them.

She closed her eyes and thanked God for bringing Slade into her life and for uniting her with her biological brother, father, and grandfather.

Diana smiled when she opened her hotel room door to find the tall, handsome, distinguished-looking man with sea green eyes standing there. "Syntel!" she exclaimed, going into his open arms.

"I hope you didn't think I'd let you and Nedwyn marry without me being here," he said, chuckling in his deep Texan drawl. "Ned called me last night and I immediately made plans to get here. I always told him I wouldn't be cheated out of the chance to be his best man."

She couldn't help but smile. Ned and Syntel had been best friends since college, and over the years their friendship had strengthened. There was nothing one would not do for the other.

When Nedwyn walked out of the bedroom and saw his best friend, he couldn't help but grin. "Somehow I figured you wouldn't let this day happen without you."

"Not on your life," Syntel said, giving Ned a huge bear hug. "And it's about time you asked this beautiful lady to share your life with you," he said.

When Diana gave him a questioning look, Syntel simply grinned and said, "Yes, I knew how he felt about you, Di. He's held it in for a long time and I'm glad he's finally let it out and admitted it. I wish the both of you much happiness."

"And what about you, Syntel?" she asked softly. She knew the woman he loved had died over thirty years ago and that she had a permanent place in his heart.

He smiled fondly and said, "I'm a man who can only love one woman, and Janeda was it for me. I'm happy these days spending time with my daughter and granddaughter."

Moments later the three friends left the hotel for the small church where the wedding services would be held.

"I now pronounce that you are man and wife."

The minister's words rang loud and clear, not just in Nedwyn Lansing's ears but in his heart as well. He stood facing the woman he had loved for so long, finally making her his.

"And you may kiss your bride, Senator Lansing."

A huge smile touched Nedwyn's lips as he leaned down to do exactly that. He whispered, "I love you," moments before their mouths touched.

When he finally released her mouth to gaze at her, her incredibly beautiful eyes sparkled with the same love he felt. "We'll probably have to do this all over again for Felicia's benefit," he heard her whisper.

"I'll do this as many times as needed," he whispered back to her. "You, Diana Madaris Lansing, are one woman worth kissing over and over."

She chuckled. "I'm talking about the ceremony, Ned."

He laughed as he pulled her into his arms. "Oh."

And then with Syntel behind them, they walked out into the dazzling sunlight, a promise that the rest of their days would be just as bright.

It's good to be home, Skye thought as she glanced around the living room of her condo. They had arrived back in Houston a couple of hours ago. With the threat removed, Justin had immediately left for Whispering Pines to get his son.

"Alone at last."

Skye turned around and glanced over at Slade. He was

leaning against the closed door. He was staring at her and the intensity of his gaze almost took her breath away.

"Our little adventure is over, so I guess it's going back to work for us tomorrow," she said, watching him slowly walk over toward her.

"Maybe," he said huskily when he reached her and drew her into his arms. "And maybe not. Taking another day off work won't hurt things. Besides, there's something important I want to do tomorrow."

She tilted her head back to look up at him. "What?"

"Take you to a jeweler to pick out your ring. Then you and I can decide on a date."

She shook her head, grinning. "Any day other than Christmas Day."

He smiled, understanding. "That's no problem." They had a chance to talk after finding Bigelow and Helen Stone together. Although Skye had told Slade she was all right, he knew both Wayne's and the woman's betrayal had to have hurt.

"I want to get married a lot sooner anyway. Would you mind having a wedding during the time of the Madaris family reunion? That way the majority of the family will be in town."

Skye lifted her arched brow. "That's next month."

He grinned. "Yes, I know, but I'm sure the women in the family will help in planning things. The sooner I make you mine, the better."

She moved her body closer to his and whispered against his lips, "I'm already yours, Slade."

And she meant every word. She could now admit she had become *his* the moment he opened the door at Justin and Lorren's home to find her standing there. And in a way she believed they both knew it.

"So what are our plans for tonight?" she asked, looking up at him.

When his eyes darkened with profound passion at her question, "Besides that," she quickly said.

He laughed. "Sweetheart, I'm a Madaris and there's little else besides that."

She smiled seductively. "Well, in that case," she said, tipping her head back and lifting her mouth as an invitation to a kiss. It was a hot, seductive, lingering kiss that beckoned them to mate their mouths until breathing became a necessity.

Slade then swooped her into his arms. She didn't have to ask where he was taking her. She wrapped her arms around his neck and rested her head against his chest. This was the man she loved. The man who would give her plenty of babies and lots of love. A man she knew she could count on when the going got rough and tough. He would erase all the bad memories in her life and replace them with only good ones.

Slade Madaris was her everything.

EPILOGUE

"So, how does it feel to be a married woman?"

Skye smiled over at Slade's great-grandmother, Laverne Madaris. "It feels simply wonderful."

"That's good, child. Slade is one that I knew wouldn't take long to know what he wanted. Now Lucas and Blade will be another story. See that young lady over there?" Great-Gramma Laverne said, looking across the yard of Whispering Pines where tables were loaded with plenty of food.

Skye followed her gaze and saw the very beautiful woman she had been introduced to earlier. Her name was Mackenzie Stanfield and she was an attorney from Oklahoma and a cousin to Ashton Sinclair. "Yes, I see her," Skye said, smiling.

"She's the one for Luke," the old woman said with confidence in her voice.

Skye lifted a brow, then glanced around for Luke. He was standing leaning against the corral taking to his aunt Diana and her new husband, retired senator Nedwyn Lansing. They had surprised everyone by returning from a trip to Savannah last month and announcing they had gotten married. Everyone was happy for the older couple.

Skye then returned her attention back to Luke. If he and the woman whom Great-Gramma Laverne had pointed out to her were an item, Skye hadn't noticed it. But she *had* noticed that most of the single men present couldn't keep their eyes off of Mackenzie. She was utterly beautiful. Christy had whispered that she was African-American mixed with Cherokee Indian, just like Ashton.

"Do you know why I say that?" Laverne Madaris then asked.

Skye's smile widened. "No, why do you say that?"

"Because I can see things regarding my grands and great-grands that they can't see themselves. Mark my word. She's the woman for Luke."

"Who's the woman for Luke?" Slade asked, coming up behind them and grabbing his wife of only thirty-two hours around the waist and bringing her closer into his arms.

"None of your business. This is woman talk, Slade," his great-grandmother quickly informed him.

"Yes, ma'am, but I just wanted to borrow Skye for a second. I promise to bring her back."

"Okay, as long as you bring her back. She and I have a lot more talking to do."

Slade took his wife's hand in his. "Come on, let's go for a walk, sweetheart."

"All right."

Both yesterday and today had been beautiful days. Yesterday afternoon she and Slade had gotten married in his great-grandmother's church. Skye's biological grandfather, Congressman Baines, as well as her biological father, Senator Baines, had been there for her. And her aunt Karen had also come. Skye glanced to where her aunt was talking to an older, handsomely rugged-looking man by the name of Abram Hawk, who was a good friend of Sir Drake and his lovely wife, Tori.

Skye couldn't help but smile and cross her fingers. Her aunt was such a wonderful and beautiful person, and it was time she found love all over again. And from what Skye could see, Mr. Hawk was as fascinated with her aunt as she seemed to be with him. One thing Skye had discovered about some of the people attending the family reunion: If they weren't a Madaris by blood, then they were connected to them by a special friendship, and to a Madaris, friendship spoke volumes.

She had invited her parents to her and Slade's wedding, but neither of them had responded to her invitation. Evidently they weren't happy about not receiving the bonus they would have gotten had she married Wayne.

She continued walking by Slade's side. He didn't say anything and neither did she. They were enjoying the quiet stillness of their surroundings. When they reached a huge stream, Slade turned to her and smiled. "Walking helps me to think."

She returned his smile. "I know. So what do you think?"

He stopped walking and put his hands at her waist and pulled her closer to him. "I think I'm the happiest man on the face of the earth right now, because I have you as my wife. And just like I said in front of everyone yesterday, I promise to love you, protect you, cherish you, and respect you for always and forever. You, Skye Madaris, are my every woman."

"Oh, Slade."

And then he leaned toward her, captured her lips to seal the words he'd just spoken. And deep in her heart Skye knew so many doors were opening to her, doors she was not afraid to walk through as long as she had Slade by her side.

She was a very blessed woman.

Courtney arrived at Sonya's home with a gigantic headache. Her cousin opened the door, took one look at her and arched a concerned brow as she pulled her into the house and closed the door behind them.

"Another migraine?" Sonya asked, reaching out and gently pressing her fingertips to Courtney's temples.

"Yes."

"Brought on by what?"

"Another episode of Ron and Barbara Andrews trying to drive me nuts," Courtney said.

Sonya released an agitated breath. "What are those two up to now?"

"They want to make their marriage work, like such a thing can actually happen," Courtney answered, tossing her purse on the sofa in disgust. "I can't believe Mom continues to let Dad use her. If that's love, then it's abusive love."

"Calm down. If you keep this up, your head will only hurt worse. You can't let what your parents do get to you. Trust me, I found that out the hard way."

"I know you're right, but I'm tired of seeing them do each other in."

Sonya grabbed her hand. "Come on in the kitchen with me. I got just the thing for you."

Courtney lifted a brow as she allowed herself to be dragged off. "And what's that?"

"Chocolate chip cookie dough ice cream. Our favorite. I was about to eat a bowl so now you can join me."

When they reached the kitchen, Courtney shook her head and grinned. "How can you indulge yourself in a bowl of ice cream less than a week before your wedding? Aren't you afraid of gaining weight to where you won't be able to fit into your dress?"

Sonya chuckled. "No. Any excess calories I take in I'll burn off later tonight with Mike."

Courtney laughed. "You're incorrigible."

Sonya grinned as pulled the carton of ice cream from the freezer. "Can't help it when it comes to Mike. He's the best there is, in or out of bed. However, I like our bedtime activities the best."

Courtney leaned against the counter and watched as Sonya filled two bowls. Standing at a height of five-nine, with medium brown skin, features that would make any man take a second look, a short and sassy haircut that emphasized her sophistication, and eyes so dark they almost looked black, not to mention her shapely figure, Courtney had always thought Sonya was simply beautiful. And although there was a five-year difference in their ages, the two had always been close. Sonya had been the big sister she'd never had and she'd always been proud of her. Sonya had always been wild and uninhibited—at least that had always been Barbara Andrews's definition of her sister's only child. But to Courtney, her cousin's *love-them-and-leave-them* lifestyle had intrigued her, made her proud there was a woman who could dish it out just like a man could. Sonya claimed there was no man alive who could make an honest woman out of her. At least that was the song she'd been singing before Mike had entered the picture.

"Hey, go easy on my bowl," Courtney said when she saw how much ice cream Sonya was putting into it. "Unlike you, I don't have a Mike to help me work off any calories later, and I need to be able to fit into my bridesmaid dress."

Sonya laughed as she slid the bowl filled with ice cream toward her. "Don't complain to me if you don't have a man. I told you a year ago you were working too hard and not giving your social life enough attention. No matter how hard I worked, I still made time for a little bump and grind. The longest period of time I went without sex was when I started dating Mike. He was determined to make me beg for it."

Courtney licked a scoop of ice cream off her spoon before asking. "And did you beg for it?"

Sonya smiled sheepishly when she said, "Like a wanton hussy. I thought I was all savvy and would show him a trick or two, but he showed me that he already knew all the tricks in the book. The man laid it on too strong and he was all smooth about it."

Courtney believed her. Sonya was too much of a woman, one who liked being in control. For her to give up that control to a man, that man had to have made one hell of an impact on her . . . her senses as well as her body, but especially her senses. Over the years her cousin had dated a number of men, but Sonya had never let one get under her skin. In fact she went out of the way to make sure she would get under theirs with no plan for any lasting results. And although more than one man had tried taming her reckless and elusive heart, each had failed miserably. "I'm glad you finally decided that race wasn't an issue and gave Mike a chance."

"I'm glad I did, too, although God knows I tried to fight it. I didn't want to get involved in an interracial affair, but I couldn't help myself. For the first time in my life I began craving vanilla with a passion. Wanted to lap it up with everything I had."

Courtney nodded. She knew the story of how Sonya had gone to the St. Laurent Hotel to confront Jesse Devereau about how he'd been treating Sonya's best friend from high school, Carla Osborne. Jesse hadn't liked finding out that Carla had given birth to his son two years earlier and hadn't told him about it, and he had flown into town intent on making trouble for Carla. When Sonya confronted Jesse that day, she'd also confronted Jesse's best friend Mike, since she had interrupted them dining together.

According to Sonya, from the moment Mike laid his soulful blue eyes on her, it had been instant attraction, the hot and steamy kind. Tall, hard, and with a body that would make any woman drool, for the first time in her life she'd wanted to find out if it was true that blondes had more fun and wanted to put Mike's smooth mouth and glib tongue to work doing something other than defending his best friend's actions.

Sonya and Mike formed a pact to straighten things out between Jesse and Carla, which eventually worked. They were now happily married, and since Sonya and Mike were the godparents to Jesse and Carla's son Craig, they began spending a lot of time together.

According to Sonya, at some point she and Mike decided to stop fighting whatever was keeping them at arm's length and give into their attraction and make things work. And they had. There was no doubt in Courtney's mind that her cousin had found her soul mate.

"It might work this time, you know."

Courtney glanced up and looked over at Sonya when her words intruded into her thoughts. "What might work?"

"This thing with your mom and dad. They must have thought it through before deciding—"

"No, and that's the problem with them," Courtney said sadly. "They never think things through, Sonya. Mom refuses to analyze and accept just what an asshole Dad has been to her when she deserves so much better. I honestly think she's afraid of letting go and moving on. She's terrified that if she gives Dad up, she'll begin acting like Aunt Peggy did in the beginning."

Sonya nodded, knowing how things had been with her mother. Peggy Morrison had become a basket case when Joe Morrison dumped her for a younger woman. It had taken almost a full year for her to build back up her self-esteem and realize that the break-up of her marriage hadn't been entirely her fault. Now Peggy had gotten herself together, was a part of the work force, and was too involved with all her charities to worry about her ex these days.

Sonya's thoughts then shifted to her father. If Courtney thought her own dad was an asshole, then his brother-in-law was an A-plus asshole. What her father had put her mother through before their divorce was almost unforgivable. How could two nice-looking, highly educated blood sisters born from the same woman—a woman who'd raised them to be strong and independent—marry such heartless and untrusting men?

"How is Aunt Peggy handling the thought that Uncle Joe is bringing his mistress-turned-wife to your wedding?" Courtney asked.

A sad smile touched Sonya's lips. "As well as can be expected. I'm thinking she's hoping he does the decent thing and not bring her, since I'm sure he knows I prefer not having her there. But we all know that he will, if for no other reason than to flaunt the fact that he has access to some young stuff whenever he wants it. I've even gone so far as to ask him to leave Suzette at home but he refused, saying he won't disrespect his wife that way. It took me less than a minute to remind him of all the times he had openly and uncaringly disrespected Mama. I doubt my words sent him on any guilt trip, so I've basically told him that if he does anything to ruin what will be the happiest day of my life, or if he allows Suzette to behave in any way to bring embarrassment to Mom, that I'll never speak to him again."

Courtney nodded. She believed her. "What about Mike's family? Will he prepare them for what could happen?"

"Mike doesn't have a family. He was given up at birth and, like Jesse, got bounced around between foster homes, usually the same ones. That's why the two of them are so close and consider themselves as brothers since they were the only constant person in each other's lives while growing up. Jesse is the only family Mike has."

A part of Courtney thought that Jesse and Mike's situation was sad, but considering the parents she'd had to deal with and all their drama over the years, the thought of being raised in a foster home held somewhat of an appeal. Now how warped could such thinking be? "It wasn't my intent to hog your entire evening since I'm sure Mike will be dropping by later," Courtney said, walking over to the sink to place her empty bowl into it. "But I wanted to check to make sure there're no last-minute details I can help you with before next Saturday."

Sonya smiled. "No, the woman we hired as our wedding planner is totally awesome. Carla used her when she married Jesse and was pleased with the results, and so far, I am as well. But I'm glad you dropped by since there's something I want to give you."

Courtney raised a curious brow. "What?"

Sonya's smile widened. "Wait here for a minute while I go and get it." She then raced up the stairs to her bedroom.

Leaving the kitchen, Courtney walked into the living room and glanced around. She thought the house Sonya and Mike had bought together a few months ago was simply gorgeous as well as elegant. She'd always admired Sonya's skill when it came to decorating and every time she visited she couldn't help but appreciate Sonya's classic taste as well as her love for bold colors that did so much to the gleaming oak floors and decorative tile walls. So far only Sonya had moved in. Mike wanted to officially take residence after the wedding, although Courtney was fairly certain he spent many nights here anyway.

And then there was the other home they were having built in Los Angeles where the corporate office for Mike's private investigating firm was located. That was where they would be spending a lot of their time since Mike's company offered professional services to law firms, prominent individuals, and financial institutions as well as major domestic and foreign corporations. Sonya would be quitting her job with a large marketing firm and would bring her marketing expertise to Mike's firms, starting with the office he had opened here in Orlando.

"Here you go," Sonya said, coming down the stairs, walking over to her, and placing a small black book in her hand.

Courtney glanced up into her cousin's smiling face with a confused look. "You're giving me your little black book?"

"Yes."

Courtney glanced down at the book. This wasn't just any little black book. As far as she was concerned, it was legendary. She'd known for years it had existed and had even watched Sonya whip it out a few times to make a hit. She had even, on occasion, run into some of the men whose names had been plucked from the book while they were out on a date with Sonya. All the men had been tall, dark, and handsome. "Why are you giving this to me?" she couldn't help but ask.

"Because I won't need it anymore and I can't think of another soul I'd want to have it other than you. Granted you probably won't like every guy whose name is listed in it even if you get the chance to meet them, but I think there're a number of pretty good prospects. The names I've lined through are guys I've met and spent time with already. The rest are guys that I met but never got around to actually checking, but there was definitely something about them that I found interesting to get their name in that book."

Curious, Courtney opened up the little black book and flipped several pages before coming to one where the names hadn't yet been lined through. The first was a guy by the name of Harper Isaac. Umm, the name sounded manly. She closed the book and glanced back at Sonya, touched that her cousin thought this much of her to pass this very special book on to her.

Dating, she'd discovered, had turned into such a horrendous nightmare that it felt good to have someone you could trust to semi-screen some of the men for you. She had found out the hard way that it was downright difficult for a woman to be certain of the type of man she would be going out with until it was almost too late.

"Thanks, Sonya. How did you know?"

Sonya understood her question. "How did I know that deep down you were lonely and wanted to meet a nice guy but were sick and tired of all the effort it took getting to that point?"

When Courtney nodded, Sonya continued by saying, "Because I was once where you're at now. There was a time when I wanted a good man to love me and all I kept fishing up were jerks. I finally adopted the philosophy that if you couldn't beat them, you might as well join them, and even then, deep down I longed for the man of my dreams to come into my life, take me away from being a bad girl, and capture my heart. Granted, I had no idea he would be of the Caucasian persuasion, but if I had to do it all over again, the only thing I'd change is having Mike come into my life sooner. The first time he tossed one of those *I'd-like-to-get-all-into-you* looks at me, I was completely lost."

Courtney couldn't help the smile that touched the corners of her lips. "You truly do love him, don't you?"

Sonya nodded. "Oh, yes, with all my heart," she said softly and filled with emotions so deep Courtney could actually feel them. "Although utilizing that little black book was fun while it lasted, I'm passing it on to you with my blessings and best wishes. I'm hoping you'll find your very own Mike among some of those names."

Courtney smiled, hoping that Sonya was right.